'Aumākua Anthology
Book3

Huaka'ipō up Pi'ilewa Point

Del Aragon

‘Aumākua Anthology
Book3

Huaka‘ipō up Pi‘ilewa Point

Del Aragon

Huaka‘ipō up Pi‘ilewa Point

Designed & Created by Del Aragon
Cover Art by Del Aragon
First printing, April 25, 2025

ISBN-13: 978-1-963531-06-0 (Paperback)
ISBN-13: 978-1-963531-07-7 (Hardcover)
ISBN-13: 978-1-963531-08-4 (eBook)
Library of Congress Control Number: 2024919191

Self Published by Del Aragon
Honolulu, HI
arts.delaragon@gmail.com

Printed through KDP

To Joe and Nani.

From my beginning and to my end, you have been there for me, shaping me into the person I am today.

I am infinitely grateful for the love, guidance and protection you've given me throughout my life.

I love you both, forever and always

Contents

Mua

"Get me a cold one, boy!"

Brandon could smell the alcohol from his father's last beer piercing the musty air of their parlor as he spoke. He stood up without a word and made his way quietly over to the icebox. He could hear his older brother, Burden, whimpering through the thin walls of their father's bedroom. It caused him to pause briefly.

"You got problems with your ears, boy!?" Mr. Alberts called out without taking his eyes off the tube.

Brandon snapped back to fulfill his task and pulled a cold can of Primo from the fridge. The bedroom door opened with a terrifying rip caused by the humidity fused door. The sound startled the already nervous child.

Brandon watched his father's friend, Chaz, step out from the room buckling up his thick leather belt, "You got one more of those for me, sweetness?"

Without hesitation, Brandon reached into the chiller for a second cold brew.

Chaz snapped both bottles away from the boy and winked, "I think I can manage it from here, son."

A shadow burst from the bedroom and dashed out of the front door. By reflex, Brandon followed quickly behind. He found Burden in the back yard whacking the trunk of a chopped tree with the busted handle of a pickaxe. Brandon knew it was best to let his brother get it all out of his system. The knocking of the redwood handle caused an anxious feeling to build in Brandon's core. He experienced the pain his brother was in by the pure force he whipped upon the lifeless stump.

Burden wiped the tears from his reddened face and flung the wooden grip to the ground, "You and me, man! It's just gonna be you and me one day. Until then, I'll be damned if I ever let anything like that happen to you!"

Burden walked over to his little brother and began beating the living daylights out of him. A sharp elbow caused Brandon to hit the ground with a heavy thud. He began choking until a tooth flew from his throat into his palm.

"What the heck are you doing!?"

Burden shot Brandon a scowl and came upon him with ferocity, but he was stopped by a strange droning noise. A massive form stood in a tall patch of California grass watching the brother's dispute from the back of the property.

Burden turned his attention to the stranger laughing at them in his odd manner, "What, fat boy? You wanna scrap!?"

The large form became silent as Burden rushed upon him. The face Burden made and the intense look in his eyes caused the peculiar teen to seize and soil his pants.

"What the hell, you pissin' your pants kid!?" Burden watched the oversized boy holding back his sobs. "Hey, take it easy, I'm not gonna hurt you."

Brandon rubbed the welt on his face as he made his way beside his brother, "Who's this guy?"

"What's your name, boy?" Burden halted Brandon from speaking.

The massive youth slowed his breathing, "Set-tah."

"Settah? What kind of fool's name is that?" Brandon scoffed just as his brother cracked him in the clavicle.

"Shut up, Brandon. He said Seth." Burden looked back at Seth, "How old are you, kid?"

Seth cowered while holding all his fingers up.

"There's no way he's my age, he's almost double our height-" Brandon spoke with an ache in his voice, but he stopped himself as Burden raised his fist up at him once more.

"Last time, Brandon. I promise." Burden took Seth's hand and pulled his body fully into their yard, "Burden Alberts... this is my little brother Brandon. It's nice to meet you, Seth."

The young giant smiled at Burden. It was the first time in his life that he ever made a friend.

'Ekahi

The voice of a nervous child vibrated out from a reel to reel audio recorder bringing chicken skin to the young man who sat listening to it. The anxious teen nestled his bottom into a couch with tight, bright red leather bound upholstery, ears open intently on the conversation that he remembered from what seemed like forever ago.

"Hello, my name is Len. A couple of years ago I lost my best friend at camp." Len couldn't believe how young he sounded when he first started his therapy sessions. "Ever since that night... I am afraid to go to sleep, I am afraid to go to school, and I'm afraid to be alone."

Len knew that therapy was the only way he would be able to deal with everything that happened at Camp Pi'ilewa in the summer of 1974. The fateful night that made it impossible for him to concentrate in class and caused him to lose all of his closest friends.

After Len's youthful voice faded, a second deeper voice chimed in, "Thank you... uh, Len. I would like to continue our first session with you telling me as much as you can possibly remember about your experience that evening. I know this must be difficult for you, but I would like you to try your best to remember the night you were hiding out in the woods. Could you please explain to me exactly how you 'lost' your friend?"

"Best friend, doctor, he was my best friend," the young patient began to sniff as he grew silent.

The dead air from the recording gave off a slight hiss. The static from the empty audio sounded like voices whispering deliriously over each other trying hard to grab the attention of anyone willing to listen. The words created by the monotonous buzz creeped out the young patient. He imagined there was some hidden message too indiscernible for his ears and brain to decode. It almost seemed as though the tone of the imagined voices mocked and ridiculed him for being so small and insignificant.

The doctor's voice cut the silence as he spoke with sincerity, "Did you want to take a moment, Len?" A few sniffs later the doctor's voice rang through the scratchy mono speakers once more, "Alright, Len. If it's too difficult to talk about, I'm going to give you something." The sound of the doctor's desk drawer could be heard sliding open. "I would like you to take this notebook and keep a journal. Write your feelings and memories in these pages. Hopefully, the act of putting it down on paper will help you to speak with me about what troubles you during our sessions. I think that's enough for one day." A loud snap caused the player to go dead.

Thoughts of that night at Camp Pi'ilewa filled the high schooler's mind. The feeling of being helpless, the feeling of being afraid. These types of worries were the ones that had tormented him for the majority of his youth. Now, more than ever, Len believed he had a better grip over his emotions. He felt ready to move forward and put all of it behind him. He desired a fresh start.

"That was our first meeting together, Len. Do you remember? Your mother brought you here to meet with me with the hope of helping you to work through your issues. Here we are today for your last session and *you* will be responsible for your own release."

A huge smile worked its way across Len's face, "Thank you, Dr. Campbell, for all the help you have given me over the past four years. Without you, I wouldn't have been as successful as I was during high school."

"You just needed an ear. I am glad that you could put your trust in me and I am very grateful for the time that we had to work through your dilemma. I feel as if I made a friend with you." The doctor smiled, "By the way, I've been meaning to ask, how was senior prom?"

Len's smile got even broader, "It was a blast! I went with Shelby. Do you remember the girl I told you about? The one I had a crush on? We danced all night long."

The doctor couldn't help but chuckle, "Yes, I do remember you mentioning Shelby once or twice. Did you tell her what was in your heart?"

Len chuckled in an awkward manner. "I did, when we were saying goodnight," the young man's smile slowly disappeared, "but, she let me know that she wasn't romantically into me, or into any guys for that matter. The only reason she decided to go with me was because her crush was going with someone else and she was trying to make her jealous."

"Oh no!" The doctor could see Len needed a little uplifting, "That's too bad, well, too bad for her because you are an amazing young man." Dr. Campbell tapped his pen on his desk twice, "Did I ever tell you about my senior prom?" Len shook his head as the doctor folded his fingers, "It didn't turn out so well for me either."

"Why? What happened? Did you get rejected like me?" Len joked.

"Actually, she accepted my offer to go to the prom, to my surprise. But, it's not like I gave her much choice. I hounded her endlessly." The doctor sat back and looked up into the air, "She was, probably still is, so beautiful… and her voice! Goodness, if there ever was an angel on earth! It seemed as though all the guys at school wanted to be near her. She was such a very demure girl. On our very first date, I was even so bold as to ask her mother for her hand. Quite silly now that I think back on it."

Len wiggled in anticipation, "So, what happened? What was so terrible about your prom?"

"Ugh, my boy, I flubbed it. The moment we arrived at the dance I just lost my marbles. I imagined a demon was trying to kill me that night. She, of course, left with her cousin and I never had an opportunity to make it up to her. One of the biggest regrets I have ever had in my life." Dr. Campbell had a look of disappointment.

"I'm sorry to hear that. It must've been very hard to come back from," Len appeared sympathetic. "Maybe you could make it up to her now? Are you two still in touch?"

"No, I believe that time has already passed for me." Dr. Campbell shook his head, "Well, if I hadn't had that experience, I wouldn't have ever dreamed of doing what it is I do today, my boy. That night moved me to find answers, to help bring light to my misconceptions. Our minds are so powerful that they can create false visions and even self harm that is veiled by fantastical delusions. It is very similar to the devout experience of those who are afflicted by the stigmata."

Len couldn't fathom Dr. Campbell being in the same situation he was in, seeing terrifying, unnatural events. It's enough to drive a person crazy. The doctor's recovery and healthy lifestyle gave Len hope he'd also make it out alright.

"I appreciate your sacrifice, Doctor. I think there was a reason I was brought here to you. It's like fate. I can't imagine there are many therapists out there who have experienced what I went through." The doctor smiled and nodded at his young patient. "So, is this truly my final session with you?"

Dr. Campbell laughed, "I only tell my demon story to my patients who have come to terms with their trauma, and you, my young friend, have done just that. If you don't have anything else to share about your prom I guess we are all finished here."

Standing in a flash with his hand propped forward, Len bid his therapist farewell, "Thank you so much, Dr. Campbell!"

Dr. Campbell took Len's hand and shook it with pride, "You're not my patient anymore, but you don't need to be a stranger either. If you want to stop by to talk, I'd be more than happy to catch up with you."

Len smiled, "Thank you, Doctor!"

Dr. Campbell stopped his former patient just before he could make his way out of the office, "Len, the next time we see each other, call me Henry."

‘Elua

“Len!? I’m back!” Mercy’s voice echoed into the entry of the apartment as she called out for her son. She struggled through the door holding a wide pizza box with her purse sitting right in the middle of the container’s lid. She dropped the pie on the counter and snatched up her bag revealing an oily stain in the spot where the cover was indented.

“Len? I’m home!” She came upon her boy sitting on the floor in the living room holding a familiar composition book with some random papers sticking out. “Hey! What’s going on? You seem deep in your thoughts.”

Len smiled back at his mother, “I think I want to apply to be a counselor at Camp Pi‘ilewa this summer.”

Mercy’s eyes popped, “Whoah, are you sure? Do you think that’s such a good idea?”

“Don’t worry, it’ll be fine. I just had my last session with Henry and I’m ready to move on. I think this is a great way for me to solidify my accomplishment. Henry practically endorsed the idea.” Len handed his mother the application and handbill for Camp Pi‘ilewa.

She slapped the flier away, “I know what the camp looks like, Len. Is this some sort of torture you’re trying to unnecessarily put yourself through?" In her own way, Mercy was trying to protect her son from regressing. "And what is this guy trying to get you to prove? You don't need to do any of this to show yourself, or me, or your therapist that you are better! Or is Dr. Campbell just showing off the results of his therapy!?" Mercy drew out a harsh breath, "And now you're on a first name basis with your therapist?"

"Henry *was* my therapist. And I am not interested in putting myself through any kind of torture." Len pulled the paperwork toward his chest, "It's to give back. It's also a way for me to get closure and honor Kawika."

Mercy understood what the guy meant to Len, but she wasn't too fond of the way her son decided to pay his respect to the memory of their friendship. She eyed the composition book resting in Len's lap.

"What's with your diary?"

"Journal, Mom!" Len nodded as he stroked the spine of the ratty book, "Yeah, I was going to toss it into the camp fire and set my fears free. I am in control of my own destiny." Mercy squished her brows together which caused Len to respond, "It's symbolic, I guess."

"Kaulana!" Mercy shouted as she scowled at the notebook. "We both know that your father was big on symbolism."

“Kaona,” Len looked lovingly at his mother. “Hey, maybe you should sit down with Henry and share your feelings about Dad with him. He’s a very good listener.”

“I don’t ever want to talk about *that* man again!” Mercy let out another huff, “And for the hourly rate the doctor charges, he better be a *very* good listener!” She folded her arms and slowly looked from the journal up to her son’s eyes, “Okay! I’ll be alright with you going if you let me take a look at your diary, erm, journal!”

“No can do, I’m taking it with me to Pi‘ilewa to burn it. Remember?” Len pulled the book away from his mother.

“How’s about you let me drive you up to camp, I can read the journal while you’re away, then I bring it up to you the night before camp is over and we do the burn ritual together?” Mercy looked at her son exposing her clenched teeth hoping it was an acceptable alternative.

“Okay. I can live with that,” Len handed the book to his mother and pulled down some paper plates from the shelf, “Shall we watch some T.V. while we eat?”

Mercy clicked through several channels at a steady pace on the remote control when a show caught Len’s eye, “Oh! *Magnum P.I.*!”

“Rerun, babes. The season ended last month.”

As she continued moving to the next channel the remote stopped responding as if taking on a mind of its own. It landed on a station with a local news reporter talking about a figure from their past.

Mercy's voice rang in panic, "Oh lord!" A photo of Seth Pedrina was plastered beside the face of the news anchor, "Baby, I'm so sorry! The remote isn't working."

She banged the clicker on the coffee table while thumbing the channel buttons, but the volume started to climb. Mercy shot to her feet to turn off the t.v. when her son stopped her movements.

"It's okay, Mom! Stop treating me like an infant. What's up with Seth anyway?" Len grabbed the remote from his mother's hand as she sat back down and they both listened to the news report.

"... Seth Pedrina, twenty, convicted murderer of two individuals at Camp Pi'ilewa in the summer of 1974, had attempted to escape the 'Āinapau Prison facility this afternoon. He made it as far as Kāo'oloa Road before he was apprehended once more. Eye witnesses say they saw Pedrina having an argument with himself on the edge of the road, which lead them to contact the police. Local authorities have stated that he will now be transferred to O'ahu Community Correctional Center some time next month. The move is to keep him from attempting to escape once more from the minimal security provided at 'Āinapau Detention Center. Pedrina was sentenced to life in prison with the possibility of parole in fifteen years which is …"

The channel flipped automatically to a station showing a colorful commercial with funny looking cartoon characters. Len's mother was in a confused state.

"What just happened?" She snatched the remote from Len and began mashing the channel buttons. She landed back on the news, but it had already moved on to a different story. "Tell me that wasn't weird… it was strange right?" She eyed her son to see if he was okay with what was just announced.

"I'm sure it was just a coincidence."

Len stared at the glass monitor with his mind locked on Seth and how insane it was that he escaped from the prison. Len thought, *As long as I don't ever have to cross paths with that psycho ever again, I'll be alright. The further he gets from me, the better.*

Len's memories of that fateful night came back in a flash. He could see himself running for his life through the dark forest, searching for a place to hide, and then being cast aside by an invisible force. He could vividly see the life of Kawika being slowly choked out of him as he floated impossibly above the ground. Len's head ached, *Those things didn't really happen the way I thought they did. It was just a way of my brain coping with the situation. Seth is to blame… isn't he?*

'Ekolu

April 1, 1978

Hello, I was told to write anything that I feel or that comes to mind. I feel hungry.

April 2, 1978

I was at the park today with my best friend Benny. He started telling me about a movie he saw the other night and the next thing I know he starts making fun of me. I told him to stop laughing at me, but he wouldn't so I socked him. I am so angry, I'm still shaking.

April 7, 1978

Another night alone. It's times like this that I start feeling like I'm being watched. I turn on all the lights to make the faces in the shadows disappear. I wish Mom was home more often-

"Hey!" Len's voice cracked as he shouted toward his mother. "What? You're reading the journal already?" The young man appeared from his room with his suitcase trailing behind him.

"Oh! No, I was just skimming the pages to see how much you wrote." Mercy sat up in her chair pressing the tattered notebook shut. "Are you sure you're ready to go? Do you have everything you need?" Len's mother had some of that kaona hidden behind her words.

Len side-eyed his mother, "Yeah, I'm ready to go. Are you?"

Mercy slapped her hands onto the armrest of her chair and stood to her feet, "Alrighty then, let me grab the keys."

***

An awkward silence hung between mother and son as the car traveled down the road. The only thing that broke through the hush was the rattle of the car's chassis as it hit a line of Botts' dots and the occasional sharp clicking of the vehicles turn signal. The old car stereo played at a low volume, just loud enough to help drone out the sound of the tires over the hot asphalt. Mercy thought about what she had read in her son's journal. That small bit was enough to make her feel insufficient as a mother.

It felt as if Len was in a better place recently, but she couldn't help that those words gnawed at her mind, *I wish I was there for Len more often too. It's not that I didn't want to spend time with him, I needed to make sure we had what we needed to live.*

Mercy looked over at her baby boy, who was now the size of a man. *You lucked out, Mercy. Your son has turned out well, even without you being present in his life. Any parent would hope for their child to end up being like Len. Smart, responsible, and helpful.*

Mercy started to feel worse about the situation that put her son into his stressed existence and the trauma he went through. “Hey, kiddo! I just wanted to say I am so sorry I wasn’t around much when all of that stuff went down.”

Len turned toward his mother and smiled, “It’s okay, Mom. You got me where I needed to be. I’m cool with it. Henry was a big a help in building my self confidence. I really think you should go sit with him to talk, you know, about Dad, or whatever.”

“Ugh! Don’t even bring the guy up!” Mercy slowed to a stop at a traffic light. “I just feel so bad that I had no real plan laid out. I know you were left alone for the majority of the time and I just moved you from place to place so that you would be safe. So I would have peace of mind knowing you were okay as I went to work. It was so difficult for me when your dead beat dad left us. I needed to work more and we couldn’t afford a sitter or nanny. Camp was one of the only places I thought you would be safe…” The news report of the Pi‘ilewa massacre came back to the forefront of her thoughts. Mercy stopped speaking and started to cry.

“Mom? Light’s green!” Len rubbed his hand over his mother’s shoulder to comfort her. “None of the things that took place at camp were your fault. You were just trying to keep me safe, no one could have predicted that any of those things would happen. I'm okay now. And besides, I met some really nice people at those places you sent me to." Len could still see his mother was hurt by her failings at parenthood, "I never said thank you for all that you have done for me. I appreciate you."

A loud, deep honk blared from behind causing both passengers inside the run down sedan to jump. Mercy let her foot off the brake and smiled through the windshield. "I love you, Len."

Mercy's son smiled back at her and brought her doubts to rest when he responded definitively, "I love you too, Mom! I'm just grateful that you decided to stop dating all those losers just because you felt I needed a father figure in my life."

Len sat in his seat watching the homes grow shorter. His thoughts brought him to his true friend and hero, *I already had the opportunity to meet the one man I needed in my life.*

Len looked at his mom and saw how all the struggle she went through in her life made her appear so much older than she was, *I bet Kawika would've been good for my mom. He could have made her happy. We could have been a happy family.*

As the mother and son duo continued onward to camp, they made their way down a lonely stretch of road where Mercy let out a bizarre squeal. Len was disturbed over the odd sound and his mother's eyes were round and twinkling, "Oh my gosh! Isn't this where the police found Seth?"

Len eyed the intersecting street sign, "Kāo'oloa Road?"

"Yup! That's the one." Mercy's eyes darted from road side to road side. "There!" She pointed out toward the side of the bridge. "That's where the newscaster was being filmed!"

Len was surprised at how excited his mother was about her discovery. "Wow, Mom. I'd have thought that it was an episode of *Hawai'i Five-O* being filmed out here with the way you're acting. Star struck much?"

She shrugged calmly at her son's misapprehension, "Your mother could've been a starlet you know! It's the reason I came all the way out here to Hawai'i in the first place. I tried out for the lead in an Elvis Presley movie. Even though I was only cast as an extra in *Girls! Girls! Girls!* Elvis himself told me I had something *special*."

She thought about the life she would've had if she hadn't fallen in love with the islands and her estranged husband. The awkward silence fell over the car once more as she contemplated her life's decisions.

Len knew that his mom harbored some resentful feelings toward his father, but he didn't care either way. Even the time his dad was there, he wasn't truly around for them. He always seemed to be making plans or scheming about the next big deal. Kawika was the only semblance of a father figure Len ever had or wanted.

***

A trail of dust lifted into the air as they made their way through the campsite's gates. Mercy was surprised at how the area hadn't changed much after all that time. She could see the shape of a stout man carrying large duffles in each of his hands heading out from the main office.

"Wait, is that who I think it is?"

Len popped his car door open, "Yeah! It's John. He's the head of Camp Pi'ilewa. He's the guy that hired me." Len jumped out of his seat and retrieved his bag from the trunk.

"Eh, howzit, Mercy!? Long time no see!" The short, wide frame of John Chun waddled up beside the car where he beamed a huge smile at the driver.

"It's so nice to see you again too, John. How time has flown, am I right?" Mercy pawed at her hair trying her best to make herself look more presentable, "Oh! Congratulations on your promotion!" Mercy eyed John's uniform. "Does Len need to wear one like that as well?"

"Oh, haha, yeah. It's a new rule." John had a proud but uncomfortable grin on his face as he looked at Len, "What are they feeding these kids nowadays? They are so much bigger than they used to be. I thought that it'd make it easier to know who's a leader and who's a camper if we wore a uniform."

Len made his way back over toward the front of the car and bid John a good morning, "Hey there, boss!"

John gripped Len's hand and gave it a tight shake, "Mornin', Len! Why don't you get settled into the Kāne's Cabin and we'll start getting ready for the arrival of the campers. Yvonne is taking care of the Wāhine's Cabin, you'll meet her later. We're still waiting on a few others."

Len stuck his head into the car's driver window and kissed his mom on her cheek, "Don't forget the journal when you come back to get me." He patted John on the back and made his way toward the cabins.

John leaned his body up against the car causing Mercy's petite form to rattle inside a bit, "I was shocked to find your son's name among the other application's. I'm not going to lie, I was actually going to decline him as a hire, but we are short staffed. We have a pretty big group this go around, thank you Jesus, and we need any help we can get." John continued since he held Mercy's attention, "Nowadays, no one really has the time to watch their own kids during the summer break. Not even the camp's bad history can scare the customers off, you know what I mean?" After realizing what he had just said, John immediately clammed up and widened his eyes expecting to get a verbal lashing.

Mercy grit her teeth and smiled through the unintentional insult, "I'm happy that you accepted Len none the less. He has been very excited to come here to give back to his community and of course pay honor to Kawika."

John lifted his weight from the small silver car, "Kawika was a good guy. He was inspiring to everyone who stepped foot on these grounds. But, don't get me wrong, I am looking out for everyone's well being here at the camp, even Len's. Which is why I was going to dismiss his application. But, if you think he's okay with being here, I'm cool with it too."

"Len has been cleared by his doctor and I have also noticed he's been less moody as of late... Hey, John?" Mercy wanted to make a formal request, "Would it be alright if I stopped by and stayed the final night of camp? Len has been keeping a kind of journal and he wants to ceremonially burn away his writings in the camp fire for closure at the end of camp."

John's eyes grew once more, "Oh! Um, yeah, sure. I mean, as long as you don't mind sharing the main cabin with me and a couple other bodies."

Mercy put her car in reverse, "Thank you, John. I'd love to catch up more, but I gotta get back to town for work. I will see you folks at the end of camp."

John watched as Mercy made her way off site and muttered under his breath, "Man! She is *still* so hot."

'Ehā

April 7, 1978

Another night alone again. It's times like this that I start feeling like I'm being watched. I turn on all the lights to make the faces in the shadows disappear. I wish Mom was home more often, I'd rather talk to her than that old guy in his weird smelling office. Tomorrow is my next session with him. I wonder if he's going to read this.

April 8, 1978

He doesn't read the journal. He said it's a tool to help me voice my concerns. We talked about Benny, but I didn't really understand what happened. Dr. Campbell said it's possible I was distracted by my persistent thoughts. I guess. It's probably why I can't remember anything from school. He says I could be experiencing anxiety. I am strong and I can overcome. I like Dr. Campbell, he's nice.

April 10, 1978

Why is math so hard? Why does my teacher give homework on the weekends? I swear, if I ever become a teacher I would promise NEVER to give homework to my students. I am strong and I can overcome.

April 13, 1978

My math teacher is giving me a second chance on my test. He said he appreciated that I took time to talk to him about why I struggled. I need to sleep early tonight. I retest tomorrow morning before school starts. I am strong and I can overcome.

April 14, 1978

I scored a passing grade, Mom made me spaghetti for dinner to celebrate. I can't wait to tell Dr. Campbell at tomorrow's session.

April 15, 1978

I miss Kawika.

April 29, 1978

Dr. Campbell was disappointed that I hadn't seen him for the past few sessions. I told him Mom was too busy to bring me. He gave me his number and told me to call him if I can't be there. It was nice to talk to someone about the creatures that lurk in the shadows and speak through the wind. Dr. Campbell is very understanding about my brain's perception.

Mercy put her son's journal down and wiped the tears from her eyes, "I'm so sorry, Len." She never realized how much pain she had put her boy through. All this time she believed she was doing what was necessary for her family to thrive, but what her family really needed was time actually being a family. She thought about her husband, Kaulana, and how he just up and left them both alone. It finally became clear to her that she had done the exact same thing to her Len, the difference being he was just a child and he had no say in the whole affair.

A cool breeze brushed over Mercy's thigh like a hand. It was odd since her home was shut tight. Her skin prickled all over and an ominous feeling of being watched fell upon her. Mercy swallowed hard at the strange sensation. She placed her son's journal down on the coffee table and stood up with a heightened sense of awareness. Her ears felt as though they had shut out all sound except for the high pitched resonance vibrating deep within her canal.

Mercy made her way out of the living room and pawed at the light switch to turn off the lamps. The darkness gave breath to something sitting maliciously still, like a hunter training its weapon on his prey. She ran into her bedroom and slammed the door shut behind her, frantically locking it as soon as she entered.

Mercy took a deep breath, laughed at how silly she was, and turned off the light on her nightstand. She went to sleep that night much earlier than usual.

'Elima

After unpacking and prepping the Kāne's Cabin, Len made his way into the main office looking for the man in charge, "What else do we need to take care of, John?"

Len froze, mesmerized by a young woman sitting at the counter looking through some paperwork tapping a pencil up against her temple.

"Oh, good!" John stood up from his desk and held the half door open for Len to enter, "I need you to help Yvonne with organizing the campers into their activity teams. We'll have a total of four groups and fortunately we have about the same amount of boys and girls." John's face had a huge smile move across it, "I think our party night is going to be *very* interesting this year. Get started on that, I'll be right back."

Len walked over to Yvonne and stuck out his hand, "Hi, Yvonne. I'm Len."

Yvonne snapped out of her deep concentration and blurted, "Hi!" She stared at Len for an uncomfortable length of time, "Oh! I'm Yvonne." She shook Len's hand and wrestled her gaze away from the young man's face. "I'm going over the list of campers, trying to find suitable teams for the activities. John said he wanted groups to be diverse."

Just as they put the final touches on the list a loud slam came from the entrance disturbing the couple, "What's up, ladies!?"

Len stood in astonishment at the very recognizable, albeit undesirable, face from his past, "Brandon!?"

"That's my name, don't wear it out. What are you girls up to anyways?" Brandon kneed the saloon door open and waltzed over toward Yvonne, "Why, hello, gorgeous. The name's Brandon Alberts, as in Alberts' Aviation." He leaned in closer to Yvonne with a hellion grin.

"Your family owns the island's air transportation?" Yvonne's expression seemed impressed.

Brandon slinked back, "Well, we share the same spelling in our name, but there's no relation."

Rolling her eyes, Yvonne snapped up the list and made her way out of the office, "I'm going to get the okay on the groups, Len. I'll be right back."

Brandon started to laugh, "Len!? You're still going with that one, huh, princess?"

Len put his hands up in defeat, "Look, Brandon, I'm not here to start drama or get into any trouble-"

"So, why *are* you here then?" Brandon interrupted Len's statement. "Are you going to call the cops and start accusing others of something that you started!?"

Len stood up taller, "I'm not some little kid that can be pushed around any more, Brandon! You know I wasn't the one who started the problems all those years ago." Len tilted his gaze at the rude teen. "Wait! Why is it that you're even here?"

A creepy smile grew across Brandon's pock scarred face, "I needed to get away from my dad for the summer. I figured I could get free food and lodging, plus I'd get paid to work here for the summer."

"Emphasis on work, Brandon." Len was not going to let history repeat itself, so he decided to nip it in the bud, "We're all here to help, so there's no slacking off."

Len awaited Brandon's sarcastic retort, but he just took a relaxed position and explained, "Look, I'm just grateful to be here. Thanks to you, I no longer have a shield from my father and his nasty friends' drunken hostilities."

Len could understand why the Alberts' were the way they were. "Look, I'm sorry about your brother-"

Brandon slapped Len's arm, "What's done is done. I just don't want you continually spreading lies about what happened that night. Yeah, my brother hated you, but I know for a fact that Seth had nothing to do with his death or the death of your pedophile boyfriend."

Len balled his fist, "You think I told the cops Seth did it!? Well, I didn't!"

Brandon shook his head in disbelief, "I was there that night too, you know. I saw what you saw and I saw that Seth was innocent. You could've always said it wasn't him. Told. The. Truth!"

Len shut down. His mind replayed the scenario over in a split second, *Yes, I didn't see Seth commit those attacks, but I also couldn't get anyone else to believe what I actually witnessed. I tried to tell the police, I tried to tell my mom and I even tried to tell my therapist.*

Henry's voice replayed in Len's head, *Our minds are so powerful that they can create false visions and self harm that are veiled by fantastical delusions.*

"Pssssh! See!? " Brandon flicked his hand in Len's face, "You probably threw Seth under the bus."

Len made himself clear, "I never, ever said it was Seth that committed those crimes. The police did their investigation and found Seth to be the guilty party, and the police knew that you would've never killed your own brother."

"Hey! What the hell is going on in here with you two!?" John had entered into the office after hearing raised voices. "Len!?"

"Sorry, John! It was just a small misunderstanding," Len looked at Brandon.

"Yeah, sorry bossman. We were just catching up, the old place gives us the nostalgic feels, am I right?" Brandon flexed his eyebrows at Len and smiled from the corner of his mouth. "See!? It's all good in the neighborhood."

"Good!" John bellowed while prodding his finger at the Alberts boy, "I don't want to see any trash from you Brandon! We are all adults here, it's time to start acting like it. I took you on because we needed the help and because I know your situation. This is the time to do right and find a direction in your life. Maybe one of these kids can help you find a passion. Now go to the ramp and lower the canoes."

Len watched Brandon make his way down to the lake, "I'm sorry, John. I had no idea Brandon was here or that he was going to dredge up the past."

"Ah, it's not your fault," John shook his head. "Look, Len, Brandon promised he wouldn't be a hassle. He told me his personal troubles and I let him know that if he starts anything, he's fired. So, let's work our way through this, okay? Keep things peaceful, Len. I'm counting on you to not start anything. We can't afford to lose a body this summer, but if I have to, I'll drop him."

Len squished his face, "It won't be necessary, John. It'll be alright. I'll just make sure to keep my distance as much as possible."

"Very good to hear!" John squeezed Len's shoulder, "Brandon will be sleeping in my cabin, so you'll be in charge of the boys at night. Is that okay with you?"

Len smiled, "Yes, sir! Not a problem at all. Thank you."

"Okay, take the cart and go check the trail before it gets too dark. Make sure there's no downed trees on the path or trash in the bins. Extra liners are in the bed of the cart. I want to make sure everything is perfect for tomorrow." John handed the cart keys over to Len, "Low gear on the way back down that trail. That little truck hauls and I don't want you losing control and crashing into anything."

‘Eono

May 13, 1978

I spoke to Dr. Campbell about the Alberts brothers. It felt so good to finally talk to someone that is supportive and could understand how terrifying these two were and how miserable they made me feel. The only other person I could confide in was Kawika. Dr. Campbell told me that the only one you need to make happy in life is yourself. Once you find happiness, you can begin to spread that to others. I am strong and I can overcome.

May 14,1978

I just woke up to a terrifying vision. I was dreaming about being chased through the forest. I could feel my heart pounding in my chest. I opened my eyes and saw the face of Burden Alberts staring right back at me. He hovered above my bed for what felt like forever. I'm not sure if I should tell Dr. Campbell, I'm definitely not telling Mom. She thinks I'm crazy enough. Maybe it's because I talked about him yesterday, maybe my mind is scaring me from being happy? Maybe the stress of finals is causing my mind to break? I need my rest! I am strong and I can overcome.

May 14, 1978

I can't believe this is happening. I woke up this morning to the face of Burden Alberts floating above my bed again. I decided to run extra laps at P.E. to tire myself out for bed.

Now that my day is over, I'm trying to go to sleep and every time I close my eyes I see his evil face staring at me through the dark. When I open my eyes and turn on the light I can hear his voice in my head repeating "kill you" over and over! My brain is sabotaging my happiness. Mom's not home and it's too late to call Dr. Campbell. I don't know what to do. I am strong and I can overcome.

May 14, 1978

I can't do it, I decided I'm staying up the rest of the night. I'm so exhausted.

May 15, 1978

It's officially Sunday morning, and I still refuse to shut my eyes, at least not until my mom comes home. Where is she?

May 15,1978

Mom burst into my room scearming at me, askeb if I was going to waist my day sleepign. If only knew I had just fallen aslep. I aked her were she was last night and it only made her more upset. I'm glad finals are almost oven. I m storng and I can overcom.

Mercy let out a quivering breath. These writings were becoming heart wrenching for her. "How could I have done this to my boy!? I'm so grateful that he had someone to protect him." Mercy laid her son's diary on her lap and drew in a deep breath, "I could have used a Kawika of my own in my life. Kaulana…"

The lonely woman's thoughts were paused when she heard the faint sounds of footsteps moving around in Len's room.

Mercy placed Len's journal on the coffee table and quietly moved over to his bedroom door. She could make out someone touching things inside her son's sleeping area as if opening drawers and containers, rummaging through them. Reaching over for the broom that leaned against her doorframe with one hand, she turned the doorknob at a cautious pace with the other. When the door's knob froze at the extent of its turn, Mercy pressed her way in and found the small space devoid of life. Nothing appeared to have been disturbed or out of the ordinary.

She stepped inside and felt a chilly air flowing about that gave her chicken skin up her arms and thighs. A loud slap from behind caught the confused woman's attention. Mercy spun around at high speed expecting to find an intruder, however, she observed no one there.

Mercy returned to the living room and was shocked to find her son's journal face down on the floor beside the coffee table. Her eyes widened to allow a larger viewpoint. She glanced around the small room as she gripped the broom handle tight and moved toward Len's journal laying eerily still on the shaggy carpet.

She bent over to retrieve the book and found that it was opened up on a particular page. Just before the apprehensive woman could read the words in the book, her telephone blared through the silence of the house causing her to scream.

Mercy closed the notebook and placed it back onto the center of the coffee table. She ran over to the kitchen to answer the call, "Hello?" The static from the earpiece told Mercy someone was on the other side, yet they did not respond to her greeting, "Yes? Can I help you? Hello?" Mercy's heart pounded deep in her chest as the hiss continued to get louder.

A small rumble made its way out of the receiver growing into an angry, deep wail. The scream was so loud Mercy dropped the hand set and bawled her fists over her ears. The sound had somehow transferred from the phone and was now screeching inside her head. She began to scream over the devilish cry and soon found that she was the only one producing any noise.

Mercy grabbed the phone and heard a monotonous hum of the dial tone, "Hello!?" Her mind started to fill with terrible thoughts. *What the heck was that? What's going on? Am I going nuts?*

An out of place slap cut through the silence once more calling for Mercy's attention. Upon investigation, she saw her son's diary laying on the floor next to the coffee table in the exact same place she had found it earlier. Again, it appeared to have opened on the same page as before. The event frightened Mercy so much she placed the book back onto the small wooden table and retreated into her room.

Mercy sat on her bed massaging her temples, "Get a grip, lady! You're starting to lose it." Taking a deep breath, she paused to collect herself. Mercy looked at her alarm clock and noticed the time. The day was still a bit young, but after what she just experienced Mercy was alright with starting her day early, "Oh well. I guess I'd rather be at work with other people than at home alone right now anyways."

After putting herself together, Mercy opened the her bedroom door to look outside. Everything had become dead silent, yet she still felt as though someone was lurking about. She snatched up her keys and purse and flew out of the front door.

'Ehiku

"Alright, Camp Leaders! Are we ready to receive our young guests!?" John hopped out of the main office rubbing his hands together in anticipation. He took a look around the grounds and smiled with pride.

Everything looks great! John thought, as he eyed his counselors lining the open area dressed in their mandatory camp uniforms.

"Looking sharp people!" He could hear the whirring of engines approaching from the highway. "Right on time!" John made his way along the wooden fence to meet the incoming cavalcade.

Two packed buses approached the camp's entry. Through the rectangular windows of the transports, the children's little heads bobbed up and down from the uneven dirt path. The orange-yellow carriers pulled up beside each other and released a flood of excited adolescents. Their voices destroyed the once quiet calm of Camp Pi'ilewa.

John jumped onto the fence connected to the camp sign and started to give his introduction by pulling out a megaphone. The high pitch shriek from the device caused the youths to turn quietly toward the noise.

"Welcome, to Camp Pi'ilewa! I am your Head Camp Counselor, Jonathan Chun. You can all call me John. Now, we need to get organized so you all can make yourselves comfortable for your stay. Camp Leader Len, please raise your hand!" Len smiled and lifted up his arm. "Camp Leader Brandon, please raise your hand!" Brandon pointed a finger above his head. "Len and Brandon will help you to offload your belongings from the buses. Once you have your bags you will meet with Camp Leader Yvonne if you are a young lady. Yvonne, please raise your hand!" Yvonne curtseyed with a large smile. "The young men will come over to Camp Leader Paula. Paula, please raise your hand!" Paula raised both arms rotating her hands at the wrist. "You will then be escorted over to your designated cabin where you can choose a bed to sleep in and a foot locker to store your belongings. We have twenty minutes before we begin our tour of the camp grounds, so please do not waste any time. You will have an opportunity to get acquainted with each other at dinner, so quickly and quietly get your things squared away. Alright! Let's move, people!"

Within a few short minutes the noise had moved from the entrance of the camp into the Kāne and Wāhine cabins. The entire experience had brought Len back to the first day he came to camp as a guest. He could see himself, bright eyed and hopeful that he'd have an amazing experience at Pi'ilewa Point. He was surprised at John's delivery. It was nearly identical to Kawika's from several years back and the nostalgia helped warm his heart.

Len felt a tug on his shirt's sleeve. He turned to see a cute red headed girl distraught with tears streaming down her face. "Excuse me, I didn't see my bag. I think someone may have taken it by accident."

"Hey, honey! What's your name?" Len leaned over to comfort the sad child.

"Mercy," the little one replied.

"Well, young lady, don't you have a beautiful name!" The girl smiled and Len could see she felt a little better. "Now, you must have rode in on this one, correct!?"

Len walked her over to the under carriage of the bus that Brandon helped to unload. He propped the storage doors open and found two bags that were slightly hard to see because of their color.

"Oh! Look at that..." Len stuck his body into the coffer, "Hmm, this says 'Andrew' and this one-"

The little girl jumped for joy, "My bag!"

She hiked the hefty pack over her shoulders and made her way back toward the cabins holding Len's hand. Len could see a young man with an odd expression searching the hands of his fellow cabin-mates.

"Mercy, this is your cabin. Go put your things away, I need to return this to Andrew." Mercy smiled at Len and ran into the Wāhine's cabin.

He looked across the walkway and hollered, "Yo! My man!"

The confused boy looked at Len's hand holding his suitcase, "Hey! Thanks! I thought someone took my stuff."

"No worries, Andrew. Go take your bag inside and choose your bed." Len presented the cabin to the young man with a sweeping of his arm.

"You can call me Andy. You're Len, right?" Andy presented his hand.

Len grabbed the hand of the tidy boy, "Yes, it's a pleasure to meet you, Andy. I hope you're ready to get a little dirty."

Andrew's face went pale, "I would hope not! That idea frightens me."

Len watched Andy make his way into the cabin and saw John walking over from the girl's side. "Nice save, Len. The young lady told me about you helping her find her luggage. I'm on my way to talk to Brandon about this."

Len stopped John, "Hey, boss, would it be alright if we just keep this between us? I don't want anything to increase Brandon's dislike of me more than he already does."

"How magnanimous of you. It's something Kawika would also do on many occasions to keep the peace around here. He'd always say-"

Len interrupted his boss' impression to finish the quote, "We do live on a small island after all." The rookie camp leader smiled as he looked toward the ground.

John could see that his young employee was still dealing with Kawika's absence, "The guy really made an impact on you, didn't he?"

"More than you know, boss. In a lot of ways, you could say he was my guardian angel." Moisture built on the corners of Len's eyes.

John tried his best to lighten the mood, "I remember watching his interactions with you. It was different than with the rest of the campers, even from previous years. He really found a kindred spirit in you. It made me appreciate each camper as an individual rather than just as a group. It's something I will always treasure."

Len could feel the heaviness lifting the more he talked to John, "I always found him to be like an older brother or like a father figure type. Something I've never really had in my life. I'll always hold those memories of him inside," Len tapped his finger onto his chest.

"Same. The guy was inspiring to say the least. We can share our stories about Kawika when we burn your book, if that's okay?" John gripped Len's arm and nodded in hopes it would be alright for him to join in.

Len smiled as a tear fell onto the soil, "That would be awesome."

'Ewalu

"Mershi? Hūi, Mershi!?!"

The loud boisterous voice of Tita wrapped around the tiled walls of the laundry mat. Mercy noticed Tita was dressed to kill as she slowly made her way down the dimly lit launderette. She already knew what Tita was going to say.

"Mershi!" Tita's voice became slithery as she spoke through her nose, "Could I ax you fo' one big fayvah?"

Mercy looked completely drained, the bags forming under her eyes told a tale of someone needing a long break. "Please, Tita, not tonight! I need some sleep."

Tita stood up offended, with her inch long fake eye lashes fluttering as if they were putting out a fire, "Girl, I didn't efen ax yayt! Why you actin' sho crayshi?"

"Tita, your shift is coming up and I can already see you're planning on going out clubbing. I can't fill in for you tonight," Mercy pleaded with the amply shaped twenty-something wearing what could only be described as form fitting circus pants.

"Look, troublemaker, I am acshually goy-ahng-ah date wid Junior Boy!" Tita rested her weight on the counter flap causing it to bow downward. "Mershi, thish ish whad I have been working up too, girl! Besidesh,"

Tita snapped her finger's in Mercy's face, "You old, you ain't got no plansh!"

The piercing in Tita's mouth made her sound even dumber than usual and her breath reeked from the infection on her tongue. Mercy made a face from the smell, "I'd love to help, Tita, and you know I usually cover for you, but today has just been-"

Tita could see her coworker was going through something serious, "Hey, shish. Ish everyding okay? Ish it yo-wah handshome shun? Ish he sheeing thingsh again?"

Mercy maintained her composure as she ignored Tita's inappropriate probing. She thought about how it wasn't her son experiencing strange things, it was actually her this time. *If I go home, who's to say I won't hear those sounds once more?* Mercy looked back down at the counter. She thought about the writing in her boy's journal and how that one night she covered for Tita was the evening Len was experiencing night terrors. *Was a slightly bigger paycheck worth my son's loss of faith in me?*

A voice even louder and more obnoxious than Tita's filled the air in the small room, "Ayargh! Tita! We gonna miss da buffet, woman!"

Junior's six foot eight, three hundred-eighty pound frame blocked out what little pale fluorescent light the ceiling offered. Mercy lowered her gaze to the counter

-top as she greeted the immense hulk of a man, "Hey, Junior."

It was always difficult for Mercy to look Junior in his eyes, not just because his cheeks made it harder to see them by pressing his lids shut, but because she always felt he was kind of into her and she was in no way interested in him.

"Wassup, Mercy? My fada says you're doing a crate chob keeping da playsh clean." Junior tried his best to wink seductively at Mercy, but he just looked gross and uncomfortably swollen to the single mother.

Tita stared at her tired, old co-worker with the face of yearning. Mercy finally gave in, "Okay, Tita, on one condition. You take my shift tomorrow night."

"Ready fo' rock, Junior boy!?" Tita did a small dance rotating her hips with her arms above her head.

"I'm ready fo' eat!" Junior clicked his tongue at Mercy as he turned. He wrapped his left arm around Tita pulling her away from the counter. The bill of Junior's hat banged into the tube light above the service counter knocking it loose, causing it to flicker. Mercy watched as the two massive forms exited the wash area.

"Damn it."

The lonely woman looked up at the ceiling light as it buzzed and flickered at random intervals. She grabbed the footstool from behind the baskets and lifted the counter-flap. After adjusting her step, she made her way up cautiously and began fiddling with the long bulb. The sound of two static pops sent a small electrical discharge outward, zapping Mercy in the wrist.

"Ow! You son of a..." the entire row of lights went dark and the air conditioner went dead. "Oh great! This is just fantastic."

Mercy made her way down the short ladder in the dark and tripped on the last step hitting her ribs against the counter. Before she could say anything, the sound of footsteps could be heard moving into the shop.

"Hello?" she called out blindly as she rubbed her side. No one answered back to the shopkeep, but the steps continued echoing inward.

"I'm sorry, you'll need to come back later, your clothes are going to have to wait until I get the lights back on."

The steps moved even closer, but when Mercy got a clear shot of the entryway she couldn't see a soul. She tried once more to caution the potential client, "Could you please give me a moment? I don't want you or anyone else to slip and fall!" The steps finally came to a standstill. She peered through the quiet darkness and everything stood uncomfortably motionless.

The hatch of an oversized drying machine clicked a familiar sound of the handle being pulled open. The silhouette of the circular door slowly swung outward with a long high pitched squeal. Mercy witnessed no one there operating the machine.

"Hello?"

The confused woman nervously walked toward the suspicious activity. Hard banging whirled around inside what she believed was an empty drum. It was as if a customer were loading the dryer with sneakers or a large animal was making a nest inside. Mercy lined herself up with the opening of the machine. Inspecting through the inky black interior conjured no visual except for two dull lights floating at the center of the barrel.

The street lamp from outside did not provide enough illumination to see what was making all of the noise, in fact it made it harder to see anything inside the shop. As Mercy squinted, she leaned forward to make out what was emitting the slight gleam. The two dull lights became orbs and began glowing brighter than a wick. Mercy stepped toward the lifeless tumbler and could finally make out a pair of intense yellow eyes glaring right back at her.

Slow, heavy breathing lurched outward flowing from the dark hole, causing Mercy to freeze in terror. Choking on her words, she tried to call out for help. She attempted to loosen her vocal chords by hemming some very hoarse vibrations at the back of her throat, but still, her words could not escape her lips. A prickly, cold sensation wrapped itself around Mercy causing her to shiver unintentionally in her paralyzed condition. She gasped for air, but fear held tight to her windpipe.

A deep growl was hurled from the opening of the dryer as a pitch black fog gushed into Mercy's face. The force of the viscous air knocked her back so hard that she hit her head on the linoleum. Mercy watched as the black smoke continued to pour out of the dryer. It flew mere feet above her, screaming an agonizing shrill, swirling and undulating throughout the laundromat. The doors on the washers and dryers began to slam open and shut repeatedly. Mercy closed her eyes and began to cry out for help.

The black fog continued its torrent of shrieks as it whipped furiously around the wash room. Mercy prayed silently for it to cease and as fast as the assault came, it stopped.

Two cold hands gripped Mercy tight at the wrists, "Leave me alone!"

Mercy opened her eyes to the concerned face of an old Portuguese woman, "Ai, Céus!"

"Oh! I'm so sorry, Ma'am."

Mercy looked around the shop and found the lights were all back on and the air conditioner was struggling to keep the premises cool. A crowd of onlookers were amassing outside. Mercy hopped onto her feet and observed that the smoke that was lashing viciously about a moment earlier had completely disappeared.

Mercy calmed the frightened samaritan, "I'm okay now, I just fell and hit my head. I'll be alright."

Mercy assisted the elderly woman from the shop and stared back inside at the empty launderette. *What the heck is going on!?* Mercy touched the part of her head that hit the floor. There was a little bit of blood on her fingers, but nothing too serious, "This is going to be a *very* long night."

Fortunately, no other odd occurrences transpired throughout the remainder of Mercy's double shift, but because she was on edge throughout the entire night she had completely exhausted herself.

The sun was already up for an hour when Mercy wrestled the door to her apartment open. It felt like someone were pressing up against the entry as she tried pushing her way in.

"Sheesh! I must be finished," she muttered as she made her way into her living space.

Mercy eyed the notebook suspiciously as it rested on the coffee table. Without taking her eyes off of it, she plopped her keys on the desk and hung her purse on a hook. She checked the hall with a fast motion and glanced back at the diary.

"It really feels as though something is pushing me to read that thing. It's just going to have to wait. I need to get some sleep first. I can't even keep my eyes open."

Mercy let out a huge yawn. She shut the door to her bedroom and fell flat on her face burying her cheeks into the bed. Within seconds she was fast asleep.

***

A loud slam on the bedroom door rocked Mercy's mattress and popped her ears. She lifted her head from her pillow and looked at the alarm radio sitting on her nightstand.

"What!? It's three already!?" Placing her hand gently on the back of her head, she began picking some dried blood out of her hair. "I need a shower…"

Mercy flopped over and found Len's diary laying on the corner of her mattress, opened up on the same page it had fallen onto earlier. She flew off the bed and immediately spun around looking for evidence of a home intruder. She reached over and grabbed the clay art piece Len made in elementary school from her nightstand. Holding it above her head she made her way slowly around her home. Checking her entire apartment and seeing that her locks weren't tampered with, Mercy shook her head and sighed, "You're really starting to lose it, lady."

After her shower, Mercy wrapped herself in a robe and nestled into her chair with a cup of chamomile tea sitting nearby. She pulled the notebook onto her lap and started to read where the book had fallen open.

January 6, 1979

Dr. Campbell is proud of my first semester grades. He said I'm doing so much better and he told me that I should start writing about the events that happened at Camp Pi'ilewa. He said it might make it easier for me to discuss at our next session. I don't think I would have been able to do it a year ago, but I believe that I am strong and I can overcome. I think I'll start with when I knew Kawika was my hero.

On our first day at camp, a girl nearly drowned at the lake. We were on the walkabout tour learning about the camp's locations. When we got to the water, I heard the girl say she didn't like the lake because she didn't know how to swim very well. The counselors took us out on the dock to tell us about rules and safety.

Burden Alberts and Seth Pedrina must've heard what that girl had said as we made our way over to the dock, because the next thing you know those two boys tossed her right off the back end of the pier where none of the camp counselors could see. Her body sank like a stone. Burden laughed the whole time with a disgusting smile on his face, and Seth just looked at the water like it was some foreign material. I watched as Kawika dove in and within seconds pulled that girl right out. She was unconscious and she wasn't breathing, but Kawika pressed her chest and the water flew out of her mouth like Nalomeli Springs.

Counselor Craig called out for anyone who saw what happened, so I raised my hand, but before I could say anything, this kid walks over and presses his shoulder hard into my chest. It was Brandon Alberts, but I didn't know the guy was Burden's brother yet. He told me that I'd be in a world of hurt if I said anything. He told me the same thing would happen to me if I snitched. That girl went home that very same day, never saw her ever again.

That night at dinner, Brandon sat with Burden and Seth. He whispered to the two other boys and then he pointed straight at me to make it clear that I nearly told on them. Burden gave me the most frightening stare I had ever seen, even till today I have never seen a look like that. A look of pure evil.

It was lights out, and I nearly fell asleep, when I felt my arms snap away from my body and pulled in opposite directions. Seth held my right arm, Brandon had my left, and staring at me from above my head was Burden. He told me that if I wanted to make it back home alive, I should keep my mouth shut and stay out of his way. He pressed a pillow with all his weight over my face and held it there until I almost blacked out. I thought I was going to die that night. All I could think about was Mom at that moment. I thought about her living at home all alone.

When the three boys finally let me go I struggled for air and I thought about that girl who nearly died at the lake and how I was the only witness. I looked around the darkened cabin and wondered if anyone saw what had just happened to me. I needed to warn them not to say anything before they get hurt too.

Mercy's heart throbbed with an intense surge. "Both of those boys deserved what they got!" Mercy's head burned, "I pray my son never has to see that other Alberts' kid ever again. I can't believe the degenerate offspring that came from that vile family nearly killed that little girl *and* my son. How could their parents not see that their children needed serious psychological help!?"

Mercy stopped herself for a short moment. "Len was heading down that same path. He was picking fights, he was skipping school, he..." Mercy hugged the diary for a short moment to catch her breath, "But, he is alright now. You got him the help he needed and he is alright now." Kaulana's face popped into her head, "Damn you, Kaulana! Damn you for destroying your family! I will never forgive you for abandoning us." Tears rolled down the distraught mother's face, "Geez, I need some air." She tossed the journal back onto the coffee table and left her apartment with her purse and keys.

ʻEiwa

It surprised many of the campers that the night air was so chilly up at the fire pit. Len could hear a small voice complaining, "It's summer, why is it so cold!?"

The entire group made a tight huddle around the large campfire finishing up with their sweet dessert of marshmallows, chocolate, and graham crackers. The teens who were done burned the tops of their barbecue sticks in the fire and wiggled the glowing tips through the sky.

A shooting star crossed above the cliffs of Piʻilewa Point, "You kids don't get views like this in the city!" John got a chuckle out of the campers as they sat in awe of the beauty of mother nature.

Brandon looked over at the big guy, "Hey, bossman, why don't you give us all a small sample of your creepy camp stories? I'm sure the kids would love it!" Brandon stretched his face unnaturally in the fire's light making a couple of girls lower their eyes with worry.

John sighed, "Well now, I'm afraid that's where I fail as a camp counselor. Unfortunately, I never was one for understanding the intricacies of story telling. Besides, I was one of those people that would hide my head and cover my ears during all the scary parts. Those roles were reserved for Camp Leaders like Kawika."

"Oh come on, bossman! You must know at least one gruesome tale!" Brandon urged John to think hard by tapping his finger on the side of his head.

"Like I said, I'd cover my ears during the scary parts, so I don't know exactly how the stories would end. Anyways, these kids don't want to hear spooky stories... do you?" John could hear a sea of groans coming from the mouths of his young guests. He raised his arms, "My mistake."

"You're losing the audience, John! They're itchin' for a fright!" Brandon wanted to meet the demands of his lowly subjects, "And, what about you... Lynette?" He snorted out of his nose awaiting another failure of a response. "Aw, let me guess. You're too scared and you don't want to pee pee your panty in front of all these children." To his surprise, Len stepped forward.

"We are all so *very* fortunate..." Len scolded the children. He picked up a decent sized twig and pushed it around at the base of the fire. The spastic movement caused embers to lift into the air where they slowly ceased to emit light. He returned his gaze up to the sky. With rounded eyes he spoke ominously, "The moon still sits plump in the sky, gracing us with her bright smile."

The kids stared up at the partially lit orb and were startled back to Len as he hollered into the night sky,

“Mahalo, e Mahina!” He cast his gaze at the bewildered audience. "We should all be grateful. It is not yet the night of Kāne, the night when the veil between our world and the spirit plane, where ghosts, monsters and all sorts of creatures dwell, grows so thin that they can travel between their realm and ours.”

Len pushed the small branch he was holding deeper into the fire pit increasing the height of the flames. The warm glow had shadows dancing across the young man’s face building terror in the hearts of the onlookers.

“The huaka‘i pō traverse the area around our camp on those nights, searching the land with reasons of their own. Maybe to even spill the blood of the innocent!” Len slapped his hands on his lap in cadence, “The sound of the pahu is your first warning! This is when you have a chance to get as far away from their path, as fast as you can!”

The young story teller started to growl in his throat, humming to the beat he made with his palms. “The oli kahiko is your second chance to remove yourself from their path and find yourself a safe place to hide…”

Len tore the ignited stick from the campfire. The flame wrestled about the tip of the wooden spike as he raised his arm up the mountain’s slope toward Pi‘ilewa point, “When you see the torches burning above head, it is already too late!”

Creating a commotion, Len cast the entire stick into the blaze and removed his jacket and slippers with force and speed, "The only thing you can do now to save yourself from 'oi'o, is get naked and prostrate yourself off of the path..." Len pointed his index finger at his crotch, "or you can suffer the humiliation of appearing simple by pissing in your pants." The troupe started laughing, but stopped when Len pulled that same finger over his lips.

"Ssssssh! The last thing you want is for the night marchers to hear you, because they will surely find you." Len slid his right arm into his sleeve without bringing notice to the campers, "And if they do find you, you better hope you have royal blood, because if you don't have an ancestor in the ranks of that procession, your life is forfeit and they run you through with the ihe!" Len pushed his right arm outward extending his uniform at his chest simulating being stabbed by a spear from behind. "Nooooo!"

The campers clapped at the conclusion of Len's exhilarating tale. The youngest of the group were in tears while the rest were rubbing the chicken skin off of their arms and legs.

John jumped to make his final announcement to conclude their day, "Alright gang, please clean up your area and make your way over to your cabin leaders.

We have an early day tomorrow so we need you all to get some rest. Lights out in half an hour."

The group sighed a breath of relief as they got ready to go to bed. Wary of the sudden appearance of ghostly torchlight, many of the campers kept a watchful eye toward the tree line running up the mountain while they packed up their belongings.

Brandon pretended to be unimpressed by Len's exhibition, but John walked over with a face of utter shock, "I couldn't look away. I may have nightmares tonight, but at least I know how that story ends." John bent over to grab some food stuffs sitting beside the fireplace, "Alright Brandon, let's get the pit cleaned up. We can't have any loose trash out here and this fire needs to be doused."

As the mass of children flocked toward their cabin leader's, Yvonne rubbed her shoulder up against Len's arm, "Gnarly story telling, creep!" She smiled at Len and it made his cheeks turn red. "I can't wait to hear more."

Yvonne was pushed out of the way by a short body, "Oh my gosh, Len! Your story was amazing!"

"Thanks, Mercy!" Len received a high five from his little buddy, "Are you sure it isn't going to give you nightmares?"

"Are you kidding me!? I'll probably never sleep again!" Mercy took Yvonne by the hand. "Let's go, cabin mama. I'm staying in the bed with *you* tonight."

Yvonne was pulled back to the Wāhine Cabin as a group of nervous boys lined up behind Len. "Alright guys, let's move it."

Brandon watched Len leading his group back to the cabins with disdain. His plan to embarrass the guy had backfired and it appeared that the children at camp now adored Len. He kicked a rock into the hearth as John collected the trash around the fire pit.

"Brandon! I need you to put out that fire. So, stop fooling around."

Brandon glanced back up at Len who caused his chest to burn and heart to thump in frustration, "Enjoy the limelight while you can, Elenor."

John gave Brandon a look of concern, "Did you hear what I said?"

Brandon shook his head and quickly grabbed the bucket of sand, "Oh right! You got it, bossman!"

'Umi

Mercy returned home with a container of won ton mein and a side order of roast pork. She saw the little red light of her answering machine flashing in the dark room as she flicked on the light switch. "Lord, I hope it isn't Len."

The machine blared a sustained high note just before the sound of an older man's voice cut in, "Hey, ah, Mercy? I'm kinda wontering wea you stay? Your shiff was at nine, putt I don't see you. Oh wait, is dat chu?" There was a moment where only static could be heard, "No, das not chu. Kimmie a call, please."

The machine beeped again, "Nine thirty-seven P.M."

"Ugh! Thanks a lot, Tita!" Mercy threw her food in the refrigerator and flew out of the apartment once again.

She came upon the laundromat and saw her boss standing behind the counter holding a fly swatter. "To'o, I'm so sorry! I thought I had the night off-"

The old man pushed the counter-flap open and stepped out from behind the work station. He looked at Mercy and sighed, "You want tah night off, I keeve you efery night off! Ms. To'o not waiting fo' me, I get home late den I no moah palusami. She eat 'em all!"

Mercy huffed, "I'm so sorry, To'o."

"You can pee sorry when I come pack hungkry." The shop owner made his way slowly out of his cleaner grumbling to himself. The moment he stepped foot outside, the fluorescent lights flickered overhead and the air conditioner made a sound as if it were about to shut down.

Mercy looked up and said a small prayer, "Please, oh please! Don't do this tonight." The lights steadied and the hum of the cooling unit decided to persevere. "Oh, thank you, Lord!" Mercy mouthed as she grabbed hold of a broom to start sweeping out the lobby.

Throughout the night people came and went as usual. Only when the store was empty, did Mercy see strange shadows moving about the shop from the corner of her eye. She thought she was going crazy, so to occupy her mind she reached over for an old magazine that had sat in the shop for months. After reading through it for the fourth time Mercy finally started to drift off. Her head bobbed, startling her awake just before her forehead could connect with the surface of her work table.

"Aruuh!"

The random outburst caused Mercy to jolt nearly giving her whiplash. The jostle gave her a shot of adrenaline that pinned her eyes wide open.

"Mershiii!!!" Tita waltzed her way to the back of the store, "Hahaha! Caught chu shlackin'! Rishe an' shine shleepy head." Tita slapped the counter with her hands as if playing the drums causing a greater ruckus. Mercy gave the stink eye to her irresponsible co-worker. "Whoah, shishtah… You look like you could yoush shum resh."

Mercy snarled, "Tita, I asked you to cover for me last night! When I got back home with dinner there was a message from To'o because you were a no show. Where the heck were you!?"

Tita started to laugh inappropriately at Mercy's misfortune, "Oh my goodnesh! I choadally fo'got!" Tita laughed even harder. "Well, ish a good ding you washent doing anyding important lash night."

"To'o threatened to fire me, Tita!" Mercy's face was sour.

"Hey, hey, hey." Tita rubbed Mercy's sleeve, "Don't look at me laddat, yo' faysh looksh chairable." The flamboyant young woman flew the counter door open and pushed Mercy out of the back area, "Go home already, you making me feel show tie-yed."

***

Mercy returned home fuming, "I can't believe it! The nerve of Tita!" She slammed her keys on the counter and threw her purse on the hook. The bag slipped from the curved arm and flopped onto the floor. “Ugh!” Mercy just left the handbag where it fell.

She looked inside the refrigerator and saw the fattened noodles in her won ton mein, “Damn it!”

She reached over for the box of roast pork but the grease from the pork made the container slippery. The package fell to the ground and Mercy watched the golden brown roast pork roll out onto the kitchen floor. Tension built in her neck and shoulders. The burned out woman slammed the refrigerator door shut which made a few magnets jump from the metal surface joining the the pork on the tile below.

The day was long and Mercy just wanted it all to go away. She stormed through the apartment making her way to her bedroom, but noticed that her son’s diary was no longer on the coffee table. She looked under the table and couch, and checked between the pillows of the furniture, but still came up empty handed.

“I know I left the darn thing right here. Where could it have gone?”

‘Umi kūmākahi

Within the next couple of weeks, things had gotten pretty routine at camp. All of the children were having a great time with their leaders as they taught the young ones all they had to impart.

Len took notice of Little Miss Mercy, a nickname the girl earned when Len shared that it was his mom’s name too, clinging to Yvonne at every step like a siamese twin. Mercy would even change her facial expressions to match Yvonne’s tone as she spoke with the other members of their group. It brought back memories of his interactions with Kawika and how he often stayed close to him. It wasn’t necessarily because Kawika was his only friend, Len had lots of pals, it was mostly because, at that time, Kawika was someone he felt filled a need in his life.

John walked over and bumped Len, “Something on your mind?”

Len snapped out of his contemplation responding with a single name, “Kawika.”

The head camp leader looked down and shared a heavy breath, "I know part of the reason you requested to work here was to get some closure, heck I'd do the same thing if I had that opportunity." John thought about how he had always wanted to tell Len's mother how he felt about her. Then he wondered if Len could see that he had a deep interest in Mercy, "I hope I haven't done anything, or not done anything, to strain our relationship in the past, Len."

The young man turned to his boss and friend, "What do you mean!?"

"Well, I know what happened all those years ago has scared you, heck it scared me too!" John tilted his gaze at his subordinate, "I wish I could've done more that night… that summer. If I weren't so involved in trying to impress Kawika, I probably would've seen the signs of that Pedrina kid." John exhaled, "That was my first year as a counselor. I saw how Kawika had the camp running like a well oiled machine. It was impressive to me. He commanded respect from his team and the campers. Well, you know first hand. Anyway, I'm sorry that I couldn't be there more for you during that time."

Len could see that John also cared a lot for him as well. He wrapped his arm across his boss' back to show how much he appreciated John too.

"You saved us that night. Me and Brandon and the others, you took care of the whole cabin. It was a lot to ask for your first camp leader gig."

"My first *job*, actually!" John pat Len on his back. "My perspective on the innocence of children changed that day. That Seth kid was enormous for a twelve year old."

Len snorted, "He had the mind of a four year old, though."

"Yeah, a psychotic four year old." John tried to make the mood lighter.

Len's eye was caught by Brandon watching them from the cereal table. "So, why'd he decide to work camp this summer? And, why on earth did you take him on as a leader!?"

John looked at the Alberts boy and spoke without moving his lips too much, "We needed the help, first of all. That and I hoped his age would have brought some maturity out of him. In all honesty, I'm not sure why he even chose to come out and apply. I thought perhaps you were both cool after all this time and maybe you squashed all the drama in school. You know, became friends after all of it."

"Friends with him!? He still accuses me of not telling the police the truth and holds it against me til today." Len winced, "Besides, I haven't seen Brandon since that night all those years ago anyways. As far as

I know, he didn't go to Lunalilo with me. I have no idea where he's been all this time."

John expressed concern with an unsettled look, "He didn't graduate from Lunalilo? His application says different."

"Never seen him anywhere around campus, and I was *everywhere* on that campus..." Len looked back over at Yvonne and Mercy, "Maybe we just never crossed paths during our time in high school. He was a couple years ahead of me." Len wanted to see the best in Brandon, "He's been a pretty big help this past week though, and he hasn't said anything offensive to me when we were together. I mean nothing like before."

"His brother wasn't a very good role model for him, but his family life was hell I hear." John shook his head, "Len, you have patience and integrity. You being able to work with Brandon without having talked to him about that night is commendable. I'm sorry that I didn't have a chance to check on you two. Maybe I should speak with him and see if he's alright. I know his brother was very important to him. He was more like his father really. Well..." John dusted the breast of his uniform and realized he was offering too much information when it came to Brandon's personal life, "You could probably gather exactly what his life was like at home.'

Len didn't want to think about the Alberts'. That family had tormented his existence long enough. Now that Len was trying to move past all of this and let it go from his life, Brandon decides that it would be a good time to step back in.

His thoughts went from self-concerned to mindful, "Maybe it's a sign. Maybe this is my chance to get closure with Brandon. Apologize and wipe the entire slate clean."

As Len watched the Alberts boy pouring milk into a bowl for a camper he saw Brandon's face shift for a brief moment into Burden's as he looked straight into Len's eyes. His heart skipped a beat. The look he received brought him back to the first night at camp, all those years ago, when Burden gave him the death stare.

John's voice ricocheted off the walls in the dining room, "Group C has K.P.! Everyone else get ready to go down to the water!"

***

Standing by the lakeshore, wearing bright rainbow colored surf shorts with his uniform top, John stood facing the campers. "We will be conducting swimming tests to see how capable all of you are in the water. Counselor Paula's group, follow me to the dock."

As Group D followed John and Paula like a line of ducklings, Yvonne wandered over to Len while their groups sat patiently on the shore, “So, you two were having a pretty deep conversation this morning. What’s that all about?”

Len’s eyes squinted from the sunlight reflecting off of the wet surface, “John and me? Nah, it was stuff from a long time ago. Nothing important.” Len’s hands flicked outward as if dusting off a sooty table.

Yvonne had a sneaking suspicion that her fellow mentor was holding out on some very juicy information, “So, you and John? You guys go way back, huh?”

Len smiled, “I came to this camp once before when I was little. In fact, it was John’s first year as a leader.”

“Wait!?” Yvonne slapped Len in the arm, “You were here during Uncle John’s first summer as a camp counselor!?”

“Yeah! Wait, John’s your uncle?” Len was in shock.

“Sorta-kinda.” Yvonne flew past Len’s question and asked, “So, you were here when the head counselor was murdered by that psychopath, Seth Pedrina!?”

“What does psychopath mean?” Little Miss Mercy stared up innocently at Yvonne.

Len stretched his mouth as Yvonne bent over to share a word, “Look, Mercy, I’m going to need you to watch what Counselor John is doing with the others so you’re ready when it’s your turn. Okay?”

Mercy’s face reflected the sun as she bounced it up and down. “Got it!”

Len rubbed his chin as Yvonne sat Mercy between two older girls, Shawna and Cheylene, "So, how exactly is John your uncle? You two don't even look anything alike." He wanted to comprehend their relation.

"My mom married his older brother after she got divorced from my real dad." Yvonne blurted her family history in a second and pressed Len again about the terrifying summer of '74. "You gotta share what you seen or what you know about that summer, dude! Uncle John still refuses to talk to me about it."

Len smirked, "You have a very dark mind, Yvonne." He could see that the sun had changed her once brown eyes to a neon green. Besides her freckles, it was another thing Len noticed about Yvonne that he found quite attractive.

"Just give me details, dude!" Yvonne begged.

Len's mind knew one story, but reality expected him to accept another. He thought, *If I want to scare this girl away from me I should be honest with what happened.*

Len's face showed a desperate struggle, he didn't want her to think he was a complete nut. He looked up at the clear blue sky and exhaled, *I can't bring myself to lie to her. If I want to build a friendship with Yvonne I should be completely honest with her. I'll share what I saw, what I really saw.*

He looked back at Yvonne's pleasant face and became lost in her emerald green pools. He felt as light as air and the fervor made his stomach a little queasy.

Yvonne grew a bit uncomfortable by Len's admiration and she broke eye contact with him. Embarrassed, her cheeks reddened as she smiled toward the lake.

"Hey ladies!" Brandon cut the silence of the pair's intimate moment, "I hope I'm interrupting." He sprayed his finger at the water's edge and his group sat without a word. Gloom hung on each of the children's faces in Brandon's troop.

Yvonne looked over at the kids splashing around in the water, "Happy to see your group made it for testing."

Brandon chortled and moved his attention toward Len, "Remember the first time we came to the dock, Ellennnn?" The Alberts boy added a cat call inflection to the way he said Len's name. "We didn't do any kind of testing back in the day. They just threw all of us in the lake and watched for the kids who nearly drowned, right, girly!?"

Len grit his teeth as he thought about the girl that flew into the water during the tour with Kawika.

Yvonne's mouth fell open, "You both came to camp together!?" Her eyes flashed in Brandon's direction.

Len's face changed. He knew that if she got the story from Brandon, his version could paint him in an unsavory light. Before he could saying anything John's voice cut through the air, "Group A! You're up!"

Yvonne called to her troop while Little Miss Mercy hopped up and jabbed her thumb at the boardwalk to inspire urgency in her peers.

"Ooh whoo whoo! Looks like Yvonne wants to get to know me a bit better!" Brandon grinned deviously, "Man, Yvonne looks like a fun one, doesn't she?" He stopped to eye Len's reaction and laughed out loud. Len's group turned to see what was so funny mirroring the look on their leader's face.

"What!?" Brandon yelled as he gave the bug eye to Len's group. "Yup, fun times. What the heck am I talking about!? You're not a dyke, are you luscious?" Brandon slapped downward hitting Len in his right nipple.

"Aagh!" Len flinched.

"Oh! Did I touch your tender vittles, sweetie?"

Len scowled at Brandon as he grew annoyed by his inappropriate chatting, "Alright, that's enough already, man! Geez!"

Brandon's mouth fell open with his tongue wagging, "Oh, how insensitive of me! I didn't know it was *that* time of the month, Ellen."

Len turned his attention back to the lake.

Unable to get a rise out of his rival, Brandon stood up appearing bored of their interaction. As Yvonne jotted notes on a clipboard, logging her kid's swimming ability, Brandon invested his gaze back toward the young female counselor, "Ripe!"

Len watched one of the boys from his group glaring up at Brandon with a dirty look. He huffed and scolded him once more, "Enough, Brandon!"

"Enough!? I will tell *you* when it's enough!" Brandon paced over the sand. "My brother didn't deserve to be remembered as a coward. You were the one being a complete baby, following your boyfriend everywhere he went and crying to him every time *we* would breathe."

John could see that Brandon was not happy about being there on shore with Len. He decided to step in, "Group C, get ready!"

Brandon flicked his arm toward the dock signifying to his team to make their way over to the deck. "This conversation is *not* over, girlie!"

Andy, wearing a buttoned up collar and slacks, sat on the ground applying more sunscreen to his already lotion saturated face, "That guy's a real weirdie!"

"Aren't we all a little weird?" Len bounced his eyebrows at the inappropriately dressed boy. "Hey, you let me know if he ever says anything strange to you guys, okay!?" His team nodded in response.

Len looked back at the dock and watched as a group of girls screamed, "Ew!"

The children created a huddle in the center of the pier as Yvonne fought her way into the mass of laughing teenagers.

During the commotion, Len witnessed a fluorescent orange form flying off the other side of the wooden deck, screaming as it crashed into the water. "Stay here!" Len shouted to his group as he sprinted to the child who was in danger.

As Len approached the point of impact, he saw a pair of pale arms sinking to the bottom of the lake. Len dove into the icy waters and within seconds resurfaced with Little Miss Mercy cradled in his arm.

"Mercy!" Yvonne ran over to the start of the dock and into the pond to help Len bring her little buddy to shore.

"Oh my God! Mercy, are you alright, baby!?" Yvonne took hold of the young one as she coughed up water from her mouth and nose. "Cheylene, run up ahead and tell Counselor Pat what happened! We'll be right behind you." Shawna helped Yvonne rush Mercy up the hill to see counselor Pat at the infirmary.

Len turned around and saw Brandon standing on the dock smiling just as his brother did when he saw Burden toss the other girl from the dock nearly killing her.

"Why did you do that!?" Len pushed Brandon in the shoulder spinning him around revealing his smug face.

Brandon swiped at Len's hands, "Do what!?"

"Hey, hey, hey!" John was fighting to pull himself out of the lake to take control of the situation.

Len screamed, "Why did you toss Mercy off the dock!?" The children looked on in a state of shock.

"Here we go again, the blame game! How dare you accuse me of throwing poor defenseless little Mercy into the lake! Why would I ever do something like that to a child who can't swim?" Brandon stared deep into Len's eyes, "It was an accident, she just fell in!"

"This was the same thing that happened when we came here as kids! Your brother and Seth tossed that innocent girl off the deck and she drowned!" Len could see the anger growing on Brandon's face.

"Don't you ever talk about my brother, or my friends like that, you keep them out of your damn mouth!"

John hopped between the young men as they were about to throw hands. He struggled to separate them, when he did his voice was louder than when he used the megaphone, "Both of you knock it off!" He pushed Brandon with a tight grip of his shirt in hand, "Len, did you see Brandon throw Mercy into the lake?"

"Not exactly, but it must've been him! They did it before!" Len gnashed his teeth as tears began to run down his already wet face.

"Mr. John!?" Everyone froze to look at the source of a soft, young voice. Sam, the slender boy who always appeared very unenthusiastic, stared in the direction of the three men, "Mr. Brandon couldn't have hurt Mercy, he was standing next to me on the dock."

John placed his fists on his hips, "You're sure?"

The skinny child nodded, "Yeah, he was the one helping me pull my swimming trunks back up. That's when everyone turned to see who was screaming."

John bounced his head in understanding, "Okay." He grabbed Brandon's shoulder, "Take your group back to the Gathering Place for games. Stay inside until I come get you."

"I don't appreciate being accused by this trash, John!" Brandon's tone was furious.

"Okay." John pat Brandon's shoulder, "Go and take your group, I'll speak with Len."

Len watched Brandon leaving the lake, taking with him his squad and any chance of reconciliation. He threw his hands in the air and blew out a deep breath. Len could already see a word forming on John's mouth and he decided to preemptively halt a lecture.

"It's just that I saw his brother and Seth do the same exact move the very first day we came out to the lake when we were here last. Look, John, I'm sorry…"

John stopped the young man from speaking, "I'm not the one who needs your apology, Len. I know that what happened just now was insane and I realize the mood flipped one-eighty in an instant, but you can't just come out and accuse people of something they didn't do. Brandon had a witness. I know Sammy's family. The Waiha'aha'a's are good, quiet people that don't like the limelight. It took a lot for that kid to speak up like he did. He probably won't speak another word until we all pack up and leave." John relaxed his posture, "I appreciate you saving that little girl, Len. I will talk to her and find the truth about exactly what happened, but for now I need you to carefully choose the next words you say to Brandon Alberts."

Len looked to the side, "I'll go apologize to him right now."

"Nope," John stopped the young counselor. "You will allow Brandon a moment to cool off and give yourself a moment to think as well. At lunch, you will apologize to everyone who was on the dock for shouting like a raving lunatic. Then, in front of everyone at camp, you will apologize to Brandon. Clear?"

"Yes, sir." Len felt like he shot back to 1974, only this time, Kawika was nowhere to provide shelter or wisdom. He took a deep breath and tried his best to emulate the man that left such a big impression on him.

Okay Len, let's take care of the group and check on Little Miss Mercy. His thoughts continued to torture him, *What if I didn't see Seth or Burden throw that girl from the dock? What if there is something wrong with my brain and it's creating these fantastical delusions that Henry told me all about!?*

Len took his team on a small walkabout around the shore, then after some time he brought the group back to the Kāne's cabin. Len yelled, "Andy's in charge!" As he retreated out the front door.

A random voice called out, "Who's Andy?"

Len made his way around the side of the Infirmary where Yvonne sat in astonishment, "Dude!"

"Hey! How's Little Miss Mercy?" The young man glanced through the screen covered windows.

Yvonne grabbed Len by the arm and spoke softly, "She's gone, Len."

"Oh no..." Len fell to his knees with a far off look in his eyes, "Little Miss Mercy, gone? Why couldn't I have just gotten to her a fews seconds faster!?" He started to feel as if he needed to throw up. He was in no way even a small bit like Kawika. He felt like a failure in every sense. "No, not Little Miss Mercy!"

"What!?" Yvonne threw Len's arm down, "Dude, her parents took her." Yvonne could see Len snapping out of his stupor, "Dude, you thought she was dead!?"

Len stood up and wiped his face moving past the embarrassing scene he had just created, "Yvonne, I am so sorry about what I said down at the lake."

"Yeah, you really need to explain yourself now! Spill the beans!" Yvonne wasn't letting Len go anywhere until he explained himself.

"I'm not even sure what the heck happened, Yvonne. I need to apologize again for not being able to tell you what occurred today or even what happened back in '74, it's a complete mess up here," Len swirled his fingers around his temples.

The young woman grew impatient, "First of all, stop saying you're sorry and chill the heck out, dude!" Yvonne helped Len up to his feet and confided, "I need your help with something."

Len looked at Yvonne and replied, "Anything!"

ʻUmi kūmālua

"Three-hundred, twenty, forty, sixty, seventy, five, six, seven and eight!" Roy pulled his hand back still holding a massive wad of bills.

"Really? I pulled a double last Tuesday! Don't you remember?" Mercy thrust her palm outward.

Gently pressing his worker's hand away, Roy explained, "Yeah! I remember. But, *you* don't remember that you took a day about a month ago, then asked me to give you your full wage and promised to pull that said double."

Mercy exhaled and rolled her eyes. "Urgh, that's right. I'm sorry, Roy. I've been going through a lot lately."

Mercy gave in and rested her hand on the counter as Roy took hold of it offering a small solution to his employee. "You know, Mercy," Roy looked into the eyes of his attractive server, "If you need the money, we could always work something out." Roy raised his brow and tilted his head at the exhausted woman. Mercy's mouth fell open, she was at a loss for words.

"Come on, Mama! Remember, you're picking up yo' son an' dropping me off. Let's go!" Cheryl shook Mercy by her shoulder as she zoomed passed their boss on her way out of the diner.

"Oh! Right, my son!" Mercy yanked her hand away from Roy, "I'd forget my head if it weren't attached." She raced after her rescuer, hiking her purse securely over her shoulder.

Cheryl called out as she opened the front door, "See you tomorrow, Roy!" Both women disappeared behind the chime of an old metal bell. "I can't believe dat, da nerve of dat creep!" Cheryl said in a gruff tone.

Mercy looked down, "And to think, I almost gave that man the goods for free."

Cheryl's face became twisted, "Gag, Mercy! You actually contemplated taking a gig like dat? I didn't know you needed da money dat bad, or are you sweet on Roy? I mean, to each her own I guess."

"No, I wouldn't and I'm not. It's just that I was going through a phase a while back. I was doing it for Len really. Now that I think of it, I may have caused more stress in my son's life because of all the men that would come and go. They weren't very good role models." Mercy stopped and looked at her work friend, "Where can I meet a guy like Charlie?"

"My Chucky Squeeze?" They continued walking as Cheryl pulled her shoulders together thinking about her man, "He's a diamond in the rough, girl. He has five brothers an' none of dem act like him. They're all trying to milk their mother out of da last of their dad's fortune, trying to buy drugs and booze… girls! So lazy, they even try to avoid working. Pathetic."

Mercy swayed as they walked through the parking lot, "Hey, you busy?"

Cheryl lifted her brow, "Chuck's taking his mom out on a belated Mother's Day evening, so I got some time. You wanna cruise at our place?"

Mercy winced at her friend, "Would you be against coming over to mine?"

***

Mercy and Cheryl sat in the living room sharing their lives over a burger and fries, "Whoo, sister! I gotta go to da lua!" Cheryl popped up from the floor.

"You gotta hold the handle down a few seconds when you flush!" Mercy cast her words through the air before Cheryl could close the door.

After a short while, Cheryl made her way back into the living area scanning Len's diary. "Hey, I was looking all over for that! Where did you find it?"

"It's da weirdest t'ing, sis. It was just leaning up against da batchroom door." Cheryl's eye's were round.

Mercy found it difficult to believe it was where Cheryl described. “I passed that door like five times and I didn’t see it sitting there.”

Cheryl shook her head slowly, her eyes still bulging, “No, sister, it was leaning up against da door from da inside of da batchroom.

Mercy’s face appeared confused, “That doesn’t make any sense. You’re saying the book was leaning against the door from the inside?”

“Right!? So, I walk in an’ there was nothing on da floor. I finish my business, start washing up an’ I hear an odd knock, you know, like somet’ing fell. I look around da sink an’ I don’t see anyt’ing on da ground, but when I walked over to da door I see dis book leaning against da door like it was blocking da way.” Cheryl turned the pages, “What is dis anyways? A diary?”

Mercy sucked the straw on her soda cup nodding her head, “That’s Len’s journal. His therapist gave it to him to help him open up about what happened when I sent him to camp…” Mercy’s voice grew in volume as she finished her thought, “That *you* told me to send him to!” She threw a french fry at her friend. “He went through some trauma at that camp.”

Cheryl immediately plopped the tasty tater into her mouth and gnashed it with her teeth, “I should have you know dat Camp Pi‘ilewa is just amazing, so says my husband. All his family sent their kids to da camp. We get family up there right now in fac'!" Cheryl continued to eye the stories written in the tattered notebook, "No lie sis, yo' son went true some ordeals! You should read dis stuff... seriously."

Mercy wiped her hands, "Yeah, Len let me read it while he's away. But I misplaced it and haven't seen it for weeks."

"Where did your son go off to anyways? Not looking for Kaulana, ah? Deadbeat," Cheryl's voice trailed at the end as she skimmed through the boy's writing.

"No, he's working."

"Eh, das how! Good for you, girl!" Cheryl winked, "Where he working at?"

"He got himself a job as a counselor at Camp Pi'ilewa." Mercy finished the liquid at the bottom of her cup.

Cheryl's eyes grew even larger, "Are you kidding me!? After what happened to him at dat place, your son went back there to work! Is he, a masochist?"

"That's not it!" Mercy wiped her hand across the air, "He's doing it to get the closure he feels he needs. And to honor his friend Kawika."

"Dat was a good man right there. If he wasn't my first cousin, sister-" Cheryl was cut off from her recollection.

"Wait a minute, you're related to Kawika?" Mercy was quite interested in getting an inside scoop, "My son fell in love with the guy."

"My maiden name is Kāne!" Mercy had a look as if it was something new to her, "Well, you would've known if you came to his funeral."

"If you're talking about that one time you asked me to cover for you at the diner all those years ago, I was a little stuck - working." Mercy rolled her eyes.

Cheryl looked up in the air, "Oh yeah, dat's right! I'm such a babooze."

"It's so weird though, Cheryl. Ever since I began reading that thing, I've started to feel as if I'm being watched, seeing shadows and hearing people moving around in my house." Mercy rubbed her arms. "I don't know if I'm going nuts or if reading what my son wrote is creating some kind of, I don't know what, to happen! Maybe it's all in my mind."

"Oh my gosh, Merse, got dis movie dat just came out, Poltergeist! We gotta catch dat one, girl." Cheryl flapped the diary on the coffee table, "Chuck hates watching scary movies. Ever since he seen da Exorcist he refuses to watch 'em."

The sound of footsteps worked their way out of the living room and traveled through the hallway. They continued down the hall ending in Mercy's room. Cheryl looked at the rooms then back at her frightened friend who was hoping that her visitor heard the commotion. "You get ghosts, girl!?"

"Oh my gosh, please tell me you heard them too!?" Mercy felt some relief, but not much, as she inquired.

Cheryl just stood up and made her way over toward the sound. Mercy slowly got up and kneeled on the couch. She watched as the sunlight from her room brightened the dark hall.

"Mercy!"

Cheryl's call made her jump. She ran over to the bedroom and saw all of her drawers wide open.

"Do you normally have yo' stuffs open laddat?"

Mercy started to shake, "I thought it was all in my head, I'm so relieved you were here to see this."

"Stop playing, sister! You set dis all up, didn't you? I don't find deez kinds of pranks funny." Cheryl crossed her arms, "Did you sneak into da bathroom while I was in there? Did you prop up dat book against da door?" Mercy shook her head, but Cheryl wasn't buying it. "You know, it took me a while to come around an' befriend you because watching you go true men da way you did made me t'ink you was one attention seeking floozy, but den I got to know you an' found out you're actually decent." Cheryl charged out of the room and snapped up all of her things, "Now, da opportunity arises to take your son's experience an' turn 'em into a way fo' get more attention?"

Mercy placed her hand on Cheryl's arm, "No, please wait. I didn't set any of this up! Honestly! This is really happening. Please don't leave!"

"You need help, Mercy. I don't t'ink I'm da one to provide you wit' dat help. You should go see Len's shrink."

"I'm not going crazy, Cheryl!"

"Get one kahu den!" Cheryl left post haste.

Mercy found herself home all alone once again. She hoped some of the light Cheryl brought into the house would stay after she had gone, but for Mercy, it only seemed to have gotten darker.

‘Umi kūmākolu

Yvonne pulled Len into the nurses office, “I’m trying to keep my calm right now Len, so I need you to explain what happened here when Seth committed those murders!”

The young man sat quietly as he tried piecing together the events without coming off as a mental case.

“Seth didn’t kill anyone that night, did he?”

Trying his best not to take the things Yvonne presumed personally, Len asked how she came about that theory. “Is that what Brandon told you!?”

“Brandon didn’t tell me jack, dude!” Yvonne took offense, “I wouldn’t trust anything he tells me anyway.”

“So, why is this so important right now? I don’t want to talk about any of this. It really isn’t something I like to dredge up.” Len pressed his fingers together, “I’m more concerned about Little Miss Mercy anyway!”

Yvonne growled, “This concerns Mercy and it concerns me too, dunce!”

Len settled himself and observed the young woman looking to confide in him, "Wait, did I miss something here? What happened, Yvonne?"

She didn't know how to start, "You see, I asked around about you and Brandon, and what happened here, with the other counselors and they had some very strange tales to tell. I couldn't believe some of the things they shared, so I assumed they were all having a laugh at my expense. But, now I know why Uncle John didn't tell me about what happened. I still need to hear it from you, because what I saw at the dock cannot be explained and it's freaking me out!"

Len was now just as confused as Yvonne, "Maybe you should tell me exactly what happened at the dock-"

"No!" Yvonne held her cheeks in her hands, "You need to go first!"

Len shrugged, "I don't know what it is you want me to say! I have spent a lot of time after that night trying to tell myself that what I saw was in no way real."

"Oh my gosh! So, the stories are true?" Yvonne's hands moved over her eyes.

Pat just returned to the medical cabin and saw the couple in the middle of something heavy, "Yvonne? Is everything alright?" The young camp counselor shot up and ran from the office in tears. Bewildered at what just transpired, Pat cast her gaze at Len who sat there with mixed emotions. "What's the deal, buddy?"

"It was Mercy. We were both worried about her safety." Len stood up, "As long as the little miss is okay. I just wanted to come check on her, but I understand she has already left."

"I think the mom was more affected by the incident than Mercy. Hopefully she'll make her return. Her father seemed understanding and knew accidents happen." Pat tried her best to comfort Len. "I hear you're the one who fished her out of the lake. I'm sure her parents will want to meet you."

"Thank you, Pat. I better get back to my group." Len made his way out of the front door of the infirmary and thought, *Accidents do happen, but what happened here today was in no way a mere accident.*

'Umi kūmāhā

"What? You're going to let a door stop you?" A dark slithery voice echoed all around the enclosed cube. "Hahahahaha, the children, they're all laughing at you! Pointing and laughing, sticking out their tongues from their smug little faces. They're saying that you can't do it, that you can't do *anything* because you're too stupid. You got caught because you're an idiot!"

There was a second voice that questioned very slowly, "Huh?" A deep baritone pervaded the dark cell.

The prominent voice returned with words that weren't so supportive. "I'm startin' to believe them. The children were right to laugh at you." Soon, thumping pulsed within the pitch black compartment. "Uh oh, gang, I think he's getting mad! Run away, kids!" The thumping turned to pounding. "That's what I'm talking about! Soon, those children are going to wish they hadn't laughed at you."

The exit started to rattle and a sliver of light could be seen at one corner of the door. An intake of air through tight nostrils created a sound like a current.

"Mmm, aaaah, can you smell it, big guy!? Fressssh aaaair."

A huge crash was heard in solitary, alerting two guards. They ran across the hall unlocking the cell block with fast beating hearts. When they came upon the disturbance they were greeted by a sizable shape, hidden in shadow, leering back at them.

An unearthly scream accompanied the sounds of bone cracking and flesh being torn from limbs. Within seconds, everything fell silent. The blood of both men covered the walls and floor like fresh paint. Now free, the murderous fiend continued his way out of holding.

Each step made by the liberated creature caused the lamps illuminating the facility to flicker and pulse. Soon the dark beast arrived at the station's front lobby, where four unsuspecting officer's fumbled for their flashlights. The sound of wood splintering and liquid splashing to the floor caused one of the officers to find his fellow guard impaled by a splintered portion of a chair right in his seat. The light from his torch was then blocked by a massive shape. The officer screamed as a sharp object swam its way through his throat, his voice instantly becoming a gurgle.

One of the officers was able to fire off several rounds, only to end up shooting the fourth guard in the head. He felt his body lift into the air as if he were flying. Smashing through the glass of the prison's front entrance, the injured cop writhed in pain from the shards of glass that pressed into his skin. The glow of the moon was strong enough for him to see his attacker.

The officer held up his gun and squeezed the trigger. The clicking of the mechanism told the brute the officer was out of luck. The pistol was snatched away, then sent hurling back, fracturing and dislocating the policeman's jawbone. The last thing he saw was a boot coming down onto his eye socket.

"Hahaha, I bet you these children won't laugh at you like that ever again!" The beast of a man dropped the bloodied gun onto the ground and made his way out of the parking area. "Let's play hide and seek, big boy!"

The broad frame, of what looked more like a monster than a man, lumbered across the highway heading toward the forest edge. A car swerved to avoid hitting the giant. As it came to a stop, the psychopath smashed his hand through the driver's side window gripping the neck of the pilot. A flex of his forearm made the woman's neck pop causing her body to fall limp.

The voice chimed in once again, "Well, that seemed a bit excessive, don't you think?" The shadow made its way into the forest and traveled the under cover of night. "I hope we can still make it to the celebration, those mean kids didn't want us to have any cake or play with the balloons, did they? Well, it's not up to them anymore, but we need to hurry before all of that chocolate cake is gone."

"Cake?" A deep nasal declaration punched out from the lips of the behemoth.

His head vibrated as the voice returned, "Yes, Seth, cake!"

ʻUmi kūmālima

After Cheryl left, Mercy cleaned up her home. She thought about the words her co-worker had uttered, echoing her son's suggestion that she see his therapist. *I may actually pay Dr. Campbell a visit. In the meanwhile, I think I'll just take a look at my son's progress.* Her intentions brought her back to the living room.

Mercy found the diary open on the coffee table. She shook her head at the book's strange proclivity and muttered, "Well, I guess since you've decided to come back, I should read you before you run off again." She made herself comfortable and sat the journal on her lap and began reading where Cheryl had left off.

May 30, 1980

I think I am ready to discuss that night. Dr. Campbell says that I need to talk about it with him. He said it'll feel better if I get it all out. I am strong and I can overcome.

I sat in the main office as Kawika called the Alberts' parents. He was trying to get them picked up from camp early because Burden threatened to kill me. It was already late, almost lights out. I remembered Kawika was mad that the number they provided was disconnected or not in service or whatever. Camp Leader Craig burst through the office doors in a panic. He told Kawika that Brandon Alberts was having some kind of seizure. Kawika flew out of the office with Craig and all of a sudden I was in that spooky office all alone.

After a minute passed, the office doors opened again, but this time it was Burden Alberts. He made his brother create a distraction so he could get me all by myself. I tried to get away, but I was too slow. Burden socked me right in the face. I hit the counter as I fell to the floor, busting my head open. Seth held my arms back as Burden punched me in the gut over and over until my dinner fell over his shoes. It seemed to have made him angrier. Seth went to help clean Burden off so he let me go. Burden yelled at Seth, but I was already on my way behind the counter. Burden tried desperately to catch me, but he couldn't get around Seth. I jumped out of the office window and ran as fast and as far as I could to hide.

The forest felt very odd that night, it was a lot scarier than usual. I must've made it very close to the lookout when my chest seized. I couldn't breathe anymore, so I took refuge at the base of a tree that had a bush big enough to hide a large animal in it.

I hid myself, wondering what to do and what Burden would do to me if he found me. Something brought me out of my imaginings. At first, I thought it was the beating of my heart pounding in my head, but as my breathing grew easier it became clear that I was hearing the sounds of the pahu.

I remained perfectly still and quiet as the beating got louder. I could hear multiple footsteps running past the tree I hid under continuing their journey up the mountain. I was ready to make a break for it back down the trail when seconds later I heard Brandon Alberts crying out to whoever he was with to run away. The sounds of their steps blazed past me once again, only they flew past going back down hill. They were trying to make their way back down the path and it appeared as though they were no longer interested in finding me. I decided I needed to run too.

I found myself in an odd situation, I was now chasing after the bullies that were once chasing me. Their shadows moved fast up ahead and I noticed one of them moving dangerously close to the edge of the cliff. I wanted to yell out a warning, but I was afraid the boys would come back and hurt me. I saw the shadow leave the earth and disappear over the horizon.

I heard the deathly wail of Burden Alberts echoing into the void of night, becoming fainter and then finally going silent. The chilly air started to burn in my lungs and the sound of chanting was growing from behind. I couldn't run any longer.

I ducked into a bush that was slightly larger than the first one I hid under. It became so cold that every exhale formed a cloud of mist. The chanting grew louder and the pahu sounded mere feet away. At first, I imagined that I was hearing someone shouting out my name. I realized when it was too late that Kawika was the one calling for me. I wanted to stand up and go to him so badly, but my fear kept my legs locked in place.

An odd sound had come out of nowhere and it didn't help me with my concealment. A faint splashing of water accompanied by a trickling sound ran nearby my feet. To my surprise I found steam rising from below. I realized that I had involuntarily soiled myself and the action had caught the attention of the ones that tracked our movements.

I looked out of the bush I was hiding in and found a pair of pale legs cut off at the knee. When I looked up, two glowing eyes stared down at me. I leaped from the bush and ran as fast as my legs could carry me, until I struck something solid and fell to the earth. In my panic, I ran into my friend. Kawika looked up toward the ghost procession and asked where the other children were. I just pointed out into the forest. I remember Kawika looking at my pants and I tried explaining that I had an accident. He shushed me and reminded me about how it was good, it was protection from the night marchers. He told me to quickly make my way back to camp and so I ran.

I didn't get very far when I felt something grip me hard from the back of my neck. My feet left the ground and I dangled midair as I was cut off from breathing. I could see Kawika struggling to pull me back to the floor and as soon I touched the ground a force tossed me off the path into something hard, a tree or rock, I don't know what.

I thought I had passed out, but I wasn't sure. I could hear Kawika urging me to stand up, but when I looked for him, his body laid lifeless on the ground. I couldn't tell if he was breathing or not, but when I looked up the trail, the procession marched right at me. I heard Kawika yelling for me to run. I turned reluctantly, leaving my friend knocked out cold on the dirt path, and ran away. When I felt I was at a safe distance, I watched the line of spirits huddle around Kawika's body like a volt of vultures.

I was so angry with myself for abandoning the man who was always there for me. One of the spirits looked me right in the eye, I turned and ran so fast it felt like I was hovering off of the road. Brandon was up ahead and I was gaining on him. We both made it back to the grounds where Counselor John helped Brandon and me into the cabin and locked us in with the rest of the campers. Many had no idea what was going on and thought the whole thing was some kind of shelter in place drill.

In the morning, reality hit the campers as everyone woke to the flickering of police lights and sounds of concerned parents. Brandon was the only kid that had no one outside waiting for him. I could see my mom from a distance and she looked distressed. She was being interviewed by a police officer and her gestures were very spastic.

When we were finally allowed to leave the cabin, each camper left one by one with long waits between dismissals. When it was my turn to go, I grabbed my bag and I was escorted over to the office. A detective asked me some questions about what I experienced. When all was said and done, I walked out of the office into the arms of my mother.

Brandon was still there sitting next to Counselor Craig and Seth was being escorted into the back of a police cruiser. My mother drove me over to the clinic so my doctor could check me out. He suggested I come see a therapist, my mom decided I just needed time. No one ever truly believed what I saw that night. It seemed as though they chose not to believe it, like it was too hard to make any sense. It made me furious.

Now that I am strong and I can overcome, I realize that what I envisioned that evening was purely created by my subconscious. My brain fought to change the pure evil I saw coming from Seth Pedrina, manifesting it into something truly inhuman, and impossible in this reality.

Mercy felt at odds. She was starting to believe Len may have actually witnessed something unexplainable at Camp Pi'ilewa. She thought, *I should definitely stop by the therapist's office tomorrow, and I think I should bring this book with me when I go.*

ʻUmi kūmāono

After lights out, Len snuck over to the Wāhine Cabin and tapped on the window nearest Yvonne's bunk. Within a minute, the form of the young woman quietly emerged from the front door. Yvonne sat on the bench next to Len, sniffing from a runny nose. She smelled sweet to Len, like pakalana, her wet hair glistened in the light of the moon and her eyes still had some pink in them.

"I'm so sorry I didn't come clean earlier, Yvonne. The trauma from that night and what my mind created make it near impossible to come out and say exactly what happened all those years ago." Len tried his best to keep a low volume while expressing how serious it all was.

Yvonne looked up at the sky and sniffed once more, "Just, please tell me what you thought you saw. I don't care if you think it was in your head or all make believe, I just want to know exactly what it was you experienced. There is something off about all of this. What I saw, what happened to Mercy, I need answers."

Len intertwined his fingers and looked between his knees at the dirt below his feet, “The last night of camp, I was chased up the forest trail.” Len pointed off the grounds toward the Pi‘ilewa Point Scenic Lookout Trail. “Seth Pedrina and Burden Alberts chased me all the way to the top hoping to hurt me, or kill me… I don’t know what. I hid in a bush and when they ran passed me I heard the sounds of…” Len stopped speaking.

Yvonne looked at the troubled young man and placed her hand on his back, “Please, Len. What did you hear?”

He looked at Yvonne’s face, her eyes reflected the stars and he could feel peace returning to his heart, “Pahu. I heard the sounds of the ancient drums. The other boys heard them too, it scared them. They charged back down the mountain to get away and so did I. I saw one of the boys running way too close to the edge of the cliff and before I could call out to them, Burden Alberts threw himself right over. His scream was so surreal. It’s a sound that I will never forget. I couldn’t believe he was gone… just as fast as that. Here one moment, then gone the next. My chest started to burn. The air that night was so cold, it was so *very* cold. I could feel my joints going rigid and I almost fell a couple of times. I found a hiding spot to catch my breath and steady my nerves.”

Len looked at his audience of one. She appeared to be accepting of his account. That trust helped him to continue on with his explanation, "I could hear the oli accompanying the beating of the drums, it was insane, it was unbelievable and it was so very, very scary." Len paused a second taking a deep breath and carried on with his recalling, "I peed my pants right in that bush."

"Oh, Len, I'm sorry!" Yvonne held his hand in hers.

"I could see a pair of legs, glowing pale, in the dark woods. They didn't go all the way to the ground and the parts I could see were kind of transparent. I guess the sound my pee made caught the attention of the ghost, or whatever, and it came for me. I ran from that bush and Kawika found me. He told me to go back to camp and he was going to find the other boys.

I could see them clearly now, the night marchers, they were coming down the mountain in a straight line. An invisible force lifted me from the ground and began choking me. If it wasn't for Kawika, I would've died. He pulled me free, but he was taken in my stead... he would still be here today if I hadn't run up that damned trail into the path of the huaka'i pō!"

Yvonnes eyes were wide, "Don't blame yourself, Len! It wasn't your fault that Kawika was taken by the night marchers. If anything, it was Burden Alberts' fault."

At that moment a scream of death came from the cliffs of Pi'ilewa Point. Both counselors jumped to their feet staring through the darkness. Yvonne took a step closer to the unexpected shriek when Len grabbed her by the elbow.

"No!" His grip caused her to stop. "That was the exact scream that Burden Alberts made when he fell off the mountain. Exact pitch, exact length and exact spot where his body was found." Len's heart beat within his throat. "Okay, that's enough. Go back inside and lock the cabin. We'll talk more about this tomorrow, when it's safer. Go!"

Yvonne ran up the steps, Len could hear the door latch and deadbolt click as he trained his eyes beyond the darkness. He swiftly made his way back to his cabin where he found a half dozen boys peering at him beside the windows.

"Why are you still up?" The latch was secured and Len moved away from the entrance.

Stu apologized for breaking the rules, "We're sorry, Len. We were just getting some tips."

"Tips?" Len asked.

"Yeah!" Andy's voice cracked, "We wanted to watch the master work his charm… you know?" Andy tried winking, "With counselor Yvonne?"

"Okay, boys, sorry to break it to you, but nothing like that is going on." Len waved his arms in the air as if herding fish into a tide pool. "It's time to go to sleep."

"Hey, Len?" Sammy spoke up.

The counselor stopped because he knew the boy was very shy, "Yeah, Sammy. Is everything alright?"

He shook his head, "What was that scream that came from Pi'ilewa Point?"

Len's eyes popped, "You heard that?"

Jeremiah looked up resentfully from his pillow and snapped, "Everyone heard it! Sssh, go to sleep!" He hid his face back into his pillow.

Sammy added, "Was it the night marchers, Len?"

The hair on Len's neck stood on end, "No, Sammy. I don't think it was the night marchers."

"My tūtūwahine, when she was one kid, said her house was built on one night mahchah pat'." Moku slipped out of his bunk and sat with the others on the floor. "She remembah her granfada wen' scold her fada, 'Eh! No build da house ovah dea! Plenty pilikia, dat!' He still no listen. About a mont' aftah da house built... BOOM! All kine shakin' an' bangin' in da hale. Knock all da photos off da walls, da dog run away and foot prints burned into da flo-wah!"

"Not even, Moku! You sucha Bulaia!" Jeremiah popped his head up again for a brief moment.

Pe'a retaliated, "Brah, try shaddap an' go back to sleep alreadeh!"

"Aaah!" Jeremiah flicked his fingers at the group and flopped over to his side.

"Das right!" Pe'a pushed his nose at the rudeness of his bunkmate. "So, when my uncle went Ka'ena on O'ahu, he remembah seeing da kine torches moving down da ridge. An' den he wen' hea' da drums beating an' one oli. Cuz, he taught he was going pupule!"

Jeremiah's voice cut in again, "All you guys, pupule! Da scream we heard was jus' one sea bird. Go sleep!"

Pe'a snapped, "How's about I put chu to sleep, Jerry!"

"That's what I'm trying to do, but you manapua mout's won't let me!" Jeremiah slapped his pillow over his exposed ear.

"I think we should all get some sleep." Len pointed at the bunks. "We've got lots to do tomorrow."

Len decided to keep watch over his boys until daylight. He sat beside the door, every once in a while he'd look out the window at the wāhine cabin to make sure it was okay. He pondered in the light of the moon, *I really don't know what to think anymore. I'm at a complete loss! Nightmarchers or Seth Pedrina? Psycho killer or procession of murderous spirits. Evil, either way. How could I possibly protect these kids from the might of an undead army or the actions of a homicidal maniac?*

The stress from these thoughts gave Len the adrenaline to stay awake through dawn.

‘Umi kūmāhiku

“Ms. Davis!? Well, isn’t this a pleasant surprise!” Dr. Campbell had just finished with a patient when he found Len’s mother waiting outside his office. “Please come in!”

Mercy sat down on a couch with tight, bright red leather bound upholstery. “I hope I’m not interrupting.”

Dr. Campbell waved his hand as he made his way around his desk, “No, no! You caught me at the perfect time. Is everything alright with Len?”

Mercy pressed her lips into a line, “Well, I have concerns, but it’s not necessarily about him right now.” She realized she wasn’t making much sense to herself and was probably getting Dr. Campbell ready to start treatment on her. “I’m sorry, doctor.” Mercy stood, “I don’t even know why I came here. Len is doing fine. He’s at Camp Pi‘ilewa working and I haven’t heard anything from him since he left. So, no news is good news, right?”

“Please, sit! I was only asking if he’s doing okay. I didn’t mean to make you feel uncomfortable.” Dr.

Campbell was concerned. He watched Mercy rest back into the couch, “So, you must have stopped by for a reason. Please, tell me how I can help.”

“Ah, okay. Where do I start?” Mercy was giving off erratic energy as she looked all over Henry’s office.

“Mercy?” Dr. Campbell assured her, “It’s okay. This is a safe place and whatever you have to share stays between us.”

“It’s about this.” Mercy pulled her son’s notebook forward, “Len has some very disturbing things written in his diary. There are things in here that he has never discussed with me or confided to me about. I’m being traumatized by this boy’s trauma!” Mercy appeared to be in a panic.

The doctor looked at the notebook that Mercy pulled out of her bag, “You didn’t read that without Len’s permission, did you?”

Mercy shook her head back and forth at a quick pace, “He actually left it for me to read when he went off to camp. He was going to take it with him, to burn it in the camp fire, but he offered it for me to read. I’m going up to get him at the end of camp to do the ceremony with him. It was to symbolize the completion of his therapy. I took it as a chance to get a better look at what he experienced during his treatment with you, but I kind of regret opening the book.”

"Well, the book *was* meant for Len to use as a tool to help him verbalize his experiences. A tool to get to the root of what made him feel vulnerable. It did it's job and I'm so proud of him for wanting to let it go in such a symbolic way. Did you read through all of it?"

"Not yet." Mercy replied, "but I don't plan to."

Henry looked at Mercy with an ease to his posture. He could see she was still experiencing some trouble. "Is there something you needed me to tell Len or do for him?"

Mercy declined, "I guess what I'm trying to tell you is that I am also experiencing something right now. Ever since I read from the book, strange things have been happening. His writing is causing some kind of break in my reality!"

Dr. Campbell now looked at Mercy in a different way, "What do you mean, 'break in reality'?"

Len's mother sighed with an irritated growl, "What is this book made of? Is it cursed!?"

"Mercy, it's just a notebook from the Woolworth! It's not cursed, I didn't pry it from the hands of a dead kahuna. It's a regular book, with regular pages in it." Henry studied Mercy from across his desk.

She tried to attack the situation from a different angle, "It must be his words then! His emotions have been imprinted in the words on these pages! You must've experienced some strange activity when you read his words, right?"

Dr. Campbell leaned forward with his elbows on his desk, hands clasped, "I've never read the book, Mercy. It's not *for* me to read, it's for Len to express himself. To make it easier for him to share his problems with me. That is all."

Mercy was beginning to understand why her son moved on from this whole ordeal, "You convinced Len that what he saw that evening was all in his mind, didn't you?" Dr. Campbell sat up straight with rounded eyes from Mercy's accusatory tone, "You listened to him pour his heart out about what happened at Pi'ilewa and then you told him it was all made up!? That it was all a lie!?"

"There are no such things as demons!" Mercy was surprised by the doctor's sudden outburst, "He needed to understand this so he could find his way in the *real* world. Did you want him to run away and hide every time his mind conjured a new allegory and just refuse to deal with what's truly happening in front of him? I'm here to help people move on, not to coddle them and watch them continue the cycle of suffering. Aren't you proud of your son's achievements? Aren't you happy now that he is happy?"

"I brought my son here thinking that you could help him with what he experienced, not to brainwash him into thinking it didn't happen. That is not empowerment, that's hiding. Hiding behind an imaginary facade. It seems like you twisted his truth into your truth." Mercy's eyes opened up fully, "Wait a minute, have you suffered from a similar experience?"

Dr. Campbell sat coughing and babbling, "Well, you see, I was not nor did I intend to brainwash! How dare you insinuate..." Dr. Campbell ceased his defense when he was mesmerized by what he witnessed. Len's notebook flew into the air from Mercy's possession and slapped onto his desk swinging open to the very last journal entry.

June 4th, 1982,

I am cured! I have finished my last session with Dr., I mean Henry. He gave me a great piece of advice that will finally help me find closure. I'm heading back to Pi'ilewa and I'm going to replace the fear and loss that I experienced there with courage and hope.

Kawika taught me about bravery and Henry helped me to get back up. Henry also thought it would be a great idea to burn this book to signify the end of my therapy. I am strong and I have overcome just as he did.

Dr. Campbell pressed his back as far into his seat as he could. Mercy looked up at the doctor, "You told my son to apply at Camp Pi'ilewa?"

“He was all for the experience… it’s not like he’s a child anymore, Mercy. He’s a man, he can take care of himself!” The good doctor seemed to be anxious.

"And what?” Mercy stood to her feet poking her finger into the diary, “You gave him the idea to burn the book, burn the evidence of your treachery!?”

“Evidence!? What now!? Are you accusing me of something here!?” Dr. Campbell also got to his feet.

Mercy’s eyes squinted toward the man who appeared to be hiding something, “Len said, ‘I have overcome like he did.’ What exactly did *you* overcome, Dr. Campbell?”

Henry dropped back into his chair. His heart raced in his chest and all the terrifying visions of ghosts and demons flashed in his mind. Tears welled up in the corner of his eyes.

“I don’t know why it happened, but before Len came to his final session I started to have some very vivid dreams, terrifying nightmares actually, of my poor granddaughter being killed by some dark entity. I would wake up every morning at three worried she was dead, I called my children to check on her safety. I knew it was becoming an issue for them, but I needed to know if she was alright. Every night, for almost thirty nights, I witnessed my poor baby dying a new and ferocious way. One morning, again at three, I awoke to a violent sequence of my grandchild’s head being removed from her shoulders, but my dream persisted. I opened my eyes and I saw a face, an evil face with an unholy smile. It hovered above me and spoke, but it never lost the evil grin it bore as the words emanated from it. It told me that it would leave me and my grandchild alone if I convinced your son to apply for a job at Pi'ilewa, and by golly it worked! I haven't had another bad dream since our last session."

Mercy was sickened by the therapist's cowardice, "You sent my son into the lions den so you would stop having nightmares!? Are you serious!?!"

"What does it matter? He has a job, he's making money and he's being independent. Isn't that what you wanted for Len?" Henry checked Mercy's face to see if she was onboard.

Len's mother thought about the night she was attacked, "This creature you saw above your bed, did it have yellow eyes?"

Henry's arm hair stood on end. He didn't want to answer Mercy in fear that he would be proven a coward and a fraud. But he decided honesty would be the most appropriate thing now, "Yes…"

Mercy asked another question, "Was its form black, an inky black, like a dense fog?"

Henry snapped a picture frame off of his desk, "Yes…" He answered as tears started to fall down his face.

Mercy's pulse began to race, "Oh my lord! Seth Pedrina was found on Kāo'oloa Road talking to himself... as if he were possessed!"

Dr. Campbell didn't understand, "What about Seth Pedrina?" He wiped the tears from his eyes with his handkerchief.

"Seth tried to kill my son at the camp. He was apprehended recently on Kāo'oloa Road... it's on the way to the Pi'ilewa Point! You know... where you sent Len, remember!?" Mercy grabbed her chest, "He was on the way to get my son! It's a good thing that psycho was taken back to jail. The police are supposed to be moving him to O'ahu soon."

Relief washed over Mercy until Henry's television set turned on all by itself. Dr. Campbell jolted, "Um, my T.V. doesn't have that feature!"

Mercy shouted, "Shut up!"

"... Seth Pedrina, twenty, the convicted murderer of two individuals at Camp Pi'ilewa in the summer of 1974, is now on the loose after successfully escaping the 'Āinapau Prison facility once more. Pedrina has killed six police officers and a thirty-two year old female motorist during his escape. He remains at large. Police are looking for anyone who knows his whereabouts. If you do see Pedrina, avoid him at all costs. He is considered highly dangerous. Should you come across Pedrina, you should not interact with him. Contact the police immediately. Local law enforcement have been authorized to shoot on sight ..."

The television went back to sleep and the room was eerily quiet. Mercy looked over at the doctor and saw him sitting there speechless with his mouth agape. "That psychopath is on his way to my baby, right now. I know it. You were the one who put him in harms way, Henry!"

It took a little more time for Dr. Campbell to finally snap out of his daze, "We need to contact the police! We have to tell them that they need to head over to Pi'ilewa right now!"

"Did you not hear the newscaster!? Six officers down! That is like half of our police force Henry! They're not going to send resources because of a hunch." Mercy grabbed her purse and Len's diary, "We're going now! We'll call the police if we see anything suspicious."

‘Umi kūmāwalu

“Rarrrgh!” A bellowing caused Seth’s head to throb, “Do you see it, Seth?”

The large mass squinted his eyes past the pine trees. A small structure gleamed in the sun as it sat in a clearing.

“We are so close! I can hear the party and it’s still going!”

The sounds of the campers playing field games and running relays could be heard. The psycho came upon the front gates, staying within the cover of shade to avoid being spotted. Waves of energy washed forth from the camp and made Seth’s ears ring.

The voice in his head began to shriek, “Back away from the grounds. It has never allowed me to come any closer.” The monster moved away from the campsite shaking his head to relieve his anguish, “The path! We must make our way up the path where we can set a trap.”

Seth looked up the Pi'ilewa Hiking Trail and frowned, "Cake!?" His dry lips yearned for the soft, grainy feeling of sweet frosting coating his mouth.

"Don't worry, Seth." A sharp hiss followed the words of condolence, "Brandon will bring us what we desire soon. We will have our cake and eat it too!"

Seth moaned deep in his throat and turned to make his way up the mountain. He hadn't seen the trail for several years, but it all came flooding back into the miscreant's mind. All the anger he had for Len powered each step up the dirt path.

"I'm going to kill him for lying!" Seth snarled in a tone of hatred.

"We… Big Guy! We are going to kill him together." A cackle vibrated in Seth's skull making the beast of a man smile with delight, "I'm going to make that piece of trash suffer for tricking us up this hill that night and for lying to the cops. He will pay for saying that *you* killed his boyfriend."

"You should have killed him at his house!" Seth smashed his palm into the side of his head.

The voice hacked with disapproval, "The further I move from this mountain, the weaker I am. I could only visit him in his dreams. But, I found a way to bring him back here. All of our patience is going to pay off. We'll throw his ass right off this cliff and I will beat him over and over again in the afterlife!"

Seth's stomach began to rumble, "Cake?" He questioned his disembodied companion.

"Patience, Big Guy. Patience."

The voice that moved Seth to kill those people at the police station and walk for miles through the forest night and day had vanished. An ease returned to the mind of the troubled man. He laid upon some leaves at the base of a banyan tree and closed his eyes to get some much needed rest.

'Umi kūmāiwa

Yvonne laughed as Len's group fell over at the tug-o-war line, "Oh! Look who's bad! We bad! We bad! We bad!" The chanting just encouraged the winning team to imitate their group leader.

Len shook his head, "Whatever, cheater! You guys had a ringer in there." Laughing playfully, Len pointed his finger at Moku. He could never belittle the sweetest gentle giant he had ever had the pleasure of meeting.

Yvonne hugged the bear of a child, "Don't accuse my little cub of cheating!"

Pat winced, "Little? Does she know the meaning?"

Len laughed, "Hey, Pat. Thanks for covering for Brandon today. Brother did not look good at all this morning."

Pat shook her head, "Sliced ham." Len was expressing a puzzled look, "We're having ham sandwiches for dinner tonight. I always keep at least two ready to go meals just in case we run into this type of situation."

John's voice could be heard blaring over the megaphone, "Alright, everyone! You're all winners in my book. Now, let's make our way down to the lake for a nice, cool swim!"

Brandon peeked out from the window of the medical cabin, watching the entire camp make their way down the hill. He cautiously snuck to the front gates and looked around the deserted area. A massive amount of pressure built within Brandon's ears and within seconds his head began to pound.

"Move, you idiot!" Screeching seared into the young camp leader's brain.

Brandon sprinted away from the camp gate squeezing the side of his head, hyperventilating. He fell to his knees in a patch of tall dried weeds, "What the hell!?"

A slithery voice chastised, "I told you, I can't be near the camp, dum dum!"

Brandon massaged his cranium, "That was worse than when Pa hit my head into the porch bannister!"

"I remember! I remember standing up to the old man when you fell down the front steps. I had scars on my back from his buckle after he whipped me. The sores looked like the belt of Orion." The voice began to chuckle at the irony.

Brandon lowered his hands and responded, "Yeah, I remember later that night, when he went back to the bar, you beat the piss out of me for it."

"You needed a reminder not to make those same mistakes, or the next time it would've been worse for you, or the both of us." There was an odd moment of abhorrent nostalgia, "You and that damned ouija board got us into a lot of trouble."

Brandon smiled, "We had a lot of fun on it too!"

"Yep, I saved your rosy cheeks from Pa that night, though." Burden's voice tingled Brandon's left ear canal.

He cried as he thought about never being able to return the favor to his brother, "I'm sorry Burden, I'm sorry I couldn't save you that night when you fell from the mountain."

"Shut up and stop blubbering you ninny. Enough reminiscing. Right now, you have a very important job." Burden spoke quickly, but concisely, "You need to bring some food out here for Seth. If he's going to help us, he needs his strength."

"Where is he?" Brandon looked at the road.

Burden's voice returned, "He's up the trail. I need to get back to him before he realizes he shouldn't be up there. He needs even more attention now than he did before. He's exhausting, but he's a damn brute! Now that I'm closer to Pi'ilewa, I'll have more control over him." Burden moved back into the plan, "Bring that son of a rat out of the camp grounds tonight, brother. It's getting easier for me to move through the veil and I should be strong enough to strangle the life from that bastard myself, just as I did to Kawika."

Brandon's eyes flashed, "Wait, *you* killed Kawika!?"

"You have no idea how angry I was that night, Brandon!" Burden's voice changed into what could only be described as demonic, "I can still see the rocks below the cliff fast approaching. When I hit the ground, I felt every nerve in my body being stabbed with hot pokers, fast and continuously until my body burned as if it were set on fire. I thought I went to hell. After a small excruciating minute, I could feel my body floating on the breeze. My body appeared as if it was torn inside out and crushed beyond all recognition. I remember that a beam of warm light fell to the earth beside the chunks of meaty remains. It's radiance called to me, I could hear Mom's voice."

Brandon's eyes watered, "Mom?"

Burden's tone resembled his earthbound voice once again, "I was distracted when I heard Len's name being called out from the cliff above. Ignoring Mom's calls, I climbed my way back up to the trail and found Len and Kawika in the middle of the path. It took me a little while to learn how to move, but you know I've always been a fast learner. After a minute, I was able to get a grip on reality, no pun intended." Burden laughed,

"I grabbed Len by his neck and squeezed. If it weren't for that pedophile creep, I would've killed the kid that night." Burden screamed causing his brother to cover his ears, "Kawika is gone! There's no one to save you now, princess! I'm going to make you experience exactly what I went through and more. You are going to pay for what you've done."

Brandon looked down in concern, "Burden, what would happen if Seth found out you were the reason he went to prison?"

"If he finds out, I'll know it was you that told him." Burden's voice did not make Brandon feel good at all. "You know what to do, so just get it done. I want to see the stupid look on the princess' face as she stands up from her fall in the afterlife."

"Okay, I'll go get some food from camp and bring it over. I need to be quick in case someone comes to check on me." Brandon urged his brother to let him go.

Before Burden left his host, he warned, "I cannot communicate with you as long as you're on the camp grounds."

Brandon assured his incorporeal sibling, "It's okay, I will make sure it all goes to plan. You just go get the big guy and tell him dinner is served. I will bring Ellen to you." Brandon could feel his body being vacated. It made him a little light headed and weak at the knees. When he he made his way back to camp he spotted a car tearing up the road. He hid from view and watched an older gentleman and a familiar looking woman blaze their way onto the premises, "Who the heck are they?"

Iwakālua

Mercy sprinted from the car and made her way over to the office. By the time Henry got out of the vehicle and found his way to the steps, Mercy returned from her inspection.

"There's no one here." She cast her gaze from left to right, "Maybe we should split up and search the entire grounds?"

Henry nodded, "That is a fantastic idea!"

"Okay then!" Mercy pointed north, "I'm going to check the lake, you stay up here and see if there's anyone up in these cabins."

The doctor watched as Mercy jogged away. Henry made his way around the main office, feeling as if he were being watched.

"Hello? Is anyone here?"

A clang came from the infirmary called out to the visitor. Henry trotted over to catch the source of the noise. He saw a shadow dart from a doorway.

"Hey! Hang on a moment, I'm looking for Len, a camp counselor. Have you seen him around?"

The shadow moved back into the doorway and responded, "Yes, I have. I'll take you to him."

***

Mercy found a large amount of young bodies peppering the waters of the lake. Len was the first to notice the woman lurking about.

"Mom!? What the heck are you doing here? Camp's not over yet."

"Len! Thank goodness, you're okay. Baby, we've got to go!" Mercy grabbed Len's hand and pulled his arm.

Len held his ground, "Whoah, whoah, whoah! Mom, what is going on? I can't leave my kids."

"Honey, I don't have time to explain." Mercy was in full panic mode. "We gotta go. Come on!"

A full framed square of a man appeared beside the couple chuckling, "Mercy! Wow, I wasn't expecting to see you so soon." John tucked his straggling hair into his hat, "Do you want me to show you to the cabin?"

Len's mother gawked at John's coordination of uniformed shirt and bright rainbow colored surf shorts. John smiled awkwardly as he noticed Mercy's line of sight.

Mercy seemed a bit in a hurry, "Hey, John! Look, I need to steal Len away, I'm so sorry. Something came up and we need to head out."

John frowned at the news, "I'm sorry to hear that, Mercy. Is there anything I can do to help?"

Mercy thought about what was headed in their direction, "I don't think you'll be much help in this matter, but thank you."

Len shucked his arm away from his mother, "What is going on right now!? You need to explain to me why you're acting so erratic."

Mercy grabbed her son's arm again, but he pulled it away just as fast, "Can you just come over here for a second? I can't tell you around all these people."

Yvonne noticed the drama playing out on shore. She watched Len reluctantly making his way over to a patch of California grass with a strange woman. "Mom, why are you acting all crazy!?"

Mercy turned her back toward the lake so no one could read her lips, "Seth Pedrina escaped prison again... and he's headed this way! He's coming to Pi'ilewa right now."

Len creased his brow, "Seth escaped and he's headed... here?"

"Yes! So, can we please go before he arrives and hurts these poor children?" Mercy pulled Len's arm once more.

"No!" Len snapped his arm back. "I have to protect these kids if he's on his way, Mom"

Mercy pleaded, "Baby, he doesn't care about the children, he only wants to hurt you. Only you!"

Len was taken aback, "He wants to hurt me? What? Nah, Mom, you're being paranoid. We'll call the cops and…"

Mercy balled her fists and spoke through her teeth, "The cops are dead! When Seth escaped, he murdered six officers *and* a motorist who was in his way!"

John's eyes got wide, "I'm sorry, what's going on?"

Mercy rolled her eyes away from her son, "Come on already."

Len, in shock, waved John closer to keep the info between the three of them. "Seth Pedrina escaped prison. Mom says he's headed here for me. She wants me to leave with her, but if he's headed here, who's to say he isn't going to hurt the children when he arrives?"

John pressed himself into the huddle, "I heard your mom say 'murdered'… who was murdered?"

"The cops, John." Mercy whispered in fear, "Seth murdered everyone at the prison, a half-dozen armed men killed by Seth Pedrina with his barehands. Now do you see why I need to take Len!?"

"Maybe we should call the parents and have them come pick up their children?" John aimed to protect everyone at the camp.

Mercy stopped the portly man, "A bus might be faster, John. You have no idea how long each parent is going to take to get up here. I'm sure some are still in the middle of work right now."

Len jumped onto what his mother relayed, "We probably want to keep the number of people up here low as well. We don't need to endanger more innocent lives, especially if this guy is tearing through the police."

"I never thought about that, okay I'll get the bus to come up." John looked at the campers and jumped on his horn, "Everyone, we are heading back to our cabins to clean up. Leaders, please be ready to move in a half hour. Leaders Pat and Yvonne, please bring up all four groups."

Pat threw a thumbs up. Yvonne tried to make her way out of the water to get back to shore to talk to Len, but he disappeared up the hill with John. She turned to look at the children and thought, *What is going on?*

Iwakālua kūmākahi

"Where the hell is my car!?" Mercy spun around in the driveway with a look of total betrayal. "I can't believe that bastard would just leave us here, high and dry!"

"Who, Mom?" Len searched for clarification.

"Henry, your damn therapist! He came here with me and the coward ran off with our car!" Mercy struggled to keep her wits about her.

John emerged from the office, "The bus will be here in an hour. That gives half of the children thirty minutes to pack up."

"Bus!?" Len's eyes bugged out, "Just one bus? So, who's going first? How do we decide who's getting out of here?"

John shook his head and placed his hands on his waist, "It's all they have, the other bus we rented is out of service until they get the new part in. They weren't expecting us to leave camp already." John wiped his forehead, "It'll be alright. We put the young ones on first. At least if the guy shows up the bigger kids can run away."

Len couldn't believe what he was hearing. "We're going to leave them to fend for themselves?"

John raised his palms, "Look, I'm sure we'll all be out of here before Seth shows up anyways. Let's keep a positive outlook here. Orderly and calm. We don't need a panic."

Len turned toward his mother, "I need you to go, Mom. When that bus gets here, you need to go with Pat, Paula and Yvonne. I don't need you getting hurt for absolutely no reason." Len hugged his mother, "I'm so happy that you came to inform us. You saved us all."

***

By the time the young ones were packed up and ready to leave, the bus pulled into the camp. John sent the four women off with the youngest of campers.

Mercy called out of the window, "Baby, please be safe! Keep an open eye, I need you to come back home!" Len smiled at his mother to help relieve her worries.

Mercy sat down and fidgeted, "Umm, sir?"

The bus operator looked into his rearview mirror and frowned, "Kids! Keep the aisle clear." The driver watched as all the little shoes disappeared from sight.

He replied to Mercy's inquiry, "Merv." Mercy appeared confused, "You can call me Merv, ma'am."

"Oh! Merv, can we get to the depot as fast as you can get this bucket to go? Let's fly like a bat out of hell!" Mercy had a very anxious look on her face.

"Please sit back and keep clear of the aisle. I can only go as fast as the speed limit allows, ma'am. Safety is the number one priority," the driver glanced up once more to make sure his aisle remained clear.

Mercy was trying to be as polite as she could under the circumstances, "I just wanted you to make it back to the camp before it gets too dark. My son is still there, I just want to make sure he gets home safe too. It's important that you get back here to get the rest of the campers as soon as possible."

The driver scowled, "Safety first!"

Yvonne moved closer to the upset woman, "Is Len your son?"

A tear fell from her eye and she sniffed, "He's my baby."

Yvonne couldn't believe this mother was dealing with almost the same thing she dealt with a mere eight years earlier, "Oh my goodness, I'm so sorry! I just wanted to say that you and your husband did a great job raising your boy. He's very hard working, caring and smart." She smiled at Mercy to help her feel better about the whole situation. "I asked Len what happened at camp when he was younger, but he never gave me a straight answer. Every time he tried, something would always come up."

"It just so happens that I, myself, have just learned a lot more than I thought I knew. Turns out I got my son hooked up to a dud of a therapist."

Yvonne saw this as her opportunity to get the answers she needed. "If it isn't too much of a bother, would you mind filling me in on all the details? After all, we do have some time."

***

Back at the camp, John worked furiously to shut down each building. Len, in the meanwhile, assisted the older kids, "When you are all finished packing, I need you to line up fronting the cabin!"

Andy stopped Len. He was trying his best not to freak out about the whole "leaving camp early" business, "Look, man! All of us are going to lose it if you don't explain what's happening. Spill!"

"Andy, I don't have time to explain anything right now. We need to pack it up, fast! The girls are almost ready to go and you guys are barely packed, hurry up!" Len was surprised when Sammy stood up beside Andy.

Sammy clutched Andy's shoulder asking, "Why are we going? We still have a few more weeks to be here. Are our parents okay?"

Len was over being nice, he didn't want to see any of these kids die, "I will explain everything once we're all packed up."

Jeremiah slammed his duffle down, "Eh! Everybody stop packing!" The room of young men looked at Jeremiah in confusion as they all froze in place. He added, "Len, if you don't start talking, pau alreadeh!"

"Okay, *fine*!" Len shook his head, "You want to know what's really going on? Here it is!"

***

The final girl from the Wāhine Cabin made her way down the steps joining the rest of her cohort. Jeremiah blurted, "Hurry up, Marian!" He watched the young lady falling in line, "What the heck took you girls so long!? We've been standing out here for five minutes." Jerry shot his attention to his counselor, "Okay, Len! We're all here, can we go now? Please!?"

John came over to the cabins seeing the last of the campers ready to ship out, "Follow camp leader Len into the cafeteria. Our bus should be here shortly." He leaned over toward his assistant and whispered, "I'm going to lock up these cabins, grab Brandon and prep for the bus. It should be here soon. Keep an eye on these little ones and we'll be out of here in a jiffy."

Len drew the remaining campers into the cafe as John finished up the lockdown. The sun was already starting to set and the light didn't last all that long in the valley.

The boys who knew the fast approaching dangers, couldn't help but tell their female peers what was truly happening. And, of course, the game of telephone made its rounds. Many of the campers now had an idea what they were on the lookout for.

Cheylene, one of the oldest in the group, squealed, "Oh my gosh! There's someone out there!"

Len looked out the door and spoke rhetorically, "Is the bus back?" He looked over toward the front gate and couldn't see or hear their transport.

Shawna called out to get Len's attention, "I see him! He's over there by the lake trail!" She pointed outside the window beside her.

Len saw the contour of a man moving through the twilight. The intruder blazed a thought in Len's mind, *That's not John or Brandon.* He grabbed a knife off the serving area and made his way out of the front door.

"Lock it!" He pointed at Andy, "No one in or out unless it's me or John!"

The young man ran toward the shadowy figure, chasing it down the lake path. The tall grass made it hard for Len to keep track of the mysterious figure, but when he caught glimpses of it, it appeared as though it were gracefully flowing rather than hoofing it down the bumpy terrain. Len pushed through to the shore of the lake and reached the beginning of the dock. He realized he made a terrible choice when the ominous figure had mysteriously disappeared. He ran back up the hill toward the cafe to protect the children.

The sun's luminescence had nearly faded, when Len returned to the campsite. The grounds had fallen dead silent and eerily still. The cafe was completely empty, the doors wide open.

"Oh no! Where are they?" Len found some relief when there were no signs of damage on the entrance. He ran across the open area toward the camp's driveway and came across a lonely figure near the refuse bins, "John! Where are the children?"

John jumped at the sudden outburst, "They are with Brandon in the cafe." The head camp leader latched the hood of the wooden box and fastened a lock onto it. "Why?" John elongated the question with concern.

"They're all gone!" Len could hear the light sound of children's voices in the distance coming from the dark path of the mountain's trail. He looked up at waxing crescent in the sky with thoughts of what Kawika told the campers many years ago, *For your safety, no one should be up in these mountains on the nights of Kāne.*

Len ran his hands over his forehead and tracked his fingers through his hair, "John, you gotta call the police, man! Brandon took the kids up the mountain."

"What? Why?" John threw his keys into his pocket. He watched as the young counselor turned toward the exit of camp. "Wait! Where are you going!?" the heavy man called out to his employee.

"Call the cops! I'm going to get those kids back!" Len shouted.

He looked up the face of the menacing mountain and could see small flecks of blue torchlight peeking from the tops of the trees. His thoughts battled against everything Henry taught him, *What in the world is going on here!?*

Len ran like a jack rabbit up the hiking path to make it in time to safely retrieve the young campers. *There's no way! It's all a figment of my imagination, isn't it?*

Len prepared himself for whatever could possibly be waiting for him up the ridge. A bully playing a terrible prank at the worst moment, a psychopath that has already murdered over a half dozen people, or a procession of spirits that could potentially take the souls of every single one of those kids just for looking upon them.

What if it is what I saw all those years ago? What if the night marchers are real?

Iwakālua kūmālua

"Shouldn't we call someone about this?" Yvonne and Mercy sat on an empty bus making its way back to Camp Pi'ilewa. The sun had disappeared behind the mountain and Merv was driving even slower on their return.

Mercy's eyes were gazing out of the front window, "Why does it feel like it's already too late. We need to pray we get back to camp in time to get everyone to safety."

Mercy looked at her new confidant and expressed her frustration with the whole situation, "I wish I knew earlier that Brandon Alberts was one of the counselors working at camp this summer. This was all too damn fishy!"

Yvonne admitted, "I wish I knew more period. Had I known Brandon and Seth were like brothers, I could have..." she thought, *What? What exactly could you have done? Are you just talking to make Len's mother feel better, or are you talking to make yourself feel better?* Yvonne felt a warm hand enveloping hers.

"Don't worry yourself over this, sweetie. It'll be okay. We all have some regret in not knowing the full story." Mercy pulled her hand back and crossed her arms over the railing in front of her seat. "I would like to know why my son's therapist just deserted us like that."

Yvonne didn't want to pry, but she was curious, "So, Len was going to therapy for what happened at camp?"

Mercy nodded, "Dr. Campbell helped Len get better, or at least I thought he did. I found out later that the guy just brainwashed my son. Instead of getting to the root of the problem, he covered it up and made Len believe he was dreaming everything up. Like the entire event was a figment of his imagination." Mercy hesitated for a moment as she confided in her young friend, "When I picked up my son from camp that day, I must admit I was also in a state of shock. In all honesty, I probably should have started seeing a therapist too, but after watching what Campbell did to Len, I'm glad I resisted."

Yvonne asked, "Did it make a difference in Len's life?"

Mercy began to realize that the situation was double edged, "I suppose it did, but at what cost? I guess we'll find out one day, but I pray that day isn't today."

Mercy's attention was brought back to the road. She noticed Merv reduced the speed of the transport to an almost dead stop. "Is everything okay with the bus?"

Merv replied, "She's fine. But, I'm more worried about the 'that'."

Merv lifted his woolly arm and extended his finger into the tree line off to the side of the road. Mercy could see a silver colored vehicle at rest in a dense thicket. It appeared to have recently smashed up against the trunk of a large tree.

"What the hell!? That's *my* car!"

***

Jeremiah walked alongside Shawna, keeping the young woman company. Sammy brushed up against the elbow of his cabinmate.

"You buying this, Jerry? Why the heck would being up here keep us safe from the psycho at camp? We're sitting ducks out here!"

Shawna let out a quiver in her breath and Jeremiah put his arm around her, "Look, Brandon said we should get as far away from da guy as possible while John an' Len go after 'em."

Sammy slapped his buddy, "There's nowhere to escape up here, you know that, right? Besides, what about the stories of Pi'ilewa Point?" Sammy looked up into the trees watching the moonlight being separated by the branches and leaves above.

Jeremiah spoke up to reassure Shawna everything was alright, "Night machas!? You talkin' about da ghost stories Len made up about da night machas? It's all fake. Created to scare da campers dat come hea fo' da summer. Shock an' awe, Sammy! You're so gullible."

"Brah, *you're* being gullible because you not even listening! Sammy's right!" Pe'a spoke out to defend his pal, "On top of all da stories, dat are indeed fo' real, we have no place fo' run if da guy makes his way up hea!" Shawna's widened eyes glowed in the dark.

"You boat need to take a chill pill. We'll be fine. He can't take on all of us at once! We bum-rush 'em all at da same time." Jeremiah looked proud of his plan.

In defiance, Sammy dragged his foot over the path scraping up some dirt and rocks conjuring a sizable scratching sound. "And who's going to lead that charge, oh fearless leader, you?" A B-52 flew up from the area of the boy's disturbance attempting to find a safer spot.

Jeremiah became uncomfortable, he knew the first to attack had a low survival rate, but he didn't want to look weak in front of Shawna. "Heck yeah, I would!"

The flying roach finally came to rest in the crook of Jeremiah's neck causing him to jump around swatting aimlessly about his face and shoulders, "Get it off, get it off, get it off!"

The spasmodic commotion finally broke Shawna. The teenage girl let out a scream that radiated out from the mountain bathing it in an uneasy energy.

***

Seth opened his eyes and exhaled a huge gust as the shrill awakened him. "What is that?"

A cackle flew around the convict's head, "Rise and shine, sweet pea! It seems as though we have a party on its way up to see you. They're bringing us cake and ice cream, isn't that nice?"

Seth's chest expanded and collapsed rapidly in excitement, "My party? Cake?"

"Yes, Seth. Cake," Burden hissed on exhale. "At least that's what I heard, but they could also be on their way here to make fun of us." Burden's voice became rasped, "To laugh at us!" He was now snarling as he spoke, "To hurt us! There's only one way to know for certain, big guy. We see if they are empty handed. If we don't see no cake, they must be here to taunt us!"

Seth got to his feet. In the dark, his form resembled that of one of the trees growing in the forest. He grumbled, "Cake."

Iwakālua kūmākolu

"Now what could *that* be?" a soft voice whispered from behind a leafless tree.

Curiosity took hold of an airborne observer. Landing gently over dried ground cover, the imp approached cautiously, to get a better view.

"Hey, watch it klutz!" A ground dwelling voice rose from the short grass and twigs, "You trying to kill me?"

A wispy laugh encircled the troll that slept amongst the weeds. It spoke in a high pitch, "I was making my way over there!"

"Oooh, what is that... who are you?" The voice ended abruptly awaiting a response.

The darkness flashed with a small pop, "I'm Lilo, and who might you be?"

"I'm Kilo."

The air pressed through the trees causing leaves to sprinkle down to the earth covering Kilo. The air sprite invited the earth goblin to join in on the investigation, "Would you be interested going on a small scouting expedition?"

"Reconnaissance!?" Kilo smiled. "I'd love to!"

Both creatures of shadow made their way over to the strange metallic object that sat hugging up against a tree.

"Hey! I've seen one of these before," Kilo said in excitement. "The last time I did, I was with a guy named Pilo. We found a very valuable treasure inside. It was a kino!"

Lilo's eyes widened, sparkling in the twilight. Kilo knew Lilo was now very interested in finding a treasure. They both wrangled their way inside the bent metal chamber to see if a kino dwelled inside.

"Ke kino!" Lilo exclaimed. Kilo fought to get to it first, but Lilo tried with all his might to keep Kilo away.

Kilo scratched at the upholstery in the busted car, "I told you about this treasure! It's mine!"

"I found it first!" Lilo pulled at Kilo's arms.

Kilo slapped at Lilo's grip, "No! Mine!"

"I invited you, Kilo! This is my expedition!" Lilo tried reasoning with the earth element, but it was too far invested in reaching the kino first.

Both creatures vanished from view when the high beams of the school bus bathed the area in white light.

Merv's abrupt call cut through the darkness ending the cricket's steady stream of chirps, "Hello! Is anyone in there? Are you hurt?"

Mercy made her way past Merv and found Henry hunched over the steering wheel, bleeding from the head. “Oh goodness, Merv! I need your help. It’s Dr. Campbell!”

The driver moved toward the wreck, “Campbell?”

Mercy pulled the driver’s side door open creating a loud, crunchy screech loud enough to wake the dead, “Help me move him into the bus.”

Yvonne watched the two pulling a body out from the wreckage. “Whoah, is that guy alive?”

Mercy placed her ear to Henry’s chest but couldn’t make out a heartbeat, “He may be alive, it’s hard to tell. He’s going to have a lot of explaining to do *if* he wakes up!” Mercy grabbed his arm. “Yvonne, help us lift him.”

They hoisted Dr. Campbell safely into the bus.

“We’ve wasted too much time. We need to get to the camp, now!”

Merv shut the door and threw the bus in gear. The large vehicle rumbled down the road continuing it’s way to Camp Pi‘ilewa.

***

The commotion of the campers could be heard approaching the lookout where Seth awaited his treat. The oppressive spirit knew it was close to party time,

"Seth, are you ready for your celebration!?" Burden relinquished his hold over the monstrosity of a man.

Seth experienced a tug that pulled at his tail bone. The sensation worked its way up his spine and finally exited out from his neck. "Haha, tickly!" Seth felt free.

"I'll be right back, big guy. Don't move!"

Burden made his way down the path and came upon the campers and his brother wandering up the trail in the dark, "Brandon!"

The unsettling voice of Burden Alberts startled his younger sibling. Brandon nodded to show that he could hear him.

"Seth is waiting for everyone near the top, but you need to make your way out of this group soon. If Seth sees you without his cake, there's no telling what he'll do to you." A course throaty laugh made Brandon's stomach nauseous. "Make yourself scarce… or not, it's up to you." The specter made its way back up the hill leaving a chill that fell upon the caravan of campers.

The frightened voice of Taylor Brown could be heard whining about how cold it was. Brandon saw this as his moment to sneak away, "Alright everyone, let's huddle together and create some warmth, yeah?" Brandon pulled stray couples and small groups into a larger mass. They lurched together as a ball of human flesh. "Stay together and keep moving. We're almost to the top." Brandon fell back behind the crowd and snuck off into the bushes to watch everything unfold.

Andy was stuck in the middle of the huddle right next to Marian and Shawna. He couldn't stop himself from expressing his opinion on their current situation, "Let me go on record as to saying I do not agree with any of this. I mean, does anyone else think that this is a bad idea?"

The voice of Pe'a rang clearly through the dark, "I t'ink wearing one bow tie wit' dat palaka shirt was a bad idea, Anday."

"My mother bought me this tie, don't you bad mouth my mom's fashion sense!" Andrew was more than mad at the unnecessary comment.

"Why? Did yoah mama tell you fo' wayah dat shirt *wit'* dat tie?" Pe'a and several other teens laughed before stopping abruptly in shock at the sight of Seth Pedrina blocking the trail. His massive shadow stood there eyeing each of the campers, none of whom had any cake.

Unassuming Andy continued to defend his mother's honor without knowing what was happening up ahead. The frustrated boy yelled out at the top of his lungs, "Not funny, you big dummy. Why don't you come over here so I can punch you in the nose!"

A gasp was let out followed by a deafening silence that made Andy very uncomfortable. The monstrous contour of the killer made itself visible to the boy. The child's knees shook and he felt his heart sink into his stomach.

Seth moved toward the group, grabbing for the closest body. He pulled a teenager in and wrapped his oversized mitts around her head squeezing it so tight that her hair tore effortlessly out of her scalp.

A horrific scream pierced Len's ears then was cut short. The sudden stillness of the forest felt eerily calm. Len's adrenaline shot through his veins. He quickened his pace as he ran up the trail.

Seth released Taylor Brown's corpse. Her eyes rolled over the soil and twigs on the forest floor, like golfballs in the rough. Her brain matter leaked from the holes in her collapsed skull. Taylor's dislocated jaw swung open exposing her tongue as it dangled out of her mouth.

The other campers were stunned by the horrific scene. Seth used this as a chance to charge in for his next victim, Stuart Takeono. The paralyzed boy didn't even know what hit him. Seth's fist slammed down onto the child's skull so hard, it pushed his vertebrae into his brain killing him instantly.

A torrent of screaming teens sent chills down Len's spine as he made his way around the bend. Len arrived just in time to see Seth drop the twisted, lifeless body of Byron Silva to the ground.

"What are you fools doing!? Run!"

Seth went in for Shawna Mako next, but before he could get a strong grip on her, a small frame of a man rammed Seth from the side.

Jeremiah yelled, "Run Shawna! Ru-" Jerry's voice stalled once Seth got his hand around the young man's throat. Seth punched Jeremiah in his face fracturing his orbital socket. Blood poured from the boy's nostrils.

Len pushed past the group of screaming teens. He swiped at the ground pulling up the only solid thing he could find as a worthy weapon. He held tight to a rounded stone that possessed cavities perfectly shaped for his fingers to clench.

The oversized psycho pulverized Jeremiah's nose and maxilla with a second smash of his fist. The boy's arms and head fell limp. Len jumped into the air and cracked the stone across Pedrina's smiling face. Seth released the battered young boy, his mass falling with a thud to the dirt.

Len did not give Seth a chance to breathe. He raised his hand up and smashed the rock against the villain's face over and over again. Hit after hit, Seth pulled himself up to recover. The brute would not yield. Len prayed the camp transport had made its way back to the campus.

"Go! Run to the bus!" Len called out to the children while continuously pummeling Seth in the head in.

Len stopped frozen in awe as the scratchy voice of Burden Albert's erupted in his eardrums, "I got you now you bastard!" The greasy cold fingers of Len's once mortal enemy held the young man's arm mid strike. Burden Alberts regained his ability to take physical hold of Len's body. He called out to Seth, "Get up you imbecile! You're embarrassing me!"

Burden wrenched Len's arm dislocating it from his shoulder. The apparition felt a surge of euphoria flow over him as Len screamed in pain. The phantom tossed the counselor into the bushes where he collided against a tree's trunk.

Len, in complete shock, fought to fill his lungs with breath. He could not believe what was happening at this moment, "Burden? How is this even possible!?!"

A slithery voice vibrated outward, "Aw, did you miss me, darlin'?" Burden began cackling and the unearthly sound brought fear into Len's heart.

"There's no way! You're not really here! You are made up!" Len struggled to find his sanity.

"I'm insulted! After all we've been through together." Burden moved closer to his opponent, "Come on, let's hang out one last time, what do you say? You, me and Seth. The thought of murdering you up in these woods in the dark, all alone... just like old times!"

Seth slowly regained his footing, Len had hoped he was out of commission, but he could see Seth was still a very real threat.

Burden Alberts? What the heck is going on brain? Whether or not he's a figment of my mind, I need to hold them off to protect those children. I can't fall apart now. But, I can't stop them with my arm like this either. I wish Kawika were here.

Burden's eyes beamed an eerie yellow toward his simpleminded accomplice. "Don't be rude, Seth. Say hi to our old friend, Princess Eleanora!"

Len's heart fell into a pit of desperation. *And now, both of them being back together to finish what was started almost a decade ago. The odds are against me, I may as well throw myself off that cliff and pray I survive the fall.*

Kawika's face flashed in front of Len's mind, *No! I need to keep those children safe, or at least buy them time to get on the bus. I may not have Kawika, but I can be like Kawika. Fight to the last breath. I'll just start with the one I know I can hit.*

Len swapped his trusty weapon into his left hand and charged at Seth screaming into the night. The black energy of Burden Alberts whipped like a flash flying right into his enemy's chest. He carried Len up the path and smashed him up against the cliff's face, knocking his head against the obsidian structure. His skull echoed in his ears from the impact.

"I'm going to toss you off the top of this mountain, Elenor! Then, I'll stop you from entering the light. You'll be mine forever!"

Len pressed the rock upward between him and Burden in an attempt to escape his attacker's grasp. His non-dominant arm did not provide enough power to create a large enough gap to break free.

"Weak! Pathetic!" Burden cackled, "I'm going to enjoy torturing you in the hereafter, little girl. Your ass is grass!"

A turquoise glow emanated from below, painting Burden's hellish face, making it easier to see his foul grin. His yellow eyes were drawn downward where the rock Len held tight was bursting with a brilliant, cool aura.

"What's this!?"

The light turned into a flame and leaped from the stone onto Burden's chest spreading like a fire over kindling. "Aaargh! Get it off me! It burns!"

Len shoved the stone into the torso of Burden Alberts where the flame began to encapsulate the dark entity. The intense heat radiating from the stone was too much for Len to handle. The blue fire singed his palm where he lost grip on his trusty weapon. Burden released his hold over Len. The shade pawed at his chest, trying desperately to douse the unearthly flames.

"You're going to pay for that!" Burden slashed at Len, tearing his claws across his chest. He swung his arm, back handing Len to the ground. "Things aren't looking so hot for you, sister!"

Seth creeped closer to Burden, but his eyes were mesmerized by the ethereal torch burning out from the bizarre rock. Burden snarled, "It was a valiant effort, princess. Too little, too late."

Len understood that the magical stone was the only chance he possibly had at defeating Burden Alberts' corpse deprived manifestation. Unfortunately, Len's hope rested on the ground just behind the floating revenant. He leaned his back against the rock wall trying his best to come up with a strategy. The earthy material burst into flame once more with an intense fire, Len thought, *What in the world is going on with that thing?*

Burden swooped down to rid himself of the cursed object and to protect his subsistence. He took hold of the stone, which caused him great pain as his hand went up in flame. Dropping the foreign object, Burden screamed calling out to his body guard, "Seth! Come here and dump this thing, will you!? Throw it off the side of the cliff..." Shining more intensely, the stone blinded the giant with its radiance and put worry into Burden's blackened heart.

"Hurry up and toss it!!!"

The sounds of the pahu vibrated out from where the stone blazed. Burden and Seth were distracted by the deep beating and monotonous droning of ancient voices flowing outward. Len eyed the rock's position to find the best route to retrieve it, when he realized it wasn't a stone at all, it was the top half of a human skull.

The drumming pounded louder and louder and the chanting became unbearable. Len's mind split in two, causing the deceit that was laid in his head over the years to go up in smoke.

"Huaka'i pō!" Len challenged, "It looks like we're *all* in for it now, Burden! There's no escape… for any of us!"

The specter laughed like a maniac, "I'm not the one who should be scared. I'm already dead!" Burden turned and looked at Seth, "Sorry about that big guy, no hard feelings?"

The skull rolled over, tooth to floor. A translucent face materialized and began to rise out from the head until the body of an ancient warrior stood above the remains. It stepped to the side to allow another koa to ascend. Over two dozen spirits poured out from the cranium surrounding Len, Burden and Seth.

Their gaze first fell upon Seth Pedrina, who began to soil himself reactively. The 'oi'o scowled at the repugnant display. They turned their gaze at the boy pressed up against the rock wall. Len's eyes watered as memories returned from the night he watched Kawika being surrounded by the spirit ranks. Len was satisfied that his last moments in life were spent doing what his hero had done all those years ago, protecting others.

The feather cloaked apparition raised his fist and extended his arm toward the young man. Len closed his eyes awaiting the piercing of a spear when out of the mass of spirits he heard a familiar voice say, "Mine!"

"Kawika!?" Len began to weep finding his friend standing amongst the procession of ghosts. Kawika smiled at Len and looked at Burden Alberts. He tilted his head toward the sickly black vapor, that stood defiantly, awaiting Len's death.

The chiefly manifestation turned his attention away from Len, arm still extended. He aimed his fist at Burden and raised his index finger shouting, "'Ō'ia!"

The spirit warriors lunged forward, each taking a stab at the demon with their ihe. Burden screamed an unearthly wail. Len covered his ears and shut his eyes as the intensity of Burden's cries grew louder and the glow of the huaka'i pō blazed as bright as a bonfire. Burden's shrieks could be heard all the way down at the camp, but were silenced as if someone put him into a pot and slowly shut the lid. The sheet of bright red behind Len's eyelids became a cool black.

Everything had come to a complete calm. Len opened his eyes and found that the night marchers and Burden Alberts had disappeared. The sound of light whimpering caught Len's attention. He stood up and ran over to a body laying in the middle of the path.

"Jerry!? You're alive!"

Sputtering, claret colored fluid shot out from the battered teen's wounds. Jerry tried to communicate, but only his choking sounds traveled through the silent forest. Garbled words forced their way out of Jerry's swollen, unrecognizable face. Len hoisted the hurt teen up with his left arm to start their descent from the mountain.

"I gotcha, man. Let's get the heck out of here." Len knew this was going to be a long walk down for the both of them.

A loud snap and searing pain caught Len by surprise. Seth Pedrina grabbed Len by his dislocated arm and squeezed. It felt as if Seth had shattered Len's ulna and radius. Jeremiah fell back to the ground as Seth gripped Len by the throat. The young camp counselor could feel his feet leaving the floor, just like the night Kawika died. He pounded at Seth's wrists with his left arm and even tried prying the beast's fingers apart. Nothing worked against his assailant. Seth had made his way to the edge of Pi'ilewa Point. He was intent on finishing his duty to Burden by tossing the guy off of the mountain.

Len's vision began to blur and his ears vibrated. A loud whirring made his brain shake. Before passing out from lack of air, Len could see two orange orbs flying out from the trail of the dark forest. Seth cast Len to the side and raised his hands in defense. Head Counselor John rammed the camp's club car directly into the behemoth causing him to sail into the air soaring off of the cliff. The huge slap from below echoed its way up the steep mountain side making John tingle in his nether region, "That was loud."

Iwakālua kūmāhā

"You're late... again!" The big man from behind the counter stabbed his pudgy finger at his employee, "I don't care how much you beg me next time, if you come walking in that door late again, you're fired!" Roy placed his thumbs into the tied strings of his grease stained apron.

Mercy smiled holding her hand out in front of her, "Mr. Adelson, you can't fire me because I quit. I'd like my final wages, thank you."

Roy was in shock. His mustache sagged even more than usual as he pleaded with his prized server, "Now, don't be too hasty, Mercy. You can't leave me like this!" Roy tried lowering Mercy's hand, but she brought it right back up again. "Just stay one more night, and we can think about it. Alright!?" Roy pushed Mercy's hand away but it returned like a boomerang, "Come on! Let's be reasonable here. There's no one else to sub for you tonight. Sarah's on vacation and Cheryl had a death in the family! I need you, babe!"

"Do you even watch the news, Roy!?" Mercy's eyes squinted at the dingy man. He shrugged his shoulders and offered a blank look. Rolling her eyes at her former employer, Mercy asserted herself, "Look, I'm leaving. I'm taking my son and we're going away. So, give me my money so we can get the frick out of here!" she swiped her hand catching Roy in the left boob.

Roy opened the til and counted out Mercy's money. He shook his head in disbelief muttering, "I try to help people and this, this is the thanks I get?"

Mercy tore the remaining wad of cash out of Roy's calloused digits, "For suffrage!" As she glared at him, he was reminded of all of his inappropriate advances towards her and nodded, defeated. "And don't call me babe!" Mercy shoved her earnings into her purse and pushed her way out of the diner.

The feeling of freedom fell over the woman's whole body. She felt liberated and as light as air. Mercy had waited for the moment to tell Roy she quit. She worked hard at the diner, but when she got home to shower, it wasn't just the kitchen grease and customer spittle that went down the drain, it was the uncomfortable stares and unnecessary comments made by that deviant that washed off as well. Her thoughts finally brought her to the doors of the laundromat.

"Mercy, if dayah ish anyfing we can do fo' you an' yoah son, you let me know." To'o handed the red eyed woman an envelope with ‘Fa‘afefai Lava’ written on it. “You did an amayshing chob keeping ouah playsh running ovah night. It’sh kona pea hahd fo’ fine someone ash kood ash you.”

Mercy motioned her head from To‘o over toward Junior Boy. He looked over at his grandson, who was pursing his lips bobbing his dome up and down. He scoffed at Junior Boy’s wardrobe of a dark tank top over a white shirt and socks in his sandals.

He shook his head while rubbing his wrinkled hand over his face, “No moah hope.” To‘o slapped the earphones off Junior Boy’s head. “Shay good pie!”

Junior Boy looked at his tamā matua with surprise at his unexpected swipe. To‘o grimaced at his big for nothing grandchild. Junior looked at Mercy and said his farewell, “Faifai Lelei! Mercy, you come pack, I take you an’ your poy to da buffet.” Junior Boy smiled exposing his golden caps and stretched his earphones back on his meaty head.

“Thank you for everything, To‘o. I really appreciate you taking such good care of me and Len.” Mercy put her envelope inside of her purse and left the washerette. She hopped into her rental to pick Len up from Camp Pi‘ilewa.

***

Len sat beside Yvonne on the bench outside of the main office. He could see her gazing up at the top of Pi'ilewa. The setting sun painted the mountain a warm orange and the air had a slight chill to it.

"It's crazy how beautiful it looks now. It was a totally different creature last night."

Yvonne looked at the wrap around Len's forearm and smiled, "I regret not getting here sooner, Len."

"No, no. If you had come any earlier, it could have been worse for you, for my mom. I couldn't live with that," Len slouched with his hands clasped.

Yvonne placed her hand on his, "I believe you."

Len turned toward Yvonne with a look of confusion, "What?"

"I believe what you experienced up there." She bounced her chin at the peak, "You saw Kawika, right?"

Len swallowed hard and his eyes started to shine, "Yeah." He thought about how he was about to die by the spear of the night marchers when he heard his voice halting the order.

"Kawika was one of them, one of the marchers. Just before they attacked he said 'mine'. They stopped for a brief moment and I was able to see him standing there. I was filled with fear, happiness, and sadness all at once. I wanted to say something, anything to him." Len smacked his fist into his palm causing pain to radiate through his forearm.

"What would you say to him if you saw him right now?" Yvonne was curious.

Len shrugged, "Thank you..." His voice trailed as he began to sniff and tears fell from his eyes. "I miss you?" He spoke softly with his face in his chest.

Yvonne rubbed Len's back and nodded to comfort him, "Is that it?"

Len took a deep breath and cast his gaze at the spot he imagined Kawika was standing near, "I love you." Len's lips quivered as he tried his best to smile at his savior.

A gust of wind swirled around the couple bringing up the dry grass and loose dirt from the ground. It moved out from the camp and seemed to be swallowed into the mouth of the trail's opening.

Yvonne's eyes widened. She smiled at the bizarre coincidence and focused back on Len, "Amen!"

Len's stupefied expression made Yvonne laugh and toward the end of her chuckle she let slip a small snort. Len eyed his pal because he wasn't one hundred percent sure he heard what he heard. Yvonne's cheeks turned pink and her eyes were circles. Before Len could confirm what she had just done, John made his way out of the office.

"Okay, you two. With that said, we should be all good." John observed his workers mid moment. "Uh-hem, well! Here are your stipends. Don't spend it all in one place." John handed an envelope to Yvonne and one to Len. Yvonne was surprised by the thickness of Len's envelope. "Oh right, yeah, so I wrote Len a letter." John smiled awkwardly at Len, "I wrote you a letter." He chuckled, "I'm not used to saying things in an emotional way, so, I wrote you some… anyway, some of it might not make any sense, well, I mean, you could call me if you have any questions about what I wrote."

Len stood up and hugged his boss, "Thank you for saving me again, John."

"Stop it! Stop." John shook his hands and blushed when Len pulled away. "You already thanked me for that, everyday in fact! For over a week!"

Len smiled, "I just wanted to make sure I said it before I couldn't."

John smiled back, "That's why I wrote the letter!"

Yvonne asked, "Why are you giving us our checks now? We have one more week and there's still a lot to do."

John looked at the couple, "Pat and Paula will be here next week. They can finish up the packing and cleaning of the main building. You guys already did most of the heavy lifting anyway. You two can use this free time to better acquaint yourselves with each other. Go to the movies! Go to the beach! Have some fun next week. Maybe it will hopefully bring you both back here next summer."

John made his way into the office. Yvonne had a very hopeful smile on her face, "So, what were you planning on doing next week?"

Len felt a bit out of his game. He was filthy and felt like he was probably smelly as well. Him crying in front of Yvonne just made things even worse. "Why don't you give me your number and we can plan something."

"Dude!" the young woman's eyes lit up, "You *better* call me." Yvonne's stepfather pulled up in his car just as Len took the young woman's number.

"Hey, Daddy-o!"

"Hey, sweetie. Let me say hi to John before we take off!" Wayne hopped up the stairs and entered the office.

Len smiled, "You know, I was having a hard time understanding how John was your uncle, but now, I'm having a hard time understanding how *that* is his brother!"

Yvonne laughed and snorted again at the end. She made a face of embarrassment as she looked toward Len. Now, he definitely knew that she snorted earlier and he found the quirk endearing. His face lit up and made her feel comfortable with the weird moment. To change the subject she whispered, "Try to imagine if you stretched John upward a few feet." They both started laughing again which made Yvonne snort even louder the third time.

Len's eyes went round in a joking manner and Yvonne pinched him in the chest in retaliation. Len tried to defend himself, jostling his busted arm, "Ow! Take it easy!" They laughed more as Wayne made his way down the steps.

"Oh! Wayne, this is Len!" Yvonne moved to the side exposing the full frame of her potential beau.

"It's a pleasure meeting you, Len. I've heard the stories and I'm very impressed by your fortitude." Wayne shook the young man's hand.

Len bowed as he released his grip, "I wasn't here alone, sir. Your brother is my hero."

Wayne smiled, "You need to stop telling him that, it's making his head big and I don't want my brother losing his balance down these stairs."

Yvonne stood up and added, "Len and I may be hanging out next week. If that's okay."

Wayne's eyes lit up, "Oh! Well, that would be nice. I hope that you rub off on Yvonne more than she rubs off on you." Both teens stood there completely in shock. "Oh, uh, geez louise! You know what I mean. Come on, Yvonne!"

Len watched as Wayne and Yvonne made their way off campus passing by his mother. Mercy pulled up past the gate and she appeared to be in a very happy mood, "You ready to party, babe!?"

Len shook his head as he got in and thought, *Uh-oh, what is she planning?*

***

Henry laid in his hospital room feeling a little restless. It was as though time had just forgotten about him. He knew he was being discharged soon, but to him, things just weren't moving fast enough. As soon as he regained consciousness, he worried about what led to him being in his current predicament. He couldn't remember much about the past few weeks. It was all so hazy.

The news reports about the incident seemed so surreal. A half dozen deaths on top of the murders at the police station. "A baker's dozen," Henry murmured staring at the hospital television that was in the off position.

His mind began to seek answers, *How could any of this have happened? These poor families, upended by one unstable individual.*

Faces that he would see at church on Sunday, were now gone forever. He felt sick to his stomach, "Was there anything that I could have done to stop all of this? What could I have done for that young man? What could I have said? Maybe he *saw* something..."

Henry thought about what he could recall from the whole event. He spent the majority of that evening on the school bus passed out. When he would come to, he would see shadows of people looming above him. He could hear them whispering, conspiring, plotting. It was like living through a nightmare, s*leep paralysis.*

Henry's mind snapped to his arrival at the infirmary on that bleak night. He could see a myriad of shadows inside the hospital, clear as day. He fought himself through the memory. *Not possible. It was a figment of my imagination. Brandon caused me to hallucinate all of it. He must've planted seeds of persuasion.*

Henry anxiously looked around the room. Paranoia was starting to take hold of the good doctor. His mind brought him back to his senior prom and his first experience with, what he believed at the time, an actual demonic entity. A violent, obscured brute that attacked him without warning. To Henry, this whole situation felt too familiar. The story played on repeat in his life and his integrity came under fire in way of doubt.

"I need to find out why I am being tormented this way." The beautiful face of his senior prom date, Keanu Haukea, popped into his mind. *Keanu must've seen something while we waited for our photo to be taken that evening. That thing that stung my wrist... she must've felt it too. We held hands!* Henry rubbed his forearms as if he could still feel the whip on his wrist. *I need to visit Keanu, it's the only way to find the truth.*

Iwakālua kūmālima

Cheryl and Mercy both sat at a round metal table with an umbrella sticking out from the middle. They shared a meal and spoke about recent events.

"How's your husband dealing with everything?" Mercy asked as she picked up her pink drink.

Cheryl rolled her eyes, "I guess he's okay. Actually, I don't know. Taylor was a lot younger then him and when the family would get together he would always talk about how she was so spoiled and how she would always annoy him. A part of me thinks that he has some relief," Cheryl saw Mercy's face contort, "I mean, he's sad about what happened, but he seems to be more concerned about his aunty. She would always dote over Taylor, plus she was the only child. They had her when they were a bit too old I think."

"Yikes!" Mercy thought about having Len when she was still in high school and thought, *Too young, too old... Sheesh, when it happens it happens!*

"Tonight, we are going to cousin Lydia's for dinner. The whole family is going to be there." Cheryl stuffed a large portion of cutlet into her mouth.

Mercy smiled, "Len and I are leaving 'Āinapau."

Cheryl's eyes bulged. She covered her mouth with her hand to avoid anything falling out, "Where? When?"

"We are going to O'ahu in a couple days. I decided we need to get away for a while. Len's going to the university and I thought maybe I'd get my G.E.D. so I can go back to school, too. After all that has happened, we need to live our lives without regrets. Am I right?" Mercy watched Cheryl wipe her face clean.

"You guys are going to Honolulu? You're going back to school… with your son? That sounds like a bad comedy. Good grief, isn't that where Kaulana went off to!?" Cheryl's questions were relentless.

Mercy looked toward the parking area, "I have no idea where he could be honestly. But, that isn't the point of going to Honolulu. I'm not letting that man back into my life, or into Len's."

Cheryl asked softly, "What if Len *wants* to see him?" She added excitedly, "What if you accidentally bump into each other on the street? It's a small island, Mercy!"

"I'm finally doing what I believe is right for my family. My son has gone so long without me. I intend to make up for all that lost time." Mercy folded her arms over each other.

"Hey, sister, I get it. I understand what you're trying to do. Just don't open the dam all the way, or you will lose your son in your flow." Cheryl jerked her shoulders and her eyes were round. "Did I just say that?"

"I get it. I worry I may smother the kid, but I'll take it slow. Besides, as much as we love it here, and this *is* our home, there has been too much tragedy for Len and me. Maybe when things settle down in our lives we'll find our way back, but for now I need this. *We* need this. Len going to college is truly a blessing in disguise," Mercy explained.

"How does Len feel about leaving?" Cheryl pushed her half empty plate away.

Mercy gazed toward the unfinished meal sliding toward her, "He knows it isn't forever. Besides, he met someone." Mercy looked at Cheryl and could see she wanted more details, "She's a girl from the camp. Yvonne is her name. She's very sweet and protective of Len. In a way, she reminds me of me when I was with Kaulana."

Cheryl smacked her knuckles onto the tabletop, "The difference is your son wouldn't just abandon someone. He's nothing like Kaulana, you raised him to be better than that."

Mercy rubbed her hands together and thought, *What raising? I left the poor kid with anyone available to watch him. Len being just like his father is probably why he came out so good. Kaulana was just as innocent, sweet and sincere when we first met. Why did he choose to leave us!?*

Mercy knew her son was a good man, but she feared he would repeat what her husband did and run off. "Well, if he does to her what his father did to me, I'll need to give him a swift kick in the butt!"

Cheryl tilted her head and raised her right eyebrow, "If only Kaulana's mom were around when he did that to you and Len all those years ago."

Mercy smiled and drank the last of her pastel beverage, "Well, if we do run into each other, I'll just have to give him a piece of my mind."

***

The soft splash of the ocean's waves rolled up over the shore. The sun had finally set and twilight made the cooling sand glow. Yvonne looked at Len who was still searching the horizon for the green flash. "I had a very nice time with you this week."

Len smiled at Yvonne, "Yeah! Everything after camp has been a complete blast."

"Oh! My mom invited you to dinner tonight, if you're interested in coming." Yvonne looked hopeful.

She could see that Len had other things on his plate. “I’d love to come, but my mom’s expecting me to be home to help pack the last of our things.” He could see Yvonne was more than a little disappointed. “I guess if you came and helped me, I could finish faster and come over for dinner.”

Yvonne was overjoyed. She jumped up and yanked the beach mat to encourage Len to get up. “Well, let’s go. Time’s a wastin’!”

Len pressed his elbow into the blanket making it harder for Yvonne to pull, “Wait, come sit for a sec.” Yvonne planted her bottom onto the rainbow striped cloth. “This is probably going to be the last time we spend together all by ourselves. I wanted to use this moment to say goodbye. A real goodbye.”

“It won’t be, like, forever though, dude. Stop being so overly dramatic.” Yvonne was also worried about not seeing Len ever again.

“Working at the camp, I have learned that it is a lot easier to accomplish anything as a team, and I thought we made a pretty good team this summer.” Len stuck his hand in his backpack.

Yvonne watched Len fumbling around in his bag, “Well, it would’ve been a lot less stressful if you didn’t bring your friends,” she responded with a joke, that may not have landed as smoothly as she intended.

Len could see the young woman was nervous. His face lit up when he found his treasure, "Here, I'd like to give this to you." Len placed a necklace around Yvonne's neck. At the bottom was a fishhook made of bone and wood.

Yvonne admired the gloss of the bone and the smooth silky texture of the wood. She laid it careful y on her chest, "You trying to say you hooked me?"

"Sweetest catch ever!" Len glanced from the hook to Yvonne's eyes, "I know I won't be here with you, and I know I'm going to be away for school, but if you would like we could still be..."

Yvonne interrupted, "Who says I'm not going to school soon!? Maybe you'll see me sooner rather than later! So, think your next words carefully. Are you sure you want to say what you're about to say."

Len thought about how his father left him and his mom high and dry. It's something he didn't want to repeat with anyone, especially Yvonne. It appeared as though he was on the same trajectory as his dad. Local boy smitten by a girl from the mainland. After all he had experienced when he was younger, he believed that he had some kind of mental disorder. Maybe something passed on to him from his father. He looked at Yvonne and believed he would never leave her. He took the anxious girl by the hands and asked, "Will you go steady with me?"

***

The sun had just reached its zenith and Henry was making his way downtown. He drove over a familiar path that filled his mind with memories. A lot had changed in his town over the years, but the road was the one thing that remained constant through it all. His car whirred up a hill and past the church he would frequent when he was younger. Within moments he pulled up to the Haukea residence. He stepped out of the car finding his balance on his cane and thought about the night of prom. His stomach grew queasy as he rang the door bell. *What if she doesn't remember me? What if I'm the last person on earth she wants to see?*

"Can I help you?" The face of an unfamiliar young man opened the front entrance.

"Hi, I'm sorry for the intrusion. My name is Henry Campbell. I'm a close friend of the Haukea ʻohana. I wanted to speak with Keanu if at all possible. Or her mother, Dolores if she's available." The doctor stood by awaiting an answer.

"Oh! A friend of the Haukea's? Hi, I'm Reed. Please come inside." Reed stepped outside the house to allow Henry to make his way in. "Make yourself at home, Mr. Campbell. Come and sit."

Henry sat at the dining room table catching the musty odor of an animal nearby. He looked under his seat and around the house as he smiled, "Please call me Henry."

"So, Henry, you're looking for Keanu, *and* you're a close family friend?" Reed sat at the table with a slightly hesitant look on his face. "It must've been a while since your last visit."

The doctor needed to make himself clear, "I suppose it has been quite a long time. Keanu and I went to school together, we were a couple." Henry didn't know who he was stretching the truth for at that point. "Is she home by any chance?"

"Henry," Reed stood up and took an official's stance, "I'm so sorry, Keanu Haukea passed away a couple of years ago. Her daughter, my sister-in-law, Kazuko, is allowing me to stay at the house as a caretaker. I'm the only one here."

Henry's brain froze over. He didn't make a sound and he didn't move a muscle for an extended amount of time. After realizing his rudeness, Henry inhaled to speak, but before he could say anything Reed placed his hand on his shoulder.

After watching the older gentleman sit there without any motion Reed asked, "Is there anything that *I* could do for you, Henry?"

Dr. Campbell thought, *Only if you've experienced the supernatural or otherworldly.* He stood, taking hold of his cane, "I'm so sorry to have bothered you, ah, Reed. I'm quite stunned and I'm at a bit of a loss."

"Well, you don't have to leave if you'd like to take a moment," Reed offered Henry some time to relax as he extended his hand back toward the chair. "I can fix something if you're hungry."

A heavy mass banged up against Henry's leg causing him to fall back into his seat. Reed tried reaching out to help Henry, but he dropped fast and unexpectedly. "Whoah! Are you alright!?"

The hair on Henry's arms stood up on end as he looked around for whatever knocked him over, but he came up empty, "No! No, I don't want to bother you more than I already have." Henry felt his mind was a lot more fragile than he originally thought. He made his way toward the front door, "I'm, ah, sorry for your loss, my friend." Henry pat Reed's arm twice as he walked out.

The young host held the door as Henry slid his footwear on, "I'm sorry for your loss as well. If you change your mind, please don't hesitate to stop by."

"I do appreciate your hospitality, Reed. You are too kind. If I should find myself here again, it would be a delight." Henry slowly entered his vehicle saddened by the news of Keanu's passing.

Reed knocked on the car window before Henry could leave giving the older man another jostle. “Hey, I just remembered. If you needed to speak with a Haukea, you could always make your way over to the ranch. I know Junior. Pretty cool guy. He comes to check on the garden from time to time. I’m not sure if that helps your need. But, I thought it may be useful to know.”

“I very much appreciate that, Reed.”

Henry waved at the friendly young man and drove back down the path that once made his stomach flutter. *I can’t believe Keanu is gone.* He thought about visiting the ranch for a second, but was overwhelmed by his past. *The only one that would truly understand my situation is gone. How would stopping off at the ranch be of any real help? I mean, I guess I could always stop by and pay my respects.* Henry turned down the highway heading south. *I owe it to Keanu. And, I owe it to myself.*

Iwakālua kūmāono

"You better be picking up some stamps if you want to keep in contact with your girlfriend, Len." Mercy smiled fiendishly at her son. "You will *not* be calling each other over the phone. That's going to cost us, big time!"

"Wouldn't it be awesome if we had super powers, Mom!?" Len looked toward his mother. Her face appeared unamused, "Yeah! Like telepathy? Then I could talk to Yvonne all the time without spending money on long distance calls!"

"Too much science fiction! Just get the stamps, okay?" Mercy made her way over to the bank to make a withdrawal. As she walked into the establishment she was shocked at the length of the line.

John noticed Mercy gawking at the end of day rush, "Sweetie!" he called out to her.

Mercy was caught off guard. She watched as John waved her over toward the front of the queue. "Hey, John!"

"I know you guys are on your way to the airport soon. I've been in this line for almost an hour." John raised his brow.

"What's going on? Why are there so many people here?" Mercy looked around at all the impatient faces.

"Just another pay day. Don't you come to the bank on pay day?" John inquired.

Mercy shook her head, "Actually, we live paycheck to paycheck mostly. Everything I bring in goes right back out. I'm only here to close out an account that was opened since Len was little."

"Next in line!" a bank clerk called out in the direction of the massive queue.

John scooted Mercy off in front of him, "Go ahead, I'll take the next one."

"Thank you, sweetie!" Mercy whispered as she made her way over to the teller.

Mercy stepped in front of the counter and was greeted by the banker, an older woman with a gray streak running through her hair, "Hello, how can I help you today?"

"Yes, I'd like to close an account." Mercy fingered quickly through her purse searching for her photo identification.

"Is there a reason for closing your account this evening, ma'am?" The clerk took hold of the woman's I.D. card.

"Ah, yes, my son and I are moving away from 'Āinapau," Mercy responded.

"Next in line!" The clerk beside Mercy called out and she could see John making his way down the walkway.

The clerk asked, "Where are you both moving to?"

"Oh, um, Honolulu... but, why is that important?" The clerk caught Mercy by surprise.

"Oh, I'm sorry ma'am." The bank agent explained, "I was asking because I wanted to see if we had any branches available to you where ever you are moving, and I believe we have three locations on O'ahu. So, if you prefer we can keep your account open and you can bank with us on that island, no problem."

Mercy looked a little uncomfortable, "Well, you see, I kind of need the money now. With the moving and all." The clerk looked a bit perturbed, but she began the process by heading to the back of the work space for the account closing slips.

John could hear what was going on from the counter next door so he prolonged his visit to make sure Mercy wasn't being treated unfairly.

The teller returned with several papers of different colors, "Okay, so I'm going to need you and Kaulana to sign these. Read and initial this one, and I'm going to need to see his I.D. as well."

Mercy's heart sank, "I mean, if Kaulana isn't here right now, would that be a problem?"

The bank clerk folded her hands over the papers, "Ma'am, you have a joint account. It cannot be closed unless the both of you agree to closing it. There isn't anything I can do in this situation. Is there anything else I can help you with today?"

"Would I be able to withdraw all of the money from the account without closing it?" Mercy asked.

"Yes, you can definitely make a withdrawal. You'll need to keep ten dollars in your checking and fifty in your savings." The clerk pulled the paperwork back and walked over to return them to their trays.

John looked over at Mercy to make sure everything was alright, "Are you ok?"

Mercy looked a bit stressed, "Yeah, I should be cool. Thank you, John."

The clerk returned, "A bit of caution, however. If you and the other joint member are not agreed to this withdrawal, it is very possible for the other member to sue you for this transaction. Is Kaulana aware of this withdrawal?" The last thing Mercy wanted was Kaulana back in their lives. She covered her face. "Ma'am, is Kaulana aware of the transaction? I'm only trying to be helpful."

John was called back to his clerk, "Sir, was there anything else I can do for you today?"

"Please give me one second," John moved over toward Mercy. "Hey, what's going on?"

"Well, it's going to be tough, but Len and I should be able to manage." Mercy looked back over to her clerk, "It appears that I won't be able to access this account after all. I'm sorry for wasting your time." Mercy thanked the teller for her assistance.

John straightened his posture as he looked at his teller, "I just need one more thing."

Mercy made her way out of the bank in tears. "Great! After the school admission, we'll have a place to stay, but we won't have any food to eat."

"Mercy!" John made his way toward the single mother as she wiped the tears from her face. "Here, this is for you." John handed a wad of cash to the distraught woman.

"Oh my goodness! John I can *not* take this from you!" Mercy looked around concealing the money as she pressed it back into the generous man's chest.

"It would be an honor if I could provide you some ease, Mercy. Please, I want to help." John grabbed Mercy's wrist and placed the money into her hand, "I don't know your situation, but I know you and your son are good people. You need it, please take it."

Mercy hid the money in her purse, "I don't feel right about this, John. How could I ever make this up to you?"

John smiled, “Well, if you feel this strongly, let’s call it a loan. When you and Len have the opportunity, you can return it. No worries about a time frame, no interest necessary.”

Mercy hugged the robust man and was surprised at how solid he felt, “I am forever grateful, John. You saved my son and now you’re saving me, thank you!”

“I hope it all works out for you and Len. If you guys find your way back now and again, I’d love to see you both,” John was interrupted from his farewell.

“Hey, boss!” Len had just returned from the post office. He could see his mother was previously crying, “Mom, is everything alright?” Len stared at her awaiting a response.

John decided to speak up, “So, did you get to read my letter?”

“Oh! No, I have been so busy with Yvonne I didn’t even open the envelope.” Len palmed his forehead.

John shook his head and looked back at Mercy, “You guys should be okay. I hope to see you again. Read that letter, Len. And take care of your mother.” John made his exit.

Mercy watched the man who saved her son over and over again walking away, “Beauty comes in all shapes and sizes.”

Len looked at his mother’s face, “What was that Mom?”

Mercy hugged her boy, "Nothing. Come on, let's get to the airport."

***

The flight was packed, and because of their cheap tickets, Mercy and Len boarded last. They found seats separate from each other, but Len found this time perfect for reading his boss' letter. He peeled the glue from the mouth of the envelope and saw a piece of note paper wrapped around a wad of bills that was double the amount that he was originally offered when he was hired. *No wonder my envelope was thicker than Yvonne's,* Len recalled. He pushed the money safely back into the sleeve and unfolded the letter.

My dearest Len,

First off, I would like to say that I am so grateful having you on as camp counselor this summer. The kids just loved you and your campfire stories. Your hard work and work ethic made it very easy to make the decision that I did. I included in your stipend the money that I was going to pay Brandon. Consider it a farewell present and a hope that one day you'll make it back to Camp Pi'ilewa to help me out again.

Secondly, I would like to apologize for what happened. In hindsight, I know I shouldn't have ever hired Brandon.

We would've been able to handle the whole summer with the crew we had, but when I think back about the situation it would have been worse had we not kept one eye on the Alberts boy.

Thirdly, I wanted to apologize that we weren't given the time to do a proper book burning ceremony. I think that it might not be a good time to do it just yet. We should come back together, you, me, Yvonne and your mom to do it the right way and let it all go properly… in the meanwhile, maybe you could add a few more journal entries in the book concerning what happened at camp this summer. It may be helpful.

Finally, I wanted to send my well wishes to you in whatever you decide to do. But, it would be a real shame if you didn't choose to work with our youth. You have a real knack when it comes to helping our keiki flourish. Keep that in mind when choosing your major.

Mahalo for everything.

Sincerely, your friend,
John Chun

P.S. Tell your mom I said hi.

Len folded the letter up and slid it back into the envelope. "Thanks again for saving me, John!"

***

When Henry pulled up to the ranch he came upon an A-frame with a sign on it that read, 'Brown 'Ohana.' It made the older man very curious as he continued down the gravel path.

When Henry reached the barn, he saw a tall, bald and rather fit older man carrying tables into the structure calling out with a rough tone in his voice, "Eh, Kukui! Take deez tables an' set 'em up ovah dea!" Henry watched the familiar looking man make his way over to his vehicle. "Wassup, braddah!?"

"Oki!?" Henry was astonished.

Junior shoved his head into the car and stared at Henry's face, "Ho, bulleh, you got old!" He yanked his head out of the window and yelled, "Pahk by da shed!"

Henry pulled his car off to the side of the shed and made his way over to his old friend. "Oki, it's so nice to see you again!" Henry hugged Oki with one arm.

"Brah, please tell me you use dat stick fo' get da girlies," Junior shook his head.

Henry's ears turned red as he squeezed the top of his cane, "Ah, well, some of us age more gracefully than others I suppose."

"Eh, Junior! Wea you like me put da serving tables?" a younger Polynesian man inquired.

Junior pointed at the back of the barn, "Trow 'em against stall eleven."

"Junior?" Henry asked.

"Oh, yeah, das right! E'rybody from skoo wen call me Oki. Anyways, aftah my faddah wen retieyah, I wen use my real name when I took ovah da ranch. Da kine business guys no can say Ka'alaikalewa, so I tell 'em fo' call me Junyah." Junior looked at Henry puzzled, "So, long time no see, cuz. Wassup?"

Henry nodded acknowledging the huge gap since the last time they saw each other, "Yes, I came by today because I recently learned about your cousin's, Keanu's, death." Henry looked down at Junior's boots.

"My fadda's shoes. Still good yet, an' da buggah fits perfs." The boots were nicely formed around Junior's calves. He answered nonchalantly about his cousin's bearing, "Yeah, Keanu stay in one bettah place. Dis world not meant fo' one person laddat." Junior stared at his unexpected visitor still unsure as to why he was there in the first place.

Henry was starting to feel a bit nervous by the look Oki shared, so he decided to cut the conversation off and move along, "So, I just wanted to say I'm sorry for your loss."

Junior wagged his head, "T'anks, Hanale." He reached out for Henry's hand.

Just as Henry put his hand up a loud scream blared from his side, “Henry Campbell!?” Lydia came running from the walkway to hug Henry nearly knocking the unstable man down. “Golly, it’s been ages! Oki, where are your manners? Invite the poor dear in!”

Junior shook Henry’s hand and motioned his face at the house, “Come insai, cuz.”

Lydia placed some ice cold lemonade in front of the doctor, “Oh, thank you so much, Lydia!” Henry could feel Oki’s intense stare burning into his forehead. He decided to ask about their history, "So, when did the both of you tie the knot?”

Lydia looked at Oki from the side of her eye, “This guy right here asked me to marry him at my graduation. Flew all the way across the pacific to find me. Such a romantic!”

Junior stopped Lydia from elaborating, “Henry, why don’t you jus’ tell us why you stay at ouah house? Fo’ real! I know you want somet’ing!” Oki crossed his arms, “I remembah from way back, you wen hang aroun’ us fo’ get populah at skoo, you wen hang aroun’ my cousin cuz you wanted her to be yo’ girl an’ now, what? Why you nevah come check on her befoah? Why now? Somet’ing stay off about dis whole visit!”

Henry began babbling, “I, ah, had so much going on in my life, Oki. When I moved back here after my divorce I needed time to get my practice up and running..."

Oki yelled while forcing his best English impression, "Why did *you* come *here* today!?"

Henry knew he needed to be frank, "I wanted to find Keanu because I believed that she was the only one who could help me."

Oki raised his hands and turned his attention toward his wife, "See!? Dis guy always about numbah one! He no kea about us, he no kea about Keanu, he no kea about anyt'ing but himself!!"

Lydia rubbed Oki's shoulder to calm him, "Henry, it's very nice to see you again, but it would be a fair assumption that you are in need of something. Just popping up out of the blue on our door step is rather odd. Now, what did you need Keanu for?"

Henry sat like a child in a hot seat, "I'm so sorry for not making myself available to my friends, to you, when I returned home."

Oki showed his discontent, "Tsa! Yoah home!? Brah, we should go talk to da Lanimainu'u's and see if day agree wit' yo' concept of home! I heard da main push fo' turn 'Ōma'o into one resort was none addah den da Campbell 'Ohana. Lucky Donna wen fine dat ana wit' all da kine ancient artifacts laddat. Recognized on da National Registry of Historical places. Sorry you never reap da benefits on dat one!" Lydia pawed Oki's shoulder and he swiped her hand away, "Bumbai today dis island would be all kine malihini dropping dea trash an' pilikia on top ouah heads! Brah, you were supposed to be a part of da movement to help da 'āina, not da one bustin' her up!"

Henry stood up, "I'm sorry for coming here, I didn't mean to start a fight." Henry made his way out of the Haukea residence.

Oki trailed behind the slow moving visitor. "Das right haole! Run away wit' yo' problems. We don't need dat ovah hea, not today. Not aftah losing ouah 'ohana to one addah pupule haole!"

Lydia tried her best to diffuse the situation, "Oki, baby, please stop! Don't do this in front of the workers."

Henry reached into his pocket to pull out his keys. His foot gripped a loose stone in the walkway causing him to fall. "Ow! Gunfunnit!"

Oki looked down at the pathetic man writhing in pain and he started to feel bad. He stuck out his hand and pulled Henry up pressing him against his car. "Brah, what da heck happened to you? You all bus'!"

Henry was out of breath, "I wanted to talk to Keanu, because I was attacked by another demon."

Lydia's eyes grew large, "Oh! No, no, no, Oki get this trash off of our property right now!"

Oki reached his arm up and pointed, "Baby, go help da boys finish setting up fo' tonight's pā'ina. I'm gonna have a small chat wit' my fren'." Oki watched Lydia gallop over to the barn. "Demon!?"

Henry wiped his face, "I know! See, this is what made me nervous. Bringing this up makes me look like a complete maniac. Just like all those years ago!"

Oki started laughing, "Brah, you talking about da prom!?" Henry nodded causing Oki to laugh even harder, "Cuz, dat night, you *was* attacked by one demon!"

Henry's face turned white, "Wait, you knew about the demon?"

"Well, firs' of all, he's not really one demon. He's my *cousin* true marriage." Oki had a wide grin. "You see, Hanale, when you was trying fo' get wit' my cousin, she was already seeing dis guy named Kaiulu. He nevah like you touching his girl, das why he wen smack yo' pūlima! Dummy." Oki looked at Henry's face and it disgusted him, "Das why hahd, you guys come down hea an' ack like you own everyt'ing, even da people. Sickening." Oki opened Henry's front door, "You get what you get an' you don't get upset. Now beat it befoah my wife come back and kick yo' ass."

Henry slid into his seat, "All this time I thought I was hallucinating, it was actually all real?" Oki stood outside his car door bobbing his head while smiling at Henry's misfortune. "So, the apparition that attacked me as I drove away from camp that evening, that was real too?"

Oki's face dropped, "What?"

"My memory is not the greatest. I hit my head pretty hard and now I can't seem to remember everything clearly." Henry looked at his old classmate and added, "I went to Camp Pi'ilewa to save a patient of mine from a psychopath that escaped the prison. An accomplice tried to jump me, so I tried to get away. A creature that was made of swirling shadows appeared in the car I was driving and it attacked me. Next thing I knew, I woke up in the hospital. That was a few weeks ago. I thought Keanu would be able to help me make sense of everything, so as soon as I was discharged from the hospital, I went to her house."

Oki shook his head, "I'm not surprised dat anadah demon wen' attack you, braddah man. So, you was up Pi'ilewa da night of da massacre?"

Henry finally calmed himself, "For the beginning of it anyway. That's why I'm all busted up."

"Come." Oki opened Henry's door, "Would you like to stay fo' dinnah?"

Iwakālua kūmāhiku

The lights in a holding cell blazed on and blinded the one that rested within. A startled male searched through the fluorescent glow trying to find a reason for the sudden intrusion. A loud voice called out, "Inmate Wilson, K., keep clear from the door!"

"Yeah, yeah! No need to shout." Ken sat up on his cot as a young prisoner made his way into his cell. "Fresh catch, huh, Jones?"

"Keep your mouth shut, inmate!" Officer Jones pressed Brandon into lockup. "Inmate Alberts, B., this will be your home for the foreseeable future. Wake up call is at seven and you are expected to follow every instruction. Do you understand?"

"Yes, sir."

"Wilson, play nice with your new friend." Detention Officer Jones and Sergeant Keala made their way out of the cell block. Brandon turned in time to see the pillow that sat on his folded blanket levitate up and over toward the bed of his cellmate.

"Alberts, huh?" Ken tucked Brandon's cushion underneath his and settled back in for sleep. "Is your name, Bea? Or was that just an initial?"

"Brandon." The young man tossed his blanket on top of his cot and laid his head on it, his eyes glued to his bunkmate.

Ken could see the teen was not very trusting, "Hey, kid, don't sweat it. I'm not going to try anything fishy. Relax. I'm Ken, by the way." He watched Brandon turn his gaze up at the ceiling. "So, Brandon Alberts. You're the kid from the camp, right? Damn, man! I would've done the same thing too. I would've left all those kids behind if I knew a psycho was around." A long silence followed Ken's statement. He decided to leave his new roommate alone to adjust to his environment.

Brandon closed his eyes and saw the enraged face of his brother fly right at him causing him to jolt up from his mattress. He screamed, "Burden no!" The terrified teen looked around the dark chamber and saw that his cellmate was fast asleep and his brother was nowhere to be found. His heart raced inside his chest. The guilty boy whispered, "Burden, I'm so sorry." Brandon laid on his side facing the brick wall and began sobbing.

Within what felt like minutes, a voice called out, "Rise and Shine! Wilson, Alberts, up, up, up! Gregory, Barker, time to move! Kamanaka and Ascension, knock that off and get up! Ready for breakfast!" Detention

Officer Palani scraped his baton over the slats of the cell block.

Ken stared at Brandon from his bed, "Rough night, kid?" The boy continued to sit in silence, "Well, you can stay in here and get some more rest for about an hour, if you like. You've got until eight, but our next meal isn't until dinner. So, eat now or wait until six." Ken watched the young man rousing. "We have about a half hour before they take us out of the cell block, so head over to the showers and get yourself cleaned up."

Brandon walked into the wash area and saw a man using a toilet. None of the stalls had doors on them. He made his way over to the sink and splashed his face with cold water. As his eyes cleared, the menacing visage of his brother leaped from the reflection of the wall mirror. The specter flew out of the glass and shot towards Brandon making him slip backwards nearly cracking his head on the tiled floor.

"Susmaryosep, you're not dat ugly, kaibigan!" The man on the toilet laughed at the boy whose head laid a mere foot away from the stained crotch of his skivvies.

Brandon turned over and stood back up with fear in his eyes. Dusting himself off, he ran out of the restroom and bumped into Ken causing his toothbrush to fall to the floor.

"You're kidding me, right!?" Ken watched Brandon snatch his toothbrush off the ground.

"Here!" Brandon offered his brush in return, "I didn't use it." He ran off back into his cell and tried to work through what he was experiencing.

***

"You can get help, if you need it. You should ask to see a psychologist if that's the kind of help you need, I mean," Ken returned from washing up.

Brandon eyed his cellmate as he hung his towel on a rail, "I'll be alright. Don't worry about me."

"Again, you went through the wringer. You shouldn't let your pride hold you back from getting help." Ken could see Brandon nod, "If you like, you could always talk to me. I'm great at keeping secrets. That's actually why I'm in here. Kept my mouth shut so tight, I became an accomplice. Isn't that crazy? All for being loyal." Ken smirked, trying his best to show his most 'likable guy' face.

"Breakfast!" A loud voice rang through the hall and into the cells.

"Well, come on, kid. Let's get some grub. We've got a long day of nothing ahead of us." Ken stood up and made his way out of their cell.

Brandon noticed that the cafeteria was very clean on arrival. There were a mix of inmates, visitors, and police eating altogether. Officer Palani called the young man over. “Alberts! Take a plate,” he jabbed his finger at the silver counter top.

Brandon grabbed a tray and took a little bit of everything. He sat on a table next to his prison pal. “I wasn’t expecting prison to be like this.”

Ken laughed, “That’s because we’re not the *real* bad guys. They’re held in a separate section away from the main part of the facility. Those guys eat, sleep, and play all by themselves. It’s where that psycho was being held before he escaped.”

“Seth,” Brandon muttered as he opened his milk carton.

“You know about the guy?” Ken asked as he bit into a crispy piece of bacon.

Brandon looked around at the commingling. Visitors sitting beside inmates and officers all talking peacefully with each other. It was an unfamiliar scene to the young man. He thought, *Why are all these people so happy?* It made his stomach wrench. Two snaps from Ken’s fingers brought the young man back to the table, “What!?”

“Earth to Brandon, yo! What’s going on up there, dude?” Ken shook his head, “Seth!? You knew about the guy?”

Brandon sank into his seat. “He was my friend.”

"Whoah!" Ken wiped his face with his sleeve. "Wait, was he trying to go after you!? Is that why you ran away?"

"No!" Brandon pounded his fist into the table.

Ken watched the visitors become unsettled and the guards placing their hands on their sidearms while staring in their direction.

"Easy, guy! I hear we're getting meatloaf for dinner and I don't want to be locked up in solitary for two days because of your outburst!" Baring a fake grin, Ken waved his hand innocently at the officers. "So, what then? You were, ah..." Ken dug his chin into his chest giving Brandon a deep stare.

Brandon knew exactly what the guy was implying, "An accomplice? Let's just say that I knew I'd make it out alive. Seth was there to take care of business. I was only trying to help an old friend."

Ken was shocked, "Cold, man. Completely frigid. You were okay with all those kids getting offed?"

Brandon smiled, "No, not at all. We were only after one guy. The guy that killed my brother. The one that framed Seth as a murderer all those years ago. If anything, *he* turned Seth into the psycho that he became. Burden and Seth, they were my brothers. My real family. Yeah, they would rag on me and punk me, but that's what family does. It makes you stronger."

Ken settled back into his seat spooning up some egg, “So, did you guys get ‘em?” Brandon looked at Ken confused, “The guy you were after! He dead?”

Brandon slammed both fists into the table causing a scene once again. An officer started making his way down the edge of the room.

“Officer Palani, we’re just talking, I promise you! The young man is just expressing his frustration with being here is all.”

“Keep it down, Wilson! You know what tonight is… meatloaf!” Officer Palani made his way back to the service counter proud of his threat.

“What did I say, kid? Don’t screw this up for me!” Ken sounded desperate as he lowered himself back to his seat. “You need to seek help, my guy. Seriously. You shouldn’t be harboring that much anger toward one person. It’s not healthy.”

“Why does it matter now?” Brandon scooped up his scrambled eggs. “My whole family is gone anyway.”

Ken looked at the troubled man, “Family can be what you make of it, Brandon. Remember that.” He stood up with his tray and walked over to the trash bins.

Brandon saw Ken speaking with a guard who immediately escorted him out from the dining area. The rest of the day, the young man found that his cellmate had vanished completely from the prison, even during the dinner he so wanted to partake in. When Brandon returned to his cell he realized all of Ken's belongings were gone.

"What the heck is going on?"

Officer Jones came by the cell just before lights out, "Well, well… inmate Alberts! It appears that your trial has moved up on a fast track. After breakfast tomorrow, it looks like we're taking a small trip to the courthouse." Jones slapped his nightstick against the cell doors, "Sweet dreams, convicts!"

The lights went out and Brandon found himself in a very strange situation. "Why do I get the feeling that I am screwed."

Iwakālua kūmāwalu

A short slender woman with jet black hair wearing a red dress spoke from the corner of the jury box, "After reconvening with our peers to review the evidence, as well as taking into consideration the recent statement made by Detective Kenneth Wilson from the Hāloa Police Department, we the Jury, find Brandon Alberts guilty on one count of terroristic threatening. We the jury, also find Brandon Alberts guilty on six counts of wanton negligence."

Judge Yamamoto looked at the young defendant, "Brandon Alberts, you are sentenced to five years imprisonment for first degree terroristic threatening of one, Doctor Henry Campbell. You are also sentenced to five years imprisonment for each of the six counts of willful and wanton negligence that will all be served concurrently. Parole will be possible after four years served. Do you understand these charges that are set upon you by this court?"

Brandon's lawyer replied earnestly over the wails of the spectators, "Yes, your honor. My client understands the ruling, thank you."

A loud pop snapped Brandon out of his day dream, "Thank you jury, for your service. You are all excused." Judge Yamamoto lowered his gavel, "Court is now adjourned."

Brandon looked around the courtroom at all the angry, tear streaked faces. His lawyer bounced his head, "Phew, you got off easy kid!" His observation moved to the crowd Brandon was paying most of his attention to, "Look, at this point they're all trying to fry anyone for what Seth Pedrina did at the camp. Since he's dead, you're unfortunately the face of this terrible incident. Listen, thirty-five years instead of life *and* you get to serve it concurrently? That's a win in my book. Things could've been a lot better if you hadn't spoken to that cop though. Keep your nose clean and maybe you'll see your freedom restored sooner rather than later. Regardless, after your time is over, your life is going to be difficult. No one's going to want to hire you, especially since everyone on this island knows the case. Find a job in the prison, make some money and move far away. You've got ten years to make it happen, Brandon." The defense lawyer grabbed his paperwork and slapped it into his brief case. He shared a wry smile and shook Brandon's hand. "God was looking out for you today, young man. Don't waste this gift."

Brandon watched his lawyer disappear out of the courtroom, "It wasn't the work of God that saved me here today. My fate is left in the hands of someone that dwells in a place a lot lower and much hotter than the so called paradise above."

"Get up, Alberts! Time to go."

The convicted teen was escorted out of the courtroom and into a squad car where he was returned to prison to serve his sentence.

***

Journalists swarmed Henry as he made his way out of the courtroom. "Dr. Campbell, how do you feel about the verdict that was handed to Brandon Alberts today?"

"Well, I must say that the tension from everyone inside that courtroom was feverishly high. Each family member and every friend of the victims at the Pi'ilewa Massacre were here looking for a face to pin the entire incident on." Henry took a deep breath, "I don't know why Brandon did what he did that night, but I feel that justice has been served. Hopefully, with time, he can see the errors in his ways."

Henry saw this as an opportunity to plug his business, "Speaking about time, I believe now is the time for healing. I am offering anyone that had immediate family at the camp during the tragic event, that struggles with trauma from that night, a free consultation with me at my office and a fifty percent discount off of my continued support and services. It's just a small way of giving back to the community."

"Thank you very much for your time and generosity, Dr. Campbell. And thank you for helping the community that was effected by the savage misdeeds of Seth Pedrina and Brandon Alberts. You're truly an inspiration to our youth and hero to our community!" The journalist turned toward the camera man, "Well, you have all seen the results of the Pi'ilewa trial and of course the mental support being provided by our own Dr. Henry Campbell for anyone that was affected by the attack during the recent …"

Oki turned the television off, "Dat fricken guy! He couldn't help himself, yeah babe? One day, he's gonna have to admit *he* get pilikia."

Lydia shook her head in disapproval. "I don't know, Oki. Times are getting harder, for everyone. Henry's just a regular guy trying to do the best he can with what he has, after all."

"Well, he's gonna face da music one day. Ignoring da warnings from da addah side is hūpō loa!

Lydia walked over to her husband who was visibly perturbed, "Promise me that if anything happens to us, we keep our humanity."

Oki squeezed Lydia in his arms, "Always."

***

"I got some good news and some great news!" Mercy made her way into the living room of their small apartment. Her son had his head buried in his books, hard at work on his studies. "Whoah! First day and already there's an assignment?"

Len smirked, "This isn't high school anymore, Mom!" He finished jotting some notes down and looked up at his mother, "So?"

Mercy sat beside Len, "So what?" Len stared at his mother unenthusiastically. "Oh, right! So what do you want to hear first?"

Len shut his book, "Let's start with the good news."

Mercy presented an odd copy of a record, "I got my G.E.D.!" Len jumped up and hugged his mom. "*And*, there's still time for me to sign up for courses this semester!"

"That's fantastic! But, I thought you were going to start your new job?" Len asked for clarification.

"Well, I'm only going to sign up for one class at the moment." Mercy watched Len's expression waiting for more details, "Theater! I'm taking an acting class!"

"That *is* great news, Mom! Wow, so what shall we do to celebrate?" Len grabbed his shoes.

Mercy crumpled her lips, "Honey, that was only the good news."

Len sat back down. "Oh! I'm sorry, what's the great news?"

Mercy pulled a newspaper article out of her purse. It had the headline of the trial of Brandon Alberts.

"The little bastard was incarcerated!"

Len grabbed the article from his mom, "Wait, it says he only got ten years? After all the Alberts family did? He should've gotten life if you ask me."

"A win's a win, baby! There's no way this guy is going to be able to show his face anywhere around here after he serves his time. He'll probably be run out of Hawai'i!"

Len nodded, "Yeah, I guess you're right, this is great news. Okay, so where to?"

Mercy grabbed her purse, "Zippy's!"

Iwakālua kūmāiwa

John observed a taxi pulling up to the entrance of Camp Pi'ilewa. "Len!" He moved over to the young man as he retrieved his bag from the trunk of the car. "You're looking well!"

Len eyed the Head Camp Leader, "Wh-what!? *You* look super, John! I almost didn't recognize you. You lost some weight." The head camp leader had a huge smile on his face. "Grapefruit diet?"

John shook his head, "No, not at all. I just stopped eating snacks and drinking sodas. Who'd've thought that it would make such a huge difference?"

"Well, keep it up! You look amazing." Len inquired, "How's the enrollment this summer?"

"You wouldn't believe the work Yvonne put into hyping up the summer camp during the off season. She promised an experience like no other." John pulled Len toward the main office, "I was worried that if we were lucky we'd get half the amount of campers we had last summer, but nope, we have nearly a full house!

Although, many returning campers had a discount due to not finishing last year all the way through."

Len dropped his bag on the counter, "That is great. I'm so happy the camp didn't suffer a loss of clientele."

"We've got a ton of work, Len." John made his way behind the counter, "Yvonne promised a lot when it came to new activities, so you're going to be very busy." John could see Len had an unnecessarily large smile on his face after he mentioned his niece. "Look, be professional, Len! I already had a talk with Yvonne, I don't want you two monkeying around during camp, okay?" John wasn't sure if Len heard anything he just said, "Ugh, she's in the Wāhine-" before he could even finish what he was saying John found Len had already flew out of the office. Within moments, he heard a high pitched scream coming from a couple doors down. John shook his head, "What have I done?"

***

When the campers arrived, Len was happy to see so many returning faces to his cabin. He saw his buddy Andy Bently who had shot up a few inches since last summer. Big boy Moku Kahuhipa had returned with a slimmer physique. Surprisingly, Jerry Gonsalves had returned as well, but initially Len had a difficult time recognizing him due to the facial reconstruction that he underwent after the attack he suffered at the hands of Seth Pedrina.

Jeremiah's transformation had many girls swooning over him with his new Rick Schroder-like appearance. Shawna Mako was stuck like glue to his arm at all times, swatting the other girls away like little gnats. Following the couple like a third wheel, was Cheylene Hikina. Whether or not she liked it, Cheylene followed the couple everywhere they went all summer long since Shawna was her best friend.

Len was disappointed to learn that Little Miss Mercy was not returning to camp. He had heard that the family had moved from the islands altogether after her near drowning. Len speculated that the craziness that ensued solidified their reasonings.

The first couple of weeks had the campers buzzing all about the events that transpired the year before. Len was over inundated by questions about what happened to him when he was little. He saved his stories for the campfire, where they had the greatest effect. The kids brought up the stories again and again when the signs of the huaka'i pō up Pi'ilewa Point would appear.

Len was tempted to make his way up the mountain trail on Pōkāne, but the thought of Kawika not being in the procession when he wanted to visit was too large a risk.

The one thing that always confused Len about his spectral saviors was that they would never leave the opening of the forest path. He saw the torches stop midway down the mountain where the pahu would halt its beating and all would go eerily quiet. It was a lot different than the stories he had acquired while in school on O'ahu. Processions could travel for miles, up the mountain ridges, down by the ocean shore and sometimes through the living room of people's homes. This group at Pi'ilewa seemed as though they were trapped behind an invisible gate.

The two months spent with the campers flew by in a flash. Yvonne and Len barely had any time to spend together. The couple awaited the end of summer, when they could finally spend some quality time.

John was so relieved when the campers all made their way off campus safe and sound. "We did it gang! We sent those kids off with memories they can share with their friends and hopefully will bring in even more visitors."

Len could see a devious look in John's eye. "Hey, John? If we get everything cleaned up early, can we leave camp earlier?"

John smiled, "Why, that sounds like a great idea!"

***

The counselor's finished all of their work with a week to spare. John came out of the office with the stipends. "You'll all be happy to hear that because we went without a fifth and sixth counselor for the summer, your pay has increased." Pat and Paula showed how very pleased they were by clapping in unison. "Don't expect this to happen every year. If we get a larger turn out next summer, we may need to hire extra bodies." John placed an envelope in everyone's hand. Len handed his envelope back to John, "This is for the loan you gave my mom the day we left."

John pushed the money back to the boy, "No, Len, I was thinking you guys would pay it back after you finished college and you were both stable." John looked into the light blue sky, "Then I'd smile at your mom and tell her I was never expecting her to pay any of it back."

"Take it John, my mom was fine with me coming up here to work this summer knowing I'd be doing it to pay back our debts and to see Yvonne." Len smiled at his girlfriend.

"Well, it was a dream." John looked down, a bit disappointed. He took the money from Len. "Well I guess since that's all settled, if you ever need help. You can rely on me."

Len hugged John, "I know, bossman. Thank you."

John flicked his hands outward, "Alright you all, get outta here already! Go have some fun."

Yvonne watched her stepfather pull up to the front gate. "Hey, how'd everything go?"

She winked, "It was a lot of work, but it was fun. Thanks for letting Len stay with us for the rest of the summer, Dad!"

Wayne smiled and helped the two youths load their things into the car. "Let me stop in the office real quick."

"Dude, did you know that the new Star Wars is out in theaters!? Maybe we should go watch, then we can stop off at the ice cream shop!"

Len smiled, "I'd love to, but I don't really have much money."

Yvonne grinned, "I'll give you a loan like Uncle John did. What did his interest look like?"

"Oh boy!" Len shook his head at the fiend.

"Are we ready?" Wayne hopped off the steps and jumped into the car, "Len, did Yvonne tell you the good news about going to the university this semester?"

The car pulled away and Yvonne's voice could be heard pouring out of the car's windows, "Dude!?! It was supposed to be a surprise!"

Kanakolu

Brandon sat in the recreational area going over how much he had lost because of Len. Even the phantom visits from his brother were much different than before. Instead of communicating with Brandon, Burden was just finding moments where his brother would drop his guard to lunge at him and scare the wits out of him.

"Burden!? Tell me this isn't you!" Brandon thought, *No! You wouldn't be this cruel? This couldn't be my brother. He wouldn't play tricks like this. Maybe he truly is gone.* Brandon wallowed in self pity and guilt.

His mind took him back to when he, Burden, and Seth would stay away from home for extended periods. How they built a makeshift clubhouse out of the chassis of a busted up '58 Chrysler Imperial.

They would often spend nights camping out in the car to avoid being anywhere near their father and his repulsive cronies. Burden would comfort him during the times it stormed. The raindrops would fall heavily on the tarp that laid over the car's roof. The noise would make Brandon anxious, and Burden would always take his worry seriously.

Footsteps echoed from behind, Brandon quickly sucked in and wiped his eyes. He turned to see who was approaching, but there was no one around. He surveyed the empty hall and something odd caught his attention. Underneath a bookshelf, that leaned against a wall on the opposite side of the rec room, sat an out of place object that called to the young Alberts boy.

Brandon stood up and made his way over to the prison's small library. A strange, slim pamphlet that was ragged and dusty hid behind the footboard of the bookcase. It was a cult manual for satan worship that looked eerily similar to the one that lived in the Ouija Board box he and his brother would play with as they grew up.

"What the heck is this doing here?" Brandon whispered to himself as he kneeled in front of the stand.

"You hab day ray-lee-djous?" Inmate Ascension blurted as he wandered into the center, snatching the television remote up off the table. "Bumbai, you ehstop by my cell por day rosa-ray?"

Brandon stood up and hid the pamphlet in his uniform. "Thanks, Manny. I think I'll pray alone."

"Inmate Alberts, where are you off to?" Officer Jones questioned the boy. "Gym hours are regulated to after three, I've told you this a dozen times."

Brandon turned around, "Oh, no I'm not headed to the gym, I was going back to my cell. Ascension is watching his soap operas again and I just needed some quiet time."

Jones nodded and allowed Brandon passage back to holding. "I'll let you know when the gym is open, Alberts."

Brandon gave Jones the thumbs up. "Thanks, boss."

When he got back to his cell, Brandon sat with his back to the door and pulled the thin reading material out of his coveralls. The title read "A Small Bite of Satanism." The hairs on Brandon's body shot straight up. He threw the booklet onto his pillow as his heart raced. He thought, *Now this is something I could see my brother doing.* "Thank you, Burden!"

Officer Jones yelled at Brandon from the cell door, "Inmate, Alberts!"

Brandon jumped up and turned toward the guard, fumbling to hide his satanic manual. Officer Jones was nowhere in sight. Instead, the large shadow of Burden's smoke-like form peered through cage and flew through the bars knocking Brandon to the floor. He sat up with sweat dripping from his forehead looking around his cell for his brother.

"Burden!?" The shadow was already gone. Brandon lifted the pamphlet up, "Alrighty, let's see what this thing has to say."

Kanakolu kūmākahi

It didn't take Yvonne long to figure out the campus of the college, but she had gotten used to Len helping her find her way during her Freshmen year. At the start of each semester, Yvonne would pretend that she still needed his help. She'd sometimes tell Len she forgot how to get around just so she could spend more time with him. Len caught on to her scheme pretty quick, but he amused her regardless.

During the summers, the couple would make their way back to the camp to help Uncle John, and each summer the head counselor's health would improve. It almost seemed as though John was deliberately trying to attract a certain someone. His first question to Len was always the same. He would inquire how his mother was doing and every time Len would respond that his mom said 'Hi!' which would bring a smile to John's face.

Mercy was happy to be active in the life that Len and Yvonne seemed to be navigating together. Being near the young couple gave her the hope that their relationship would endure. At first, she wasn't sure how she felt about Yvonne coming to Honolulu for school, but they worked out a plan as a family and everyone seemed to be benefitting from the arrangement. Mercy decided that Yvonne should stay with her in Len's room and Len could sleep on the pullout in the living area. Yvonne helped where needed, but mostly they all pulled their weight and acted very much like a small family. Mercy loved how respectful Yvonne was of her. The young woman treated Mercy as if she were her own mother.

As the years moved on, Mercy started spending more time at the theater. She started landing larger roles and even picked up the lead a few times. When Yvonne and Len had a moment, they would stop by the production to support her. Things really started to click for Mercy, except in one particular department.

***

"Mercy!" Damien, an actor from their play, shot over beside her at the end of their final showing of, '*It's Not Over, Maureen!*'. "Hey, the group is headed over to Hell to let loose, you wanna come along?"

Mercy eyed her children, "Oh, sorry Damien. I'm on my way home with my kids. We've got plans."

Len knew she was lying but, he played along, "Yeah, we have a fun evening planned."

Damien's face grew long, "Okay then. Maybe we can do get together some other time?"

Mercy pushed Yvonne and Len to get them moving, "Oh, yeah, haha maybe."

"Sheesh, Mom! What was that all about?" Len asked, as his mother shoved him along the walkway.

"For an older dude, that Damien guy was cute. Didn't you want to go out with him?" Yvonne made an attempt at making Mercy feel comfortable.

"No, it's okay. We are doing just fine as is. We don't need the drama, well *that* kind of drama, in our lives right now. Besides, dating an actor?" Mercy shot her gaze between the young couple, "Don't get me started."

Len was indifferent about his mom dating. He had seen it hundreds of times, and besides, he had other things on his mind. "By the way! Speaking of drama, there's this professor that teaches history that stopped by our English class today to promote his course. The guy is pretty far out. He came all decked out, just like you are now, Mom. Anyway, he was so animated and passionate about his craft. I was interested in taking his course next semester."

Mercy squished her face, "Wait, you already took Art History to fulfill that credit, why would you want to waste money on the same credit?"

Len shrugged, "It felt like something that could help me in the future, like when it comes to story telling, Mom."

"Len is an amazing storyteller! You should see the kids' faces at camp when he tells his ghost stories. They are completely captivated." Yvonne hugged Len's arm.

"See!" Mercy shouted, "Yvonne says you're already good! What would be the reason for taking that silly course? It seems frivolous. You already have the talent in your genes!"

Len felt that this was something his mother was not going to budge on. Yvonne looked at her disheartened beau and kissed him on the shoulder, "Where to?"

Len sat quietly in the car as they made there way over to the Sizzler. His education was locked behind the paywall of his mother. He thought, *Maybe I can stop by the guy's office to chat before everyone leaves for winter break. He might offer some ammunition in way of convincing Mom that taking his course is a good idea.*

***

Monday morning, Len made a trip to the professor's office in hopes he'd find the eccentric history teacher. He looked around the dim hallways, but there was no one to be found. “Ugh, I suppose he’s gone. I missed him already.”

“Missed who?” The history professor stood wide-eyed, staring back at his confused visitor.

“You, Professor!” The young man thrust his hand outward, “My name is Len. You stopped by my English class last week promoting your history class.”

“Ah, yes! I’m pretty informal so just call me Dale!” The free spirited man beamed. “So, will I be seeing you next semester then?”

Lens face dropped, “Unfortunately, I took Art History already. My mom doesn’t want to waste time and money on a class that I already gained a credit for. But I was so impressed with your presentation, I just wanted to introduce myself and tell you that I wanted to sign up for your class.”

“Well, Len, it’s not an entire loss. I’m pretty busy at the university, but if I have a moment, I wouldn’t mind spending time speaking with you about… wait, what exactly were you interested in talking about?” Dale squinted.

“Oh, it was just the way you presented yourself. I thought it was very captivating.” Len continued to share, "I’m actually getting my degree in teaching, and I really enjoy story telling because the kids I work with respond positively to them, especially spooky tales around the campfire.”

"Oh my goodness, I love a good ghost story!" Dale became very animated, "Ever since I came to Hawai'i I have been fascinated by the legends and tales of the various cultures that live here in these islands. It is so amazing to me that all the different peoples that come here have their own strange tales to share, but so many sound so similar."

"Have you ever heard about the Night Marchers?" Len asked.

"Terrifying! Yes!" Dale slapped his thigh which echoed off the walls of the empty hall, "A procession of phantom koa and high ranking ali'i that travel across the darkened landscapes during a particular phase of the moon! Chilling! And, *quite* deadly may I add."

"I've seen them frequently up Pi'ilewa Point, on 'Āinapau!" Len was completely geeking out.

"Really!?" Dale looked closely at Len, "What's your last name?"

Len was puzzled, "Elenor Kahi is my full name."

Dale smiled and snapped his fingers, "That's why you looked so familiar. You *must* be related to Kaulana Kahi?"

Len's heart stopped a beat and he stood staring blankly forward. Sweat trickled slowly down the side of his face. "Kaulana Kahi?" he repeated.

"Yeah, you have the same eyes and build. Is he an uncle or older cousin?" Dale asked innocently.

"No, he's my father. I haven't seen him since I was a kid." Suddenly, Len had hopes of finding his dad. He could ask him why he abandoned his family and his mom could express her frustrations with him. "Has he come around here recently?"

Dale pawed the air, "Heavens no! It's been years. He was very interested in the night marchers too. He even mentioned Pi'ilewa a few times in his stories. Sheesh, it feels like I am actually experiencing déjà vu right now." Dale's eyes roamed around the office, "So surreal!"

Following up, Len asked, "So, it's been a while then? Was he a student?"

"No, he said he was looking for answers and he was referred to me because of my knowledge about the history of Hawai'i." Dale rubbed his chin, "We would talk off and on. Finally, he told me that he was going to search for the night marchers. He asked what locations were the best to come into contact with them. I believe that was the last time we spoke."

"Do you remember the locations you gave to my dad?"

Dale shrugged, "Yeah, the typical hot spots. Kalihi Valley, Ka'a'awa Valley, Kamananui Valley and Nu'uanu Pali."

Len became discouraged, "How would I know which location he decided to go to? Four different places and these were just the ones nearby!"

Dale pointed his finger at Len, "My bet would be the Nu'uanu Pali location. He asked me which one would be the least perilous. I told him that the Pali would be the easiest place for emergency responders to make their way in and out of. He let it be known over and over that he was very worried about getting stabbed in the butt by a boar."

"I cannot believe I found someone who knows the whereabouts of my dad. Maybe he's been living like a hermit in the forest all these years!" Len smiled at his fortune.

Dale looked at his watch, "Well, I've got to get going, Len. I really hope your mother reconsiders you taking my class. I believe you could benefit from joining in on the fun, truly." Dale locked his office door, "Good luck finding your father. Come back and tell me the story when you finally do reunite with him. I have a feeling it's going to be *very* interesting."

Kanakolu kūmālua

"I'm so sorry that I can't go with him this time, but he is just obsessed with these hikes and I'm afraid if he goes alone something bad might happen. Please force him to take you with him today, Ms. Kahi!" Yvonne was practically on her knees trying to convince Mercy to go on the hike with Len.

"I don't know why he doesn't just wait for you to be free to go out again. Why is he hiking during the rainiest season anyways?" Mercy pulled her flannel closed and shook as she saw the gray clusters swirling above Punchbowl.

"I can't stop him!" Yvonne cried. "I've never seen him so fixated. It's scary! He won't even tell me why he's all of a sudden so into hiking. We have gone on several trails up Nuʻuanu and it honestly feels like he is searching for something."

Mercy pulled her attention away from the T.V., "Searching?" She stared at the foot of the chair across the room as if looking for some hidden runes carved into the wood. Mercy stood and took off her soft robe. "Okay, I'll go with Len today."

Yvonne hugged Mercy, "Thank you! Believe me, if it weren't for my cohort celebrating finals this afternoon, I'd be there like white on rice. Besides, his hikes aren't usually longer than an hour anyway."

Mercy watched her boy come out of the bathroom, "Hey, good lookin'! Where you off to?"

Len stopped and smiled, "Hey, Mom! I'm gonna go hiking up Nu'uanu."

"Nu'uanu, huh? Sounds interesting!" Mercy awaited Len's invitation.

Her son nodded as he changed the batteries in his walkman, "Yup!"

Mercy, not being totally satisfied with her child's response, shook her head and decided to be a bit more direct, "I heard Yvonne has to go to some finals relief party…" Len smirked. "So, I don't know, did you want some company?"

Len looked at his mom. He worried that she would scold him for the reasons he was going out on all these jaunts. *I can't lie to Mom about looking for Dad. But, if she doesn't have a chance to ask, I won't need to lie.*

Len looked at the shoe rack, "Do you have a pair of shoes you don't mind getting muddy?"

***

The clouds were getting heavier and darker as mother and son made their way up the mountain. Mercy was afraid to ask Len to turn around in fear that he would just go it alone.

"Looks thick up there-" Len cast daggers at his mom. Him squinting his eyes slowly at her, made the woman feel uncomfortable. "I'm just saying we should be mindful of flash flooding, that's all." Len returned his attention to the road ahead. The tree tunnel they rode through made it appear as though it were midnight instead of late afternoon. Mercy's son pulled the car over to a narrow shoulder. It confused the woman that half of the vehicle still jutted out onto the road, "Are we going to be safe parked here?"

Len hopped out of the car, pretending he hadn't heard his mother saying a word. He disappeared into the bush as Mercy ran behind to catch up. The speed Len moved kept Mercy watching her footing instead of asking any more unnecessary questions. It was the exact desired effect Len hoped would've come about.

It felt as though they entered into a brand new world devoid of other humans. As Len pressed his feet into the mud and rocks he thought, *If my dad is out here, I can only imagine how much he's eating all of this beauty up. It's so peaceful.*

High pitched buzzing flew past Mercy's ears, "Well, this is nice." Mercy flailed her hand around smacking mosquitos out of the air. "Len, exactly how far are we going up this trail?"

Len picked up the pace going up a steep hill with tree roots serving as stairs. He needed to move faster to get his mother to run out of breath, "Come on, Mom!"

The top of the hill gave Len a nice vantage point. He cast his gaze wide to find any signs of his father.

Mercy finally gave up conversing with her son to avoid being stranded and alone as she fought to catch up to him. She slipped on a tuber and scraped her knee against a gnarled root.

"Owie!" She looked up hill and called out, "Len!"

As if by magic, rain poured down drowning out her call for help. She got back up while being pummeled by the torrent.

Len moved toward a tall tree, finding the rain less fierce near its trunk. He spotted his mom making her way near a nook that fell off into a stream. His heart jumped.

"Mom!"

A substantial amount of runoff appeared from out of nowhere heading right toward Mercy. Len ran as fast as his feet could carry him down the hill to save his mother from the flash flood.

"Mom!"

Mercy looked up just in time to see a large cascade of water rushing right into her face. The funnel of water ran vigorously into Mercy's mouth until she lost her grip and was knocked back.

"Mama Lucy!" she screamed.

Len grabbed his mother's hand just in the nick of time.

The young man tried to help his mother find her footing, but Mercy squirmed around until she slipped on a moss covered rock and cracked her shoe into Len's shin. They both slid down the falls and crashed into the raging stream below.

Len fought to keep his mother's head above water by holding her up by the only thing he could grip, her neck. He kicked his feet vigorously to move away from the current of the plunge pool. Mercy's eyes rolled toward her forehead as her son strangled the life out of her and drowned himself at the same time.

When Len's feet hit a deposit of silt and stones he was able to push himself out of the water to catch his breath. Len tossed his mother off to the side of the stream as he gasped for air.

"Oh my goodness! Mom!? Mom are you alright?"

Mercy flipped over on her side coughing. She was speaking, but it was difficult for Len to understand her.

"Mom, are you choking?" Len patted the battered woman on her back, "Let it out. Get it all out."

"Were you trying to kill me!?" Mercy flopped over and swatted Len, "You dummy! You were strangling the tofu out of me, dodo head!" Mercy massaged her neck. "What the hell was that all about!?"

"I'm sorry!" Len threw his arm around Mercy's back. "I was so scared that you were going to drown."

"So, you decided to strangle me instead!?" Mercy gave Len the real stink eye. "This isn't a hike is it, Len? You're out here looking for something aren't you?"

The guilty young man sighed and nodded his head, "Yes… I thought I could find Dad."

Mercy screeched, "Your father!? The reason you've been coming out here is because you're trying to find your father!?" Mercy's arms shook with anger, "What in the sweet lord's name makes you believe he's even out here!?"

Len rubbed his face in a circular motion, "I don't know! I just had hope that … I don't know!"

Mercy waited, but Len didn't elaborate, "Hope? You really need to give up hope in that man. He gave up on *us* a long time ago!"

Len's tears dripped down disappearing into his soaked shirt. He thought about how fragile the human mind was and how his dad could have experienced something life altering just as he did as a child. "Maybe he didn't give up on us, Mom!"

Mercy was alarmed by her son's outburst. Her mind exploded into thoughts and questions that made her heart ache, *Does Len think Kaulana left us because of me? Maybe it was better that I stayed away from my boy as he grew up. Maybe he would've left me too. Maybe I'm driving him away now. What does he want with Kaulana anyway?*

Len tried to rationalize, "Maybe something pulled him here. Like how something otherworldly convinced Dr. Campbell to get me to come back to Camp Pi'ilewa after all that time. Why else would he be out here? Traveling into this strange forest all alone?"

Mercy was relieved that Len's concerns did not put into question her parenting. She knew she could have been a much better mother to him. To keep the heat off of her shortcomings, Mercy used this time to further berate her estranged husband.

"There was something off about him the last few days he was around, Len. I always believed it was something he was avoiding, like an illegal debt or even a second family."

Deep inside, Len always believed it was just one thing that sent his father away. He finally confided out loud to his mother, "Was it because of me?"

The young man finally let go of a long hidden and deep-seated fear. His tears began falling faster than the rain.

"Listen!" Mercy propped herself directly in front of her son, "You need to stop this anguish over your father. I've been harboring more than enough hatred of the guy for the both of us ten times over. I didn't work my butt off trying to keep you safe, just so I could lose you to some fool's errand! Why on earth do you believe that he is even out here!? Who planted this thought into your mind?"

Len calmed himself and answered his mother, "The history professor. He said he met Dad. He said Dad was looking for the night marchers." Len could already see disappointment in his mother's face, "I'm sorry, Mom! I just feel like after Dad left there was a huge hole in my life. When I met Kawika, it felt as though a cover was built over that pit and I found a new person to help me continue my growth into manhood. That was up until he was taken by the night marchers. Now, there are two giant holes, Mom. What Dale told me gave me hope that I could at least fill one of them back in. I'll never get a chance to thank Kawika face to face, but maybe, maybe I can get closure with Dad. Tell him how I feel."

"You don't need him!" Mercy's voice echoed above the forest canopy and caused the rain to stall to a mist. "You are a beautiful person and such a strong and handsome young man. Yvonne would not be hanging around you if it weren't true. You only need to look into her eyes to see how important you are to her. I'm telling you how important you are to me and that should be enough. Don't you think doing something like this could be dangerous for you? I want you to remember me, and remember Yvonne, and all those little kids who love you back at camp. Think about us the next time you put your life in jeopardy. You don't think you made an impact on any of our lives? Well you did! And you do!"

Len thought about the young faces that looked up to him at Camp Pi'ilewa and he smiled, "Thanks, Mom." He stood up and reached out for his mother, "I'm sorry it took nearly getting us killed to realize it."

"It was a long time coming, Len." Mercy grunted on her ascension, "The longer you wait to express your feelings, the bigger the damage done in its wake." Len smiled and kissed his mom's disheveled hair. "I'm sorry that I wasn't enough for you."

"It's not that at all. I was just being selfish. I'm so grateful to have such an amazing mother."

Mercy's heart felt as if it were going to explode. She hugged her son and thought, *I guess you did alright lady.*

Len cast his eyes into the sky and saw a beam of sunlight breaking out a pinhole of a massive cloud. "We are truly blessed to have one another. It's okay that we never found any signs of Dad, now that I think of it. It probably would've just made things worse for us."

"Maybe, but to hell with it, good or bad. Your dad made his choice."

"Mercy!"

Mercy jumped when she heard the familiar sound of her husband's voice beckoning to her from across the stream. It was unmistakable to her ears. She found that the odd ray of sunshine illuminated a small circle at the edge of the water, across the rapid flow of the stream. She squinted to see through the beam and noticed a man glowing in the sun's ray. It was Kaulana. He waved at her with his oh so charming smile. Mercy became worried that her son might discover that there may be something seriously wrong with the integrity of her psyche. She thought, *Is my brain fried? I must be hallucinating!*

Len called out, "Hey, Mom! Isn't that Dad?"

Kanakolu kūmākolu

Len helped his mother over a tree that crossed the width of the water. It took a long while, but they made their way back upstream to Kaulana's campsite. When they arrived he was already gone.

"Where the hell did that man go now!?" Mercy was filled with anger, "Kaulana!? Kaulana, this isn't funny!"

"Mom, look!" Len poked around his father's tent. "It doesn't seem like he's been here for quite some time. Look at the debris. Maybe he has another campsite or shelter nearby?"

Mercy could already see that it was starting to get dark and it would take a while for them to make it back to the car. "Ugh, well I guess we're camping out here tonight."

Len was surprised at how willing his mother was to stay out in the forest over night. "Alright, I assume because of how glad Dad was to see us, that he'll be back shortly." Len started cleaning off the tent making it more habitable. "Hey, Mom! You hungry?" Len tossed some sealed snacks at his mother.

"Of course!" Mercy shook her head, "Your father always loved these things." She yanked the package open and found the snacks' aroma delectable. As she was about to chow down on the makeshift meal, Len laughed.

"Whoah! These things expired like three years ago, Mom," Len watched her chew on the pastry. "I'll eat it if you think it's okay."

Mercy looked down at her goody and took a quick sniff, "Meh!" She shrugged her shoulders and downed the rest of the sweet treat.

***

It wasn't long before the both of them fell fast asleep waiting for Kaulana to return. Mercy's snoring kept them both safe from random wild life that thought about getting too close.

A few hours had passed when Len was roused by a deafening quiet. No longer breathing deeply, his mother was as silent as a mouse. Her body didn't even reflect that she was breathing. She appeared as if she were a corpse. The crickets and frogs had all fallen silent as well. It started to get uncomfortably warm inside the tent. Len reached over to check on his mother when a voice startled him.

"Leave her, son. Come."

Len's hair stood on end, his father's voice was so clear and out of place. He watched as his dad's shadow stepped away from the tent. The curious young man unzipped the door and noticed the stream had also become very calm, creating light sounds of faint trickling. Len zipped up the tent to keep his mother safe before following his dad to a tree he was resting his weight upon.

The light from the stars and moon gave a nice glow to the forest canopy. The woods became a sort of fairy-like village. Green colored eyes, hiding in the treetops and low lying shrubs, could be seen watching both men as they traveled by. Len continued to keep a steady pace behind his father as they both moved deeper into the still woods. He began to feel a bit nervous about the whole affair. His father hadn't spoken another word since calling him from the tent. Len watched Kaulana running his hands against the trees as he passed each one until finally he made his way to one that had fallen. The tree was the perfect spot for them to sit and talk.

Len smiled at his father, "Dad! What's going on?"

Kaulana knew he had a lot to explain, "I thought it would be better to talk out here so we wouldn't bother your mother. How has she been? Is she okay?"

Len shook his head, "She *hates* you right now, Dad. But something tells me she wants to find peace with you. Otherwise we wouldn't have waited for you to come back around."

"Your mother has always been the best part of our marriage." Kaulana massaged Lens shoulder, "You were the next best part." Len felt the stress of a decade melt away. A heavy weight lifted from the spot his father gripped his arm. Kaulana called out in surprise, "Wow! I've never seen that before!"

Len tilted his head, "What?"

"I saw a beam of light shoot up from your neck and shoulders." Kaulana fixed his eyes on the area the light shot into.

"Hey, Dad, why did you leave us? If you loved Mom and me, why leave?" Len skipped over the catching up.

"First, tell me, how are things with you son?" Kaulana crossed his legs and placed his hands on his knees.

"I'm going to school and I'm dating a very nice woman, her name is Yvonne," Len smiled

Kaulana copied Len's expression, "That's good, boy. Very good. I always hoped one day you, me and your mom could come out into nature and camp like this. I didn't expect it to be under these conditions or even take this long."

"Dad, I know you want to play catch up, I do too, but what is this all about? You gotta give me something! Mom has been working her butt off trying to keep us fed and sheltered. She needed to work around some pretty unsavory people. She sent me to places to keep me safe so she could make more money, and I have always felt like half a man because I had no one to emulate." Len demanded answers, "How could you leave!? You abandoned us!"

Kaulana clicked his tongue, "That's not true, son." Kaulana lowered his leg and straightened his back, "You had Kawika. To me, it seems like you chose a very good man to emulate. I *am* sorry for how things turned out with our 'ohana. You need to remember son, that you met the people you met because of our dysfunction. Your life moved up this path for the better."

Len wouldn't accept his father's disappearance as a good thing, "That's bull, Dad. You owe Mom an apology. She went through a ton and she's still going through it. All those disgusting men that she thought would help me grow up normally!"

"How many men are we talking here?" Kaulana joked with his boy.

Len wrung his hands, "Bad taste, fo' real! You better be honest with Mom, that's all I ask. I don't care how selfish it paints you, you need to come clean. She deserves it."

Kaulana did not see his boy in front of him anymore, he saw a full grown man. "I feel a pride inside me I did not earn coming from you, Elenor. I cannot tell your mother the truth. She would not hear it."

"Ugh!" Len was growing tired, "Just tell *me* why you left us then? I'll tell her. We'll be out of your hair come sunrise. Was it drugs? Did you have another family?"

"It wasn't drugs and I don't have a second family." Kaulana bounced his head believing that his son was ready, "Okay, before I explain what happened, I want to share a story with you first, if that's okay."

Len got comfortable looking directly at the reflective light bouncing out from his father's eyes.

"Long ago, two beings of incredible mana fell in love, Luna and Lalo. They would come together in their human form for a few days each month to make love and share their magical works and deeds with each other. When their time came to an end, Lalo would return to the streams as fresh water and Luna would become the rays of light on the peaks of Nu'uanu.

Lalo was very attractive in her mortal form, and when they were apart, Luna feared someone would try to steal her away from him.

On one visit, Luna told Lalo he wanted her all to himself and offered her to hide in a cave nearby. She refused. She said she was meant to flow so the land could prosper. Without her mana, the balance would be thrown off and catastrophe would follow.

Luna spent his time away from Lalo conjuring up a plan. He came up with an idea that he knew Lalo would not reject.

Luna walked with Lalo deep into the forest where he presented a gift. Luna had created a nest in the center of an enclosure of tall trees. He explained to Lalo that the basin was made of a fine, smooth stone that had tiny holes which would allow Lalo to flow through. He connected the vessel to a multitude of underground pathways that could reach under the entire forest. Lalo seemed very pleased with the gift. She agreed to stay in the basin until he returned for her. Luna would hide Lalo in the nest he made for her using fine earthly materials after every visit.

At the end of their final visit, Luna laid Lalo in her pit of soft river stone and moss where she awaited his return. She watched her husband ascend into the sky becoming the morning light. Luna did not know that a stranger watched Lalo waving to him from her pool.

The stranger came upon the sight of a beautiful, naked woman adoring the sky above. The stranger wanted to take the woman for himself, so he ran over to her. When he got to the small luawai all he found was a pool of pristine, fresh water.

Believing he was in need of a drink and a bath, the stranger decided to bathe himself in the exceptional waters and drank of the bowl's contents. The stranger felt so invigorated after his bath that he wasn't upset about missing his opportunity to possess the lovely enchantress.

Weeks went by and the beautiful girl never returned, but the stranger continued to make his journey to the pool to take a dip in the refreshing waters.

During one visit, the stranger sat unwinding in the pool and fell asleep. He sat in the pool through the entire night. As dawn broke, the stranger found the water had all disappeared and in his arms was the beautiful woman he once saw in slumber. The stranger couldn't believe his luck. He decided to take advantage of the innocent creature as she slept. As he drew himself onto Lalo she opened her eyes believing that Luna was already with her. As day broke, Luna descended from the clouds above and found his beloved in the embrace of the strange man. He grew so angry that his body illuminated with a blazing intensity. The heat scorched the flesh from the stranger, turning his bone to ash.

Luna's rage had caused Lalo's mortal form to evaporate into a fine mist. Luna had lost his ability to take hold of his beloved forever more. The evil that had fallen over Luna had completely shattered him. Luna's mind flipped that day. He no longer offered the dawn's early light that would kiss the peak of Nu'uanu. He now accompanies an army of ali'i in search of evil that lurks the land during Pōkāne. Luna brings his radiance to the path of the night marchers. He provides his torchlight to the huaka'i pō."

Len was confused, "I don't understand. What does that have to do with you leaving me and Mom?"

Kaulana looked up and saw dawn approaching, "Son, I was the stranger in the story and I needed to find a way to say sorry to Luna."

"You're talking metaphor, right?" Len was still so confused.

"Son, we don't have a lot of time. Behind me is the future. Please help me to make things right again." Kaulana jabbed his thumb toward his back repeatedly in a very inhuman way. It was like he was on repeat and his motion played over and over.

"Dad? Is everything alright?" Len started to grow in fear.

"Ask Kawika, then come back and visit me after you make things right, okay?" Kaulana reached behind the log they sat on and whipped something hard at Len's face.

Len fell back and hit his head on the root of a tree. He opened his eyes and saw the sun was fully up sparkling through the tree tops.

"Good morning! I thought you were going to sleep all day!" Mercy was sitting up with the tent door open.

"The stream is so beautiful when it's not trying to kill you."

Len thought about Luna. He rubbed his head, "Man! I think those snacks are bad! I had a terrible dream last night."

Mercy frowned as she took a sniff of her refined breakfast, "I slept like a baby... What's your problem anyway? What'd you dream of?"

"Dad?" Len looked around, "But, it all seemed so real."

Mercy opened a second package. "Tell me about it, maybe your father will reappear as you share" Mercy raised her voice, "So, he can see what a *failure* of a father he is!"

Kaulana's voice repeated in Len's head about his mother not being ready to hear his truth, "Well, I woke up in the middle of the night and he called me out of the tent. We went through the forest and chatted."

Mercy dropped her face and eyed Len from the top of her brow line, "This was a dream?"

"It felt so real, but how did I get back here if it was real?" Len was perplexed.

"Well! Get on with the dream then!" Mercy spat crumbs at her boy.

Wincing at his mother's repulsive display Len started to discuss his strange experience, "Okay, so, first we talked about you."

The story teller was halted by his mother making a huff. "He asked about me?" Mercy added, "I hope you told him how I felt!"

Len addressed his mother's words with a look of contempt, "Did you want to hear what I have to say or not?" Mercy held her hands up in submission. "He told me a story about Luna and Lalo and a stranger that came and took advantage of Lalo. Dad said he was the stranger."

Mercy screamed, "See? Ganfunnit! I knew it! He started another family with a married woman! Now he's in hiding, lying rat!"

"Dad threw a stick or a rock at my face and I woke up." Len waited for his mother to respond.

She just sat there waiting for more, "Oh! That was it?"

Len nodded, "Yes, I said I woke up, didn't I?"

Mercy laughed, "I thought you were having some kind of epiphany, I'm sorry son." Mercy stood up, stepped outside the tent, and stretched. "I don't know how it could be real anyway, the forest was pitch black."

"No Mom, the stars and moon gave everything an ethereal glow, fo' real!" Len's eyes were round.

Mercy smiled, "Now I can see why those children loved your campfire stories. That was pretty good kid." Mercy looked around, "I think the bastard just decided to run away. Another thing to be angry at him about. As long as he stays out here in the wilderness, I'm happy." Mercy wiped her hands on her pants and yelled out loud, "Good bye, Kaulana! Thanks for nothing!" Mercy called out to Len, "Come on son, let's go see if our car is still there."

"Wait, Mom!" Len pointed down at the mud. "Foot prints!" He lined his feet up with the print, "Different shoe and too big to be your feet." Len followed it behind the tent. "Um, Mom!"

Mercy made her way over, "What is it?"

"I remember seeing these trees in my dream!" Len took off following the path his father showed him, carefully locating each trunk his father rubbed his hands upon.

"Len! Wait up!" Mercy could feel the expired pastries bouncing around in her stomach giving her a side pain. Len would disappear and reappear behind the forest growth as Mercy struggled to keep up.

"Slow down, son!"

She came to a point where Len had completely vanished from view. She spun around and found herself all alone. Her heart raced in fear that she was lost.

"Len!" she cried from the top of her lungs.

"Yes?" Len observed his mother's odd behavior as he sat on the fallen tree he remembered from the so called dream.

"Oh my goodness! I thought I lost you." She sat beside her son feeling a little embarrassed. "So, what was that all about?"

"Mom! This is where Dad and I had our talk. This place is exactly as I saw it in my dream." Len's eyes flashed, "What if I wasn't dreaming!? What if he came for me during the night and called me here!?"

Mercy watched a spider drop down beside her from its web, "Why here? What makes this spot so special?"

"Wait! I remember Dad saying that 'Behind me is the future' and he pointed his thumb behind him." Len thought about what happened next. "Then he threw that thing at my head."

Mercy hadn't really taken her eye off of the spider completely. She watched as it traveled over the log and behind Len's back.

Leaping to her feet with lightning speed and eyes bulging, she called out, "Len!" The frightened mother's arm was outstretched pointing at the forest floor.

Len stood up and found the rotting carcass of a human being just behind the log he sat on. It looked as though it had been laying there for years.

"Oh no!"

He inspected the remains. Len could see a puncture in the base of its back. "Mom, I think *this* is Dad! It looks as though he was stabbed and he tried crawling back to camp."

Mercy lost strength in her knees falling onto the log. She began crying uncontrollably. Len carefully made his way over to her and held his mom in his arms. He gripped his mother tight and rocked her to ease her pain. It took a long while, but finally Mercy was able to speak.

"It's him. I don't know how I know, but that is Kaulana." Her heart beat irregularly as she looked upon her husband's remains. "How is he in such good condition?"

Len couldn't really see anything that identified the body as the person he spoke to mere hours ago, but he explained what he knew, "Apparently, if there aren't many decomposers, like flies, a body can take years to break down completely. It's too cold up here for flies so…"

Mercy rubbed her arms from the chill in the air, "They don't call it Nu'uanu for nothing." She looked longingly at Kaulana and sighed, "I think it's time we called someone for help."

Kanakolu kūmāhā

As time went on, Brandon had become even more reclusive during his incarceration. He spent a lot of his time studying his satanic guide book, looking for ways to get even with everyone who scorned him and his family. Every time Brandon would open the pages of the evil manual, there would be some new incantation or recipe of darkness that he overlooked. It was like the vile pages read his mind and produced the curses he required. He even used a spell of dark energy projection, sending it to his first cellmate. He prayed that Kenneth Wilson would come to a young and horrific end.

"Family is what you make of it huh, Ken? I think I'll take Wilson's words to heart and conjure me a brother."

The bars of Brandon's cell gave off a strange tapping sound that grew closer and louder. Brandon widened his eyes to see what it was that created the sound. Nothing was there, physically.

"Burden? Burden is that you?"

The pillow from Brandon's bunk flew off of his bed and wrapped itself around his face. He fought to remove the down-filled cushion. Brandon's voice was muffled but his screams were clear. He cried out for Burden to stop and begged his brother for forgiveness.

The pillow fell from Brandon's face and revealed prisoner Ascension's disconcerted face. "Bro-dare, ip you're hong-gray, I suppose maybe you eat day break-faust!"

Brandon stared out of his cell doors at Ascension as he gasped for air. He watched the confused witness make his way out of the holding area.

Brandon began his preparations to bring his brother back from the other side. It was the only way to stop the daily torment Burden inflicted upon him.

"Blood sacrifice! The life force of an innocent spilled on the ground where the one you intend to resurrect was taken from this world." Burden understood that his hands would get messy from the ritual.

"An unholy recitation made over the sacrifice to call forth the soul of the damned… Burden, when I get out of this place I will bring you back to me and we can deal with Len together. We will make him suffer." The troubled inmate could hear footsteps approaching his cell.

"Inmate Alberts, B., two visitors to see you!" Officer Palani invited two men in suits into his cell. Brandon quickly stuffed the tattered booklet under his pillow.

The short younger man spoke first, "Hello, Brandon Alberts. I'm Larry Cott with the Board of Parole and this is my associate."

The man with silver hair nodded, "Hello, young man, I am Victor Clegg."

Larry continued, "We are here to evaluate you for early release. It appears that your behavior has been quite exceptional, even helpful to an extent. This could be very good news for you if you continue to keep your peaceful disposition."

"You have a very good chance of getting out of jail sooner rather than later. We have you scheduled for a hearing in a couple of months." Victor offered wonderful news to the detainee.

Brandon smiled, "I would really appreciate that. I'm sorry that you two even needed to be in here to speak to me about this. I promise if given a chance, I won't make the same mistakes."

Larry smiled, "We'll see you very soon, Brandon. You will have a hearing within the next several weeks. In the meanwhile, keep doing whatever it is that you're doing now. I'm very excited to see you make a return as a law abiding citizen once more," he thrust his hand toward Brandon.

"Thank you, Larry." After shaking hands with the first man Brandon reached out toward Mr. Clegg, "Thank you for your time as well, Victor."

Officer Palani escorted the men out of holding. Brandon shoved his hand under his pillow and retrieved the manuscript. He became absorbed once more in memorizing the words written on those hellish pages.

"I'm going to have to study a lot faster!"

Kanakolu kūmālima

"Dude! That is so fricken crazy!" Yvonne was just completely amazed. "So, what? Your dad just wanted you to find his body and put it to rest?"

Len sat on the couch beside his girl, "It doesn't feel like that... Honestly, it seemed as though there was something bigger going on, but I don't know if the whole ordeal was a dream or if it was, like *real*, real! This is so confusing." Henry's words came back to haunt the young man's mind. Len thought, *You shouldn't doubt yourself! Not anymore.*

Yvonne snapped him out of his insecurities, "We know that the guy was only saying that to avoid his own personal issues, babe. I think the conversation with your father was *very* real. How else could you have found him? You need to get to the bottom of this. How often do people come back from the dead to ask their loved ones for help!?"

Len nodded, "You're right. My dad needs me. He said 'Behind me is the future' and that's where we found his body. Maybe there's more to what was there.

But, I looked all around the area for clues after they took my father's body away." Len twirled his fingers over his temples, "Why does everything need to be so mysterious when it comes to my father!?" Len sat still with intense concentration.

Yvonne offered some ideas, "Maybe he was being literal, what if you need to find something deeper within the forest behind, where you found his body? Maybe there was something else he was trying to show you?"

"This whole thing could be nothing." Len attempted to brush it all off.

Yvonne tried to keep his doubts at bay, "Or it could be everything!"

"Wait! I just remembered something!" Len turned and looked at Yvonne, "My father also said to return after I fix his mistake."

"Well, what mistake did he make? Leaving you and your mom?" Yvonne didn't have much to go on.

"Dad said he was the stranger from the story. He needed to make things right with Luna and Lalo." Frustration started to take hold of the young man. "Why was he so dang cryptic!?"

"Wait, what did the stranger do in the story again?" Yvonne tried to help Len pull what he knew together.

"He stole someone else's wife," Len shrugged.

"How would you make up for taking advantage of someone though? I don't think Lalo represents an actual person. It all seems like..."

"Kaona!?" Len's eyes popped, "My dad was all about kaona! The stranger taking Lalo for himself sounds like she represents something mystical, something that has to deal with the night marchers? My dad took something that didn't belong to him and he wants me to return it!" Len laid his hand on Yvonne's lap, "Would you be willing to come with me? Back to the site of my father's murder?"

Yvonne was a little more than afraid, but she wanted to be there for Len, "Sure thing! When should we go?"

"Tomorrow?" The young man wanted to finish this task before he got bogged down with his final semester of college.

Nodding in agreement, Yvonne rubbed Lens hand, "Okay."

Ending a call concerning her deceased husband, Mercy made her way into the living room with a large bowl of popcorn. "Were you two planning on going somewhere tomorrow?"

Len squeezed Yvonnes thigh, "Out to shop for some Christmas presents!"

"Cool," Mercy plopped onto the couch next to Yvonne. "Could I tag along? I need to stop by the hospital. The Medical Examiner wants to give us your father's belongings."

Len looked at his mother because she seemed a little off to him, "Are you okay, Mom? Was there anything you wanted to discuss? Anything you needed to get off your chest?"

"I'm fine, Len. I just want all of this to go away already. I'm ready to move on from this whole ordeal." Mercy eyed her son, looking at her with a face full of concern, "It's all good, son! I've already shed more than a few dozen tears for that man. In fact, it's more than all good! Now that we have a death certificate, I can finally close that joint account we opened for you all those years ago. We can stop by the bank while we're out."

Len looked at Yvonne perturbed, signaling that their trip to the forest was a bust, "Okay, Mom. So, did the coroner tell you what kind of belongings Dad had? I can't imagine that he wanted to give you his mud stained, blood soaked sweat pants and matching shirt."

"No, they aren't giving us your father's clothes... come to think of it, I don't really know what they found. I mean besides all those outdated danishes," Mercy squished her nose.

Len could see his mother was genuinely doing alright. "Okay, Mom. We'll find out all about it tomorrow."

"Then there's the whole cremation thing. Ugh, we'll have time to discuss this all later! We can talk about where you'd like to scatter your father's ashes at another time. For now, let the show begin!" Mercy picked up the remote and pressed play on the Betamax.

Kanakolu kūmāono

Mercy sat in the waiting room chatting with Yvonne and Len when a woman in a white lab coat approached them holding a small bag.

"Good morning, Ms. Davis, I'm Dr. Robin Takamori, the forensic pathologist who examined your husband." The middle aged doctor handed a plastic bag with mysterious contents to Mercy. "Please follow me into my office. I'd like to discuss something with you."

The small group made their way through a couple of double doors until finally making it to a small white room with a black metal desk.

Mercy sat down in a chair and asked, "Is everything alright, Dr. Takamori?"

"There were some anomalies in the state of your husband's remains when he was found." The doctor took her seat in front of the family. "So, we know your husband was stabbed in the lower back, but the puncture wound wasn't what caused his death. Although, he probably would have died from blood loss without acquiring medical aid."

Len wasn't the least bit surprised, "Do you know what stabbed him in the back, doctor?"

Dr. Takamori flexed her brow, "Well, it looks like Kaulana was pierced with an object that had a long, flat, tapered head lined with small serrated protrusions."

Yvonne was completely puzzled. She had never heard of such an intricate weapon being used to kill someone in this day and age. "I'm sorry, but what kind of object do you believe it to be?"

The doctor pulled out photos from the exam and showed the damage that was caused. "See, the puncture point tears the skin here…" the doctor pointed at a darker picture, "and these lesions were caused upon exit. The tissue was shredded here, there, there, and there." She left the visuals for the family to look over. "The only other kind of material that would simulate these kinds of injuries are sharks teeth."

Yvonne was fascinated. She scooted closer to inspect the photos. Len already knew what kind of weapon was used in the attack of his father. "Ka ihe."

Dr. Takamori smiled, "It's what I thought as well. Fine build too. None of the teeth came off during removal of the spear's tip. Also, no particulates of wood fiber were found inside or outside of the wound."

Mercy was confused, "So, how did Kaulana die exactly?"

The doctor looked at the plastic bag that stuck out from Mercy's purse. Mercy pointed her fingers toward the bag the doctor had handed her earlier. "This?"

The doctor smiled and added, "We found that inside Kaulana's mouth. We didn't know exactly what it was that was in there at first because the object framed his tongue. When we finally separated the flesh from the bone we saw the rest of it had made its way down his throat cutting off Kaulana's air supply."

"Dad suffocated to death!?" Len wasn't ready for that revelation. He thought about the odd coincidence, *Kawika and my father died the same way?*

Mercy wiggled her tiny hands around the plastic bag and removed some jewelry. Len eyed the piece and was mesmerized. Mercy looked at her son and explained, "This is your father's niho palaoa. He said it would give us luck, good fortune." Mercy scoffed, "The only thing that happened after he brought this junk home was his ego inflated and he disappeared."

Len elbowed Yvonne and threw his eyes at the necklace. Misunderstanding what Len was trying to convey, Yvonne gave him a *what's so funny?* look.

Pointing to the artifact, Len mouthed the words, "Future behind me!" Yvonne's face lit up.

"I'm not sure why your husband made that choice after being attacked. Perhaps he was trying to keep the heirloom safe?" Dr. Takamori rationalized, "I probably would've done the same thing seeing that it is a very ancient, and expensive, piece of history."

Mercy tossed the lei back into the bag as if it were trash. "So, when can we cremate Kaulana's remains?"

The doctor looked a bit shocked. Len jumped in, "Mom has had her ups and downs with Dad. This is just another thing she needs to take care of because of him." Len wasn't sure if that explanation helped matters or made them worse.

"No, I totally understand, Ms. Davis. You're ready to close the door on this chapter of your life. I just wanted to present all available information, even if strange, before we released Kaulana."

The doctor sat looking at the well adjusted woman as she stared right back at her. An uncomfortable amount of time went by with the two women looking at each other in complete stillness and silence.

Len stood up and took the bag from his mother, "Thank you for everything, Dr. Takamori, and I do mean *everything*." Yvonne stood up and Len yanked on Mercy's shirt, "Come on Mom, we should let the good doctor get back to work."

Mercy snapped out of her daze and shook the doctor's hand, "Thank you, Dr. Takamori. I appreciate you taking such good care of my husband."

***

Driving toward the bank, Len had a large smile across his face. “Mom! Do you know what this is!?”

Mercy quickly passed air through her pursed lips, “More headache from your father?”

“Mom! This is what Dad wanted me to return! To fix his mistake!” Len’s smile disappeared, “But, where was Dad’s mistake made?” Len lamented in his mind, *One step forward, two steps back.*

“Turn Len!” Mercy’s hand waved in front of the distracted man’s face. “The bank is in the shopping center.” Mercy stabilized herself as the car went over some speed bumps. “Well, where ever he made his mistake, it was on ‘Āinapau. That’s where he got that thing. He went with his friend to scout some locations for this unsuccessful local cop drama one day, then he came home with that.”

Len grimaced, “I didn’t know Dad worked in show business.”

“It’s how we met.” Mercy shook her head, “He would try to find jobs in entertainment, constructing sets and other grunt work. He was a hard worker. I remember after we started dating how he would annoy the big wigs with my head shot. He was always trying to find me an acting gig. He knew I wanted to be in front of a camera.” Mercy smirked and chuckled, “Too late now. I’ve passed my prime to get my foot in the door. But, I’m perfectly happy with the theater at the university. It scratches the itch."

Len watched his mom disappear through the glass doors of the bank. He leaned back and rested his head on the seat. "We need to find out where this thing belongs. I don't understand why Dad even went to the night marchers up Nu'uanu in the first place. He chose that area out of convenience... But, why did he confront the huaka'i pō?" Len couldn't find a clear solution, maybe neither could his father. "He might have gone there seeking some answers, but what does this lei mean to a group of ghosts? It doesn't make any sense. It was such a huge gamble, dealing with 'oi'o, it cost my father his life. Dad came to me because even after death he wants his mistake to be resolved."

Yvonne was at a complete loss. "He got it on 'Āinapau!? So, that's where we look. It's a small island, but even a small island is a needle in the hay stack situation!"

"I know." Len looked in the rear view mirror to see Yvonne's eyes, "We have to be smart about this. What else do we know?"

Yvonne spoke in a panic, "Virtually nothing!"

After a long moment of quiet thought, Len felt he may have found the missing key, it was going to be a gamble in a game his father played just before he died.

"Kawika! Dad mentioned Kawika. He didn't even know the guy... or did he? Anyway, the night marchers are known to spare the lives of those who have family in their ranks. Kawika spared *me* that night on the mountain. I need to go talk to Kawika. He's the key. He will have the answers-"

Mercy pulled the passenger door open, startling the couple inside. "We did it, baby! We live to see another day."

Len looked at his mother smiling like a fool who just won the lottery. "Mom, did Dad know Kawika at all?"

Mercy stopped and thought for a moment. "Hmm, you know what? I actually have no idea... maybe? Why?"

Len shrugged as he reversed the car out of the stall, "He mentioned Kawika a couple of times during our conversation. How else would he have known him?" Len's neck started to itch as his hairs rose, "What if Dad saw Kawika the night he was attacked, just as I did up at Pi'ilewa!? You know and I know that he was stabbed by the huaka'i pō. What if Dad met Kawika in the procession?"

Yvonne questioned, "Why did they stab your father if Kawika conversed with him? How do we even know the night marchers on this island are the same on every island? Or if they're the same on different parts of an island? How do we know that the same survival rules apply to every single one of them!?" Yvonne slammed her back into the seat with a very displeased look on her face. She scowled at Len in the rear view mirror. "I know what you're planning, Len, and I do *not* approve!"

Mercy had never seen this side of Yvonne before. She was proud of the young woman for expressing herself.

Mercy thought, *I wish I was as strong as this girl when I was her age!* She decided to stick up for the disheartened young woman, "Why are you upsetting your sweetheart, Len?"

"It's not my intention. But, I believe that Kawika is the key to fixing all of this and helping Dad find peace." Len thought about how to involve everyone in his mission. He thought it would be best if all three of them did it together. "Mom, remember when you asked me what I wanted to do to celebrate after graduation?" Len asked.

Mercy slid her bank note cautiously into her purse, "Yeah, why?"

"We should all work this summer at the camp! I think the kids would love to do a play, and you could run the production!" Len smiled deviously. "But, I would like to go up a week or two earlier if that's okay with you."

Mercy thought about the possibilities of becoming a theater director and how adorable it would be to get the kids interested in the stage. "Okay, just as long as I don't have to wash any dishes." Mercy inquired. "Why do you want to go up early?"

Len came to a stop at the traffic light, "I thought we could take Dad's ashes home and spread them up at Pi'ilewa Point."

Kanakolu kūmāhiku

After his early release, Brandon went hunting for Len. There was only one thing running through his mind the entire time he was locked up. It was seeing Len in an agonizing amount of pain.

He searched all the places he believed the young man could be and came up empty handed. "I can't keep wasting my time moving aimlessly in hopes that I'll find him." Brandon's stomach began growling, "I should find a bite to eat."

Brandon tried to find a food stand or a diner that would serve him, but everywhere he went they treated him like a second-class citizen. He came across a diner where a waitress recognized him immediately and she began shooing him away before he could even make his way through the door..

"Brandon Alberts! Get out!" Cheryl pointed at the door. "You are not welcome at this restaurant!"

Roy came out from the back with a look of concern, "What's going on out here!?" Roy could see the young man who got her cousin killed at the Pi'ilewa massacre. "Cheryl, relax! If the kid got money, seat him!"

Cheryl snarled, "You know who this is!?"

"I do! But, he is here as a free man. Stop being so bitter! He paid his dues, now let him pay for some food," Roy slapped his spatula on the counter.

Cheryl looked at the seat closest to the door. "Sit!" She made her way around the counter and yelled, "I'm not waiting on that. You serve him!" Cheryl continued to help the other customers.

Roy called toward Brandon, "What'll it be, kid!?"

"Your special, please." Brandon sat innocently in the booth with his head lowered.

"Great!" Roy wandered back into the kitchen.

Cheryl decided to express her anger to the patron who had just made his way in. She chanted, "Eddie, Sammy, Stu, Byron, Charity and Taylor Brown!!!" The waitress slammed a glass of water on Brandon's table, tears welling in her eyes. "You remember those names, the names of the slain under *your* watch. How could you have abandoned those kids? You're just as much a monster as Seth Pedrina!"

The other patron's, fighting to enjoy their meals in the presence of Brandon Alberts, screamed back in agreement, "Yeah!"

"It was lucky for you that Len Kahi and John Chun were there to stop that animal! They both saved your ass from spending more time in jail. You should be grateful!"

Brandon looked up at Cheryl, "I'd love to repay them, and all the families affected by my negligence. The only one I have no clue to his whereabouts is Len. How is it that I can personally thank him?"

"Hmph! You're going to have to wait until summer when he comes back to help at the camp. He's going to college off island... You better come up with a good reason as to why you abandoned everyone, mister!"

"Cheryl! Leave that kid alone..." Roy slid Brandon's breakfast in front of him. "Go! Go serve everyone else." Roy glanced back at the reformed young man, "You need anything else?"

Brandon shook his head, "No, sir. Thank you."

Roy nodded and thought as he walked away, *Good kid.*

Brandon cleaned his plate in record time and snuck out of the diner without paying his bill. He continued to make his way around the towns of 'Āinapau looking for ways to earn some money, biding his time, awaiting Len's return. No fortune came to the young criminal. Everyone rejected his help and shunned his needs. He found himself desolate, living on the street.

A large truck that smelled of sweet cut grass pulled up to a store that Brandon slept in front of. The engine whirred and knocked causing the young man to awaken. He heard the sounds of heavy boots stomping onto the sidewalk. He tried his best to go back to sleep, but felt a kick under his foot.

"Hey, you! Get the hell away from my shop!" The store owner scolded Brandon for blocking ingress.

The delivery man looked at the downtrodden kid and his heart broke, "Ho, Bulleh!"

Brandon turned around and saw a tall Polynesian man calling to him. "Yes, sir?"

"You da kid dat wen' run away, yeah?" The raspy voice of the man was unique to Brandon's ears.

"Um, yes, sir." Brandon slowly turned around and started walking toward the road.

"Eh! You like one job, oah what?" the stranger called out to Brandon again.

Brandon ran over, "Are you serious!? Yes, please! Thank you, sir!"

"Call me Junyah!" Oki pointed at the bed of the truck signaling to the guy to jump in. "I get one moah delivery. Come help me drop 'em off an' I'll take you to da ranch."

***

Brandon worked as a hand on Oki's ranch. He drove deliveries to the shops and farms. Lydia wasn't too comfortable with having Brandon around during business, so Oki made him delivery boy to keep him off site for most of the day. It also gave others a chance to see that the boy had changed and his one mistake should not define who he would be for the rest of his life. Oki found him to be a valuable addition to his workforce. Brandon stayed on the ranch patiently waiting for the summer months to arrive.

Kanakolu kūmāwalu

Len, Yvonne, Mercy and Kaulana's ashes sat on a plane headed toward ʻĀinapau. Yvonne was excited to go home to see her mom and stepdad, and Mercy was happy to finally put an end to a drama that played out for nearly two decades.

"I'm so proud of you, Len," Mercy shared a loving smile with her son.

Len placed his palm on his mother's hand, "There's no way I could've done it without you, Mom. Thank you for believing in me."

Mercy reached into her purse, "Here!" She handed the ancient artifact back to Len. "I know you'll be alright. I can feel it in my gut."

Mercy was giving her son his wings, finally. She knew she held onto him too long, most parents would've let their children soar much younger, but Mercy couldn't resist keeping him near to her. Whether she did it for his sake or hers, she was now ready to let him make his own choices and honor his decisions.

"Of course he'll be alright," Yvonne interjected, "He's going to be with me after all."

Mercy thought it was funny that even though she set Len free, he was now bonded with a woman that appeared to be even more enveloping than she was.

Len disagreed with Yvonne's appraisal, "I think it best if you stay behind, Yvonne. Unless you want to soil your brand new shorts, I need you to stay back. The only reason I am still alive is because Kawika claimed me. I'm not even sure if he is going to be there again or if he still has the power to make such a request twice. This is all new territory for us. I can't risk your safety if I'm wrong… I mean, it would be nice if you could meet Kawika. I just don't want to chance it."

Yvonne didn't like the sound of what Len told her, but she understood the situation. "Fine, I'll be with my mom and stepdad until you get this all sorted."

"That sounds awesome!" Len checked his seatbelt as the loudspeaker sounded. The plane began its ascent into the night sky.

***

Len pulled the car around to pick up Yvonne and his mother who were sitting near the car rental office. They first made their way to drop off Yvonne at her house and then to the hotel where they checked in for a week long stay.

"Everything here seems so different to me," Mercy commented as she pulled up a slice of pizza.

"How do you mean?" Len asked through a mouth full of dough and cheese.

"It's not the place. Everything looks the same. It's a feeling." Mercy shrugged, "I don't know. Like, *I* feel foreign? Like I don't know what I'm really doing here, now."

Len could understand his mother's meaning, "It seems as though you found your calling on O'ahu, Mom. You know definitively that Dad's gone. The jobs you had here, the people you acquainted yourself with in the past here, were all ways to keep us safe and weren't places you would have naturally made friends. You can now pursue your passion."

"Passion… You're right, son. I found my passion when we went back to O'ahu." Mercy looked at her boy who seemed a bit at odds. "What's the matter?"

"Well, there have been some huge changes and revelations recently, and they are all pulling me in a direction that I feel would benefit me in the long term." Len tried his best not to disappoint his mom.

"You're not coming back to O'ahu with me, are you, son?" Mercy was saddened.

Len elaborated, "Yvonne is special to me, Mom. You know she's good for me and this is where she wants to live. This is where her mom is and she loves the island, it's where we met, and it's much slower paced than Honolulu."

"But, she still has three more years of schooling!" Mercy tried to reason.

"I know! But, I was thinking I could start working out here so we can get our own place together after she graduates. I thought that's when I would ask."

"Oh my goodness! Len are you going to propose!?" Mercy leaned over the pizza pie and hugged her son. "That's so sweet!"

"Well, we'll see how things turn out. I have high hopes that everything will work out. I'll save it for when she graduates." The young man smiled, "I am also applying to all the schools in the area. I want to teach here and share everything I know with the children of the kids I grew up with. These people, this community, helped raise me. I know almost everyone around here from all the places you sent me to as you made our living. They helped you and I want to pay it forward."

"I couldn't be more proud of you," Mercy winked at her son as she scooped up another cheesy slice. She turned the T.V. on and yelped, "Ooh! Murder She Wrote!"

Len rolled his eyes and snuggled next to his mother.

Kanakolu kūmāiwa

The air was unusually still and warm during this particular morning. Cheryl made her way from the employee parking area of the diner, lit by a single street light. An odd sensation of being watched fell over her and the shadows that laid on the asphalt made it look like evil creatures were circling her like a shiver of sharks. She looked through the mostly empty lot for any signs of life while quickly entering the diner.

From an out of the way area, Brandon Alberts watched the skittish woman seeking shelter inside the illuminated eatery. He thought, *She'll regret speaking to me that way. She'll be the first of many sacrifices I make to Burden.*

He patted the outside of his pocket where the evil instruction manual was held. It was so important to his conquest of reviving his brother.

"I'll be back for you at lunch."

Brandon cycled Cheryl's schedule through his mind. He had memorized her car, where she parked, where she'd take her breaks and lunches, her route home and even where she'd stop on occasion before going home. It was nearly time for him to pounce.

A short while before Cheryl's lunch break, Sarah made her way in to start her shift. "Hey, girl!? What's the four-one-one?"

Cheryl smiled, "Not much, except for Roy being Roy."

Sarah rolled her eyes as the front doorbell chimed.

"Sister!"

Cheryl turned around to see her friend, Mercy, making her way into the diner.

"Oh my gosh! It's been so long, what are you doing here? You coming back!?" Cheryl was so excited her voice carried over to the cooking area.

"Oh! Hey, Mercy." Roy stuck his head out from the kitchen, "How's my girl?"

"Not your girl!" Mercy answered without looking at the man. "But, I'm doing fine, Roy." She shook her head and spoke quietly to her friend, "Why does he always sound so creepy?"

Roy strained his ears, "What's that, Mercy?"

Mercy waved her hand, "I said I still feel so sleepy!"

"Feel free to take a nap in the backroom if you like," Roy offered while bouncing his bushy eyebrows. He looked over at Cheryl, "You can go on your lunch break now."

The two women sat at a booth in the back of the diner to converse.

"So! What's the scoop!?" Cheryl was desperate to catch up.

Mercy spoke as if she were going away and never coming back, "So, Len graduated and I've found a new life at the theater. He wants to stay on 'Āinapau with his girlfriend and I will be back on O'ahu... like, living there."

Cheryl's face was a mixture of sadness and pride. "I can't believe your little boy is all grown up, and look at you! You seem different. Like you have purpose. I'm actually really digging this side of you Mercy."

"There's probably a reason for that." Mercy let the drama flow, "We found Kaulana."

Cheryl's eyes bulged, "Oh my gosh! How did it happen? Tell me *everything*!"

Mercy smirked, "Not much to tell. He was killed in the forest up in Nu'uanu. Len found his body up there when we went camping. He was dead for a while."

Cheryl was getting mental whiplash from all the unexpected emotional changes. "What!? You guys just stumbled upon his remains!? What are the odds? Do the police know what happened?"

"Yes and no. See, he was out in the forest for some reason and came across some people that didn't approve of him being there. Other than that, we don't have very much to go on." Mercy sat back in the booth trying not to divulge any crazy sounding details.

"That's insane! All this time he was gone, it's because he was dead?" Cheryl put her fist under her chin.

"Well," Mercy added, "at least it wasn't for the reason's we presumed. He had no secret family and he didn't abandon us, per se."

"I guess that's one point for his character. How did Len handle it?" Cheryl inquired.

"Len is currently on a mission to redeem his dad. He always felt Kaulana was a light in his life, even when I'd rag on the guy for deserting us. I'm just glad that I won't have to worry about Len doing the same thing to Yvonne." Mercy had a far away look in her eye that beckoned back to her hurtful past.

Cheryl decided it was time to change the subject, "So, how long are you in town for? Do we have time to catch a movie?"

Mercy smiled, "Well, I decided that I'd spend the summer at Camp Pi'ilewa with Len and Yvonne."

Cheryl started laughing, "You're going to be a counselor? That would be something to see."

"I just wanted to have fun with my son for once. I owe it to the both of us. After we found Kaulana, I just felt like I shouldn't let my life mean absolutely nothing. Len isn't a burden, he deserves to experience me as a friend too. I think after all he's been through, he needs something positive to remember." Mercy was adamant about fulfilling her desire to be more than just a safe haven.

"Mercy, you've always been a fantastic mother to your boy. Don't doubt it for a second. I admire that you've come to see him as more of an equal though, like a friend." Cheryl shared, "I believe it's what a parent transitions into."

"He's a good kid, I mean a good guy," Mercy smiled.

***

Brandon sat in the heat of the parking lot awaiting Cheryl's typical lunch excursion to the fish market, but for some reason time moved on without showing hide nor hair of his prey.

Brandon sighed, "Something's up. I'll try again later."

Just before he could leave, he saw a familiar face exit the diner. He started his vehicle and quickly drove off the lot and cut in front of Mercy on the sidewalk.

"What the hell! Are you blind!?" Mercy kicked the passenger door of the vanilla colored sedan.

Sarah looked out of the diner to see Mercy in an altercation with an unstable motorist, "Cheryl, Roy! Look at this creep, he nearly ran Mercy over!"

"What?" Cheryl ran out of the diner to check on her friend only to find a car flying down the street. She looked down at the gutter and saw Mercy's purse lying in it.

"Oh no!"

***

It didn't take long for the diner to turn into a complete circus. After a few calls, the restaurant was buzzing with law enforcement and journalists. Many patron's stopped in to sneak some info or gossip about what was going on. Roy was happy with the rise in business, but because his waitresses were being interviewed he needed to run the entire shop by himself. Cheryl was able to contact Mercy's boy and he made his way over to learn what happened to his mother.

Len was in hysterics as he spoke to a cop, "I don't understand why anyone would abduct my mom!"

Cheryl stood nearby watching Len give his statement to the officer.

The policeman asked, "Was your mother here for any particular reason?"

Len nodded, "Yes, she was here to visit Aunty Cheryl. Mom used to work here a few years back."

"Okay, I have already gotten her statement. She said a light beige car sped off and she found your mother's belongings in the gutter there." The officer asked, "Do you know anyone that would want to hurt your mom? Does she have enemies?"

"No, never! My mom was always nice to people, officer." Len's heart raced. Every second she was missing meant another second of her being hurt by her abductor.

"Is there anyone that wants to see you hurt? Do you have any enemies?" The officer stroked a thought from the young man's mind.

"I mean, Brandon Alberts, but he's in prison." Len felt a hand pulling him at the shoulder.

Cheryl looked at Len with fear in her face, "Did you say Brandon Alberts?"

Len looked at Cheryl's worried eyes and nodded, "Yeah, Brandon. He has always hated me, I'm surprised you didn't know that Aunty."

"Oh gosh, sweetie! Brandon isn't in jail anymore. He was released early for 'good' behavior." Cheryl began to shake, "He's been working at the Haukea Ranch since he left prison. Jerk stopped in here and didn't even pay for his food." Cheryl folded her arms as tears fell from her eyes.

The officer ran over to his radio to call in an A.P.B. on Brandon Alberts and the cream colored vehicle. Len decided to get help from Yvonne. She understood the urgency of this predicament more than anyone. After leaving his statement with the police, Len made his way over to the Chun residence.

Yvonne's stepfather was throwing water over his dried up grass when Len pulled up to house, "Hello, Mr. Chun! Is Yvonne around?"

"Oh! Hey, Len. Yeah, she's inside getting her things ready for camp." Wayne watched Len exit his car flying over to the front door. "She's dropping her things off later on today. John's already at the camp setting up."

Len knocked on the door. "Thank you so much!"

Yvonne made her way out. "What are you doing here? Is everything alright?" Yvonne asked in concern.

Len's eyes turned red, "Brandon Alberts abducted my mom this afternoon!"

"Holy mackerel! What should we do!?" Yvonne's tone made Wayne a little upset.

"Yvonne? Is everyt'ing alright?" He watched both Len and his stepdaughter run past him jumping into Len's rental. "Hey! Yvonne!? Where are you two off and running to!?"

Yvonne was afraid that if she said anything Wayne would forbid her from leaving with her boyfriend. Len pulled out of the driveway and zoomed away.

Wayne shook his head, "Kids these days. You never know what's going on up in their heads."

Kanahā

Mercy woke up when her face smashed into a hard, scratchy surface. Pain radiated from the left side of her jaw where Brandon punched her. She opened her eyes and found herself locked away in a dark box with pin holes letting in the light of the sun. She could hear the sound of a car door opening.

"Someone! Help me! Please help!" Mercy called out in hopes of getting anyone's attention.

A loud slam vibrated throughout the dark, hot box and was accompanied by quick successive banging, "Shut up!" a strange voice called out. "No one can here you out here! You're just wasting your breath," Brandon punched the side of the vehicle once more.

Mercy followed her abductor's footsteps on a gravel path, moving away. She tried to remove the bindings around her wrists without success. She squirmed over to one of the holes, trying to get her bearings, only to find she couldn't get near enough to see out. An unintentional, prolonged scream of frustration escaped her. No one could hear her, no one knew where she was, and no one would be able to save her.

The thoughts of her life only just beginning enraged Mercy. She began to thrash about uncontrollably while crying out. After a while, the abductee calmed herself by thinking about Len. She needed to keep her wits about her. Her turbulent outburst would only serve to help her kidnapper by wearing her down. Mercy took long, slow breaths to calm herself and conserve her power. She lie in wait for a chance to break free from her captor. Mercy just needed to wait for her moment.

She drew in a long slow breath, "Patience."

***

Len and Yvonne traversed every street through and surrounding the town searching for any signs of Mercy, Brandon, and his car. The police began to notice the couple making their rounds.

"Hey, you two! Where are you headed?"

"Oh, sorry officer. Just looking for a place to picnic," Len tried to think on his feet.

The officer turned his ear toward his radio listening to the chatter, "Look, go to the beach. If I see you two moving down any of these streets again I'm arresting you for obstruction." The cop turned his light bar on and pulled away.

"I don't know, Len. I think it's time we made our way home. We covered a lot of ground and the entire police squad is looking for Mom. We should stand by and wait for word at the house." Yvonne didn't believe spending the night in prison would be all that helpful to their cause. "Besides, the light will be gone soon."

Len didn't like the idea of leaving his mother, but Yvonne was right. There was too much land to cover and there was no sense in being arrested for checking an extra street or two. Yvonne and Len were silent the entire drive back to the Chun's.

Wayne came out from the front door and walked over to Len, "I'm so sorry, son. I heard on the news."

They made their way into the house and sat in the living room. "Wayne, I'm sorry I hadn't said anything when we left, but I didn't think you'd let me go if I told you what happened," Yvonne apologized.

Her stepfather had a look of worry, "You're probably right. But, I want you to understand that I would've understood. Please, for the sake of my, and your mother's, sanity, let us know what's going on. Maybe we could help."

Len shook his head, "That's the thing, I don't want anyone else to get involved. Brandon Alberts is only after me. He wants to hurt me. That's why he took my mom and that's why I can't let anyone else get too close. Me being here may not bode well for any of you."

Yvonne squeezed Len's hand, "Stop, stop. You're building up Brandon Alberts as if he has some kind of supernatural ability. He's not God! He is only human, and he can be stopped."

"He's more like the devil!" Len had a difficult time sitting still. "Wayne, I am so sorry. There's no way I'm involving Yvonne like that again. It was careless of me. I'm going back out to look for my mom."

Yvonne grabbed the handle of her suitcase. "Good, when you go, you can drop me off at Pi'ilewa."

Kanahā kūmākahi

John started to clean up after a long day of prepping for the summer. He filed his paperwork and grabbed his keys. On his way out the door he spotted a strange Chevy illegally parked alongside the Pi'ilewa Point trail. He made his way back into the office and called the city to send someone to regulate the car's current infraction.

As he stuck his key into the door, John thought he heard the sound of a woman in distress. He turned and looked toward what he thought was an abandoned jalopy and had his fears realized. The sharp scream of a distressed woman blazed toward the camp offices and was strangled short. John picked up a bat and ran over to the perilous sound.

On his approach to the off-white Nova, John found Brandon Alberts standing above the body of Mercy Davis. He held a bloody knife in one hand and his malignant manual in the other. John could hear Brandon chanting something as he got closer. He pulled his arms back and swung his weapon at the malicious man. Brandon turned in time for the bat to miss his head by an inch, catching him in the hand instead. His brochure fell to the ground and the psychotic jerk took off onto the Pi'ilewa trail.

Len and Yvonne had just pulled up to the camp when they noticed the cream colored car matching Aunty Cheryl's description.

"Is that Brandon's?" Yvonne asked.

As soon as they drove passed the car, Len saw his mother covered in blood, laying in John's arms. John looked up and yelled toward the sound of the humming engine, "Help me! Please, help me!"

"Uncle John, it's me!" Yvonne screamed, jumping out of the car before Len could stop it. "Is she alright!?"

"I don't know! When I got here she was already like this." There was a quiver in John's voice. "Please, Yvonne. Help her!" Tears flew from John's eyes as he watched his niece tend to the woman he secretly crushed over for years.

Len screamed, "Mom!" He looked at his boss and asked, "What happened?"

"Brandon! It was Brandon Alberts! He was doing some kind of evil ritual, he was reading something from that brochure. After I hit him, he ran up the mountain..." John turned and started making his way back to the offices, "I'm calling the nine-one-one!"

Len picked up the wad of paper from the ground and saw that it was just an old take-out menu from a fast-food restaurant. He looked at Yvonne, "Is Mom going to be okay?"

Yvonne shook her head, "We need to stop the bleeding, she's already lost so much blood!" She could see the look in her boyfriend's eye, "Don't do it, Len! He's trapped up there. Let the cops take care of it. They'll be here soon!"

"Take care of my mother, Yvonne, please. I love you!" Len ran up the trail after Brandon Alberts. The sunlight began to disappear at an extraordinary rate as he made his way up the mountain. "I'm really getting tired running up this damn path!"

Near the top, Len took a corner and was knocked to the ground by a swinging branch.

Brandon cast a tree's arm to the forest floor. "You came alone? What an idiot! I knew you were dumb, but hot diggity, you've out done yourself this time." Len was impressed by how large Brandon had gotten. "You checking out my guns, Eleanor?" The psycho jumped onto Len and threw a left hook at his face. "I always knew you were sweet on me, faggot!"

Len's vision blurred for a second when he saw Brandon's right hand incoming. He dodged the blow as Brandon ground his fist into the dirt. "Faaaaaa!!!" Len lifted his knees rolling Brandon off.

"You crazy bastard! You tried to kill my mom!?" Len got up to his feet.

Brandon cupped his right hand in his left and raised himself to one knee, "Killing your mom wouldn't even equal the loss of one half of my brother! If your mother hadn't saved that doctor he wouldn't have testified to seeing me talking to Burden, he would've died in that crash and our plan to kill you would've been kept a secret!"

"Why do you hate me so much!?" Len was trying to figure out what transgressions amounted to their current situation, "All because I saw your brother and Seth throw that girl off the peer!? That's why you stabbed my mother?"

Brandon wailed, "You killed my brother! You convinced everyone it was Seth that did it, but it was you!"

"Burden fell from the cliff because you three chased me through this forest!" Len couldn't believe Brandon's botched memory.

"We chased you because you humiliated Burden!" Brandon groaned, "Everyone laughed at him, everyone disrespected him because of you!"

"It was a piece of chocolate cake, for crying out loud! No one truly believed your brother took a dump in his pants, Brandon!" Len lowered his fists. "Your brother's death didn't need to happen. Seth breaking out of prison and killing all those innocent people didn't have to happen. This, this right now! It doesn't need to happen! Why couldn't you have just left me alone?"

Brandon smiled, "It's too late. We will never leave you alone, right Burden!?"

Len looked around the forest in fear that Burden had returned, but no one came to Brandon's aid, "Look, I told everyone who asked, the truth about what I saw, but no one believed a word I said! I tried. Even the therapist I saw thought I was lying about it!"

Brandon was looking around the tree tops in hopes that his brother was near. He looked at Len. "Wait! Your mother's dead! I stabbed her to death and I read the incantation from the manual. Where's my brother!?"

Len took a few steps closer to his attacker and lowered his tone, "Brandon, it's okay. I can help you. We don't need anyone else getting hurt today. Please, let's go back down and talk. My mother will be fine, you won't need to go back to jail and I'll be sure to tell the police everything. We're adults now, they'll believe me this time."

"Your mother's alive?" Brandon's face eased up, "Hu! That was a close one, am I right?"

Len nodded and leaned over with an extended hand, "Yvonne is taking care of her, you won't need to worry about taking someone's life, because you're not a killer. You're not a murderer."

Brandon's face changed and appeared evil, "You think Seth was able to kill Chatty Charity, Earnest Eddie and Skinny Sammy while he was busting in the face of Dreamboat Jerry? I hate to break the news to you, Len, but I killed those other kids. I tried to kill more, but you had to show up, you had to stop my brothers." Len's face expressed dread and confusion all at once. "After I kill your mom and your pretty girlfriend, I'll bring Burden back to torture you for all eternity!"

Brandon whipped a handful of dead leaves and soil into Len's eyes. Len struggled to recover as Brandon ran from behind, cracking the young man in the back of his head with a stone. Len crawled through the path trying to escape the lunatic.

"I spent the last four years busting my butt in the gym and reciting those satanic rituals for this very moment!" Brandon turned Len over by kicking him in his ribs. He mounted him and began pummeling him with his left hand. "You're lucky this isn't my strong hand, Ellen. I'd have already killed you." Brandon halted his flurry of punches when a strange sound blared from behind him. "What was that?"

Len laid on the ground trying to focus his eyes on Brandon. He started to hear the pahu beating in slow rhythm. "It's the night marchers!"

Brandon shook his head, "No, not possible!"

Len laughed as blood trailed along the corner of his mouth, "That's what everyone else said when I told them that."

Brandon got up to his feet, "Well, I have a date with your mother, Ellen my dear. My brother will be back to clean up whatever the night marchers leave behind. Assuming they are real!" Brandon shot his foot across Len's face and made his way down the mountain as fast as his feet could carry him.

Len was sprawled out on the dirt drifting in and out of consciousness. The drums sounded in his head and the vibrations pulsed through his body. He could see the flame of Luna illuminating the trees of the forest. He prayed that Kawika walked with the marchers once more. He prayed his mother, Yvonne, and John would be able to protect themselves from the incoming threat of Brandon Alberts. Everything began to overload Len's senses. The torch light blazed in the reflection of his eyes, the drums burned inside his ears. It almost drove Len mad when all went silent at the whisper of one word.

"Mine!"

Kanahā kūmālua

John made his way back to the mouth of the Pi'ilewa trail. He could hear the faint sounds of the pahu from up the mountain. He stood watching like a hawk and after a short while came face to face with the man who stabbed the woman of his dreams.

Brandon's breath was fast and heavy, but it didn't stop him from speaking, "John, you look great, man! We should work out together one day."

"Nah!" John replied, "You wouldn't want me to spot you. I'd probably leave the weight on your neck. Where's Len?"

Brandon could see John was not in a good mood. He looked down at the floor and saw the knife he had dropped when he ran, "We had a chat. He decided to stay up there with his new friends." Brandon watched John crack his neck, "There's no way you'd be willing to let all of this go, is there?"

John unbuttoned his shirt, "Not a chance, Alberts. If you want to leave you'll need to get through me."

Brandon smiled, "Sounds fun!"

***

Len sat up and Kawika took hold of him in his arms. Shaking his head, Len wiped his face and looked the apparition in his eyes, “Am I dreaming?”

Kawika laughed, “No, boy. I’m here.”

Len hugged his former counselor, friend, and father figure, “I missed you so much, I can’t believe this!”

“I missed you too, Elenor. I’m sorry that you had to go through all of these nasty things.” Kawika eyed the young man who had grown a lot since the last time he saw him, “Those Alberts brothers are something else, yeah?”

“They hate me, Kawika,” Len felt the pressure of his father figure squeezing him closer.

“The Alberts don’t hate you, Elenor. Intolerance is a terrible thing. They hate what you stand for. They hate anyone who has happiness in their lives because they weren’t afforded that same happiness. They hated those who could not do the things they could do. They felt superior, they would pressure or push people that couldn’t do what they could no matter if it hurt others.

Remember the girl you saw being tossed into the lake? They thought she was weak for not knowing how to swim. That’s how they were raised. They did not have the values you were brought up with. Instead of a mother who worked hard everyday to protect them, they had an alcoholic dad who would beat them for disturbing his drunken stupor. Instead of being brought to places to care for them, they were dumped on others to put up with their terrible behaviors. Your situations were very much the same, but the difference is you were offered love and safety. Your mother gave you the foundation to be who you have become today."

Len's eyes were filled with tears, "I appreciate you, always have. I always wanted to thank you for being there for me. To show me what a real man is."

Kawika tilted his head, "And what is a real man?"

Len was a bit confused. To him, Kawika was the definition of a real man. He thought deeper, "A real man is someone who cares for others."

Kawika beamed a huge smile, "Like your father."

Len felt the hairs on his arms rise, "Did you know my dad, Kawika?"

"Kind of." Kawika replied.

"I don't get it. How did you kind of know my dad?"

Kawika explained, "Well, I remember a movie crew coming up here to film some big Hollywood movie in the late sixties. They wanted to catch the view from the lookout point. Your dad was here with this pretty little thing following him around holding onto the cutest little kid."

Len blushed, "That was probably me and Mom."

"No! I knew it was her. I recognized your mother the day she brought you to the camp. My new guy was smitten. He wouldn't stop talking about your mom. I kept telling him, in your dreams, Johnny!" The specter laughed, "I never actually spoke to any of the crew that came that day. But, like I said, I saw your dad, I saw your mom and I saw you."

"My dad didn't stick around for very long after that." Len chuckled, "He made a huge mistake that cost him his life." Len looked at the night marchers who stood at attention mere feet away. He inspected their spears to see if he could find the one that gored his dad. "My father wants me to help him make things right, but I don't know how. He mentioned that you would know."

Kawika was puzzled, "I don't know how I can help you. I've only recently become part of the procession. I don't have much say in what happens. Really, none of us do... except these two." Kawika presented a set of conjoined men each wearing feather helms and a large singular feather cape. "This band of marchers are run by these two ali'i, they run the show."

Len was confused, "What do you mean?"

"Well, the huaka'i pō are lead by their ali'i," Kawika began to explain. "Unfortunately, these two take turns leading our procession. They share a sacred trinket that would go between them each Pōkāne." Kawika could see that Len was straining to follow his story. "Let me start from the beginning... Huaka'i Pō have a bad reputation for being terrifying and murderous, which they are, but not how you understand them. You see, they protect the 'āina from evil. Mostly shades and demons that think they can infiltrate our world and prey on innocent people. Huaka'i Pō stop these creatures by walking the lands and punishing the evil."

"Whoah! Okay, now this is very fascinating. All this time I believed they were out to collect souls to build their ranks, but they are actually peace keepers!" Len blinked and saw the phantoms as spiritual heroes.

"Yes! They found my spirit after Burden Alberts murdered me. They offered me a place among them in the procession-" Kawika was stopped in mid-sentence.

"And you took them up on the offer because you are a hero!" Len couldn't resist.

Kawika smiled at the young man, "I had no idea I made such an impact on you, Elenor." Len's eyes watered. "Okay, so, getting back to these two guys. One brother believes that most of the evil comes from the mauka side of the island and the other believes it comes from makai. Every march they take turns leading. Depending on which brother wears that sacred item, they will take the procession mauka or makai."

Len asked, "So, without the object, they don't know who leads?"

Kawika rubbed Len's head, "Bingo! We've been stopping at the base of the mountain for years during our Pōkāne. It's actually pretty embarrassing."

"I think I know what it is they lost, and I believe I know what happened to it." Len revealed the niho palaoa that was in his pocket. "Is this what they were missing?"

Kawika's eye's burst into blue flames. He pulled Len's hands up toward the twin ali'i. Their faces lit up. They raised their arm pointing up the hill. "Follow me, Elenor." Kawika lead Len to a crack in the wall of the mountain. "Here, look inside."

Len could see human remains bound in the small cave. "Is this a burial mound!?"

"Yes," Kawika answered. "These are the bones of the twins. One is unfortunately missing his head."

Len ran toward a tree and pulled a skull up from the brush, "I got it!" He looked at the ali'i, "I'm sorry, but I believe I used your head to fight Seth and Burden a few years ago."

He made his way back to the hole and placed the niho palaoa on the neck of the body missing its head, then placed the head back over the neck. Len watched as the twins split apart from each other becoming two entities instead of one.

"Elenor, you did it! Now we are free to go. Free to protect the 'āina from dark entities that would try to commit terrible acts on mankind." Kawika stood up to join his ghostly brothers.

Len wasn't ready to see his friend go, "Wait! Will I ever see you again?"

Kawika smiled, "You know where to find me. But, don't waste your time on the past, Elenor. Live, move forward and share yourself with other's who need your inspiration, like what I have done for you." Kawika made his way downhill with the rest of the night marchers. He turned back around toward Len, "I love you, boy. Remember that."

Len's eyes filled with tears, "I love you too, Kawika!" The young man began to feel faint. His head spun and he passed out in the dark of the woods.

***

Brandon was knocked to the ground for the umpteenth time. John stood above him with a bloody nose, "You had enough yet?"

The Alberts boy landed right beside the knife he used on Mercy. "I yield! Enough, I yield!"

John gazed out at the main highway. The flashing blue and red lights reflecting off of the trees down the road and squeals of the sirens calmed the victorious man. "Looks like the calvary has arrived just in time. Another minute with me, Brandon, and the paramedics would have nothing to take back to jail." John turned to wave down the emergency responders.

Brandon grabbed the knife from the grass and jumped up to kill his ex-boss. He pulled his arm back to jab the blade deep into John's spine.

A loud scream caught the camp leader's attention.

"'Ō'ia!"

John's eyes widened as he witnessed the huaka'i pō press their spears deep into the back of Brandon Alberts. Tearing their ihe out of Brandon's ribs, his lifeless body fell into the dirt. John watched the ghost procession head down toward the lake path. The police arrived just as the last flicker of blue torchlight disappeared below the hedge line.

"Hands where I can see 'em!" The voice of an officer called out toward John. He ran over and patted the camp counselor down, up until he pawed at a wet spot. "Ugh!" The cop pulled away quickly from the bloodied man. "Where's your I.D., sir?"

John pointed at his shirt that was laying on the ground, "Left pocket."

The officer pulled the shirt off the ground wiping his hands on it. He found John's badge right where he was told it would be, "John Chun. You run the camp?"

"Yes, sir."

"You can drop your arms." The officer continued, "You want to tell me what happened here, sir?"

"I would love to tell you everything, but, there is someone up that trail that may need our help." John had an intense worry in his eye. "I can tell you right now that this man here..." John pointed toward the skewered Alberts boy, "is the psychopath you were called out here for!"

The E.M.S. made their way over to Brandon's body.

John scolded them, "No! No! This guy's already dead. You need to head into the main office. There's a very attractive woman in there who needs your help."

The police officer flicked his flashlight up the dark trail, "Let's go!"

John ran in the opposite direction pointing his finger up in the air. "One second, officer!." He popped his trunk open and pulled out a rainbow colored piece of cloth. John suggested, "Let's use the cart!"

Len could see the lights of the camp's club car making its way up the path. He smiled at the two men as they jumped out of the cart.

"John! I was so worried. Is my mom alright?" Len attempted to stand, but slid back down onto his side.

John grabbed Len, "Your mom will be okay."

"Easy, kid!" The officer hoisted Len up with little effort. "What happened to you?"

Len chuckled, "You wouldn't believe me if I told you."

"Huakaʻi Pō?" John sighed with a heavy breath.

The cop made an uneasy expression as Len smirked, “You saw them!?”

“Who do you think killed Brandon Alberts?” John shook his head. “They killed him just as he was about to drill me with a knife!”

The officer was now very confused, “So, the guy at the base of the trail was Brandon Alberts?”

John nodded.

“And, the night marchers were the ones that ended his life?”

Len nodded.

“How the heck am I supposed to write this in my report?”

“Just be honest about it...” Len leaned up against the bed of the cart, “How were you able to survive the night marchers, John? Did Kawika claim *you* as well?

John’s face turned red as he looked down at his legs.

Len followed John’s gaze and saw that he had changed into his rainbow colored swimming trunks. He laughed and winced through the pain.

“Hey man, whatever works.”

Kanahā kūmākolu

A few weeks later, the camp started to buzz. Kids from all over the island came to enjoy Camp Counselor Yvonne's summer activities and anticipated the addition of Camp Counselor Mercy's theater troop. Unfortunately, the children were more than a little disappointed to hear that the production was canceled due to the new counselor's health condition. Mercy still stayed at camp, tucked away in the staff cabin, healing from her wounds sustained by Brandon Alberts. John was happy to have her near and Len was appreciative of John allowing his mother to stay the duration of camp.

"I love this so much," Len smiled as he witnessed the return of several familiar faces. John stood beside Len as they watched the rookie counselors assisting the children with their belongings. Len made a face of concern, "I don't see many of our old timers."

John glanced at Len, "The survivors of the attack? I thought you heard. A few haven't returned because they went missing this past year. The one's that are still around are too traumatized from the incident to make their way back."

Len's eyes were wide, "What the heck? What is happening to Hawai'i!? It's bad enough that there are crazy people killing our kids, we need to worry about them going missing too!? As if all these spirits and demons weren't enough. It's a real circus nowadays!"

"It's all 'end of the world' kine stuff, no doubt." John thought about everything that happened with Brandon, "Kids are resilient when they have the right support at home. They bounce back rather quickly, you should know that." He gave Mercy an implied five star rating for her parenting skills. John looked at his niece in the mass of people. She was so excited greeting them all. John added, "Besides, with time, I'm sure we'll see our old friends again. One way or another." He pointed toward Yvonne with his chin.

Len could see his girlfriend hugging a pretty teen that was only slightly shorter than Yvonne. He squinted his eyes and the young woman finally sparked his memory, "Is that Little Miss Mercy!? Looks like it's just Miss Mercy from now on."

John thought about the woman resting in the cabin just behind them, "Your mom is pretty resilient too, Len. You don't need to worry about her when it comes to her decision to stay on O'ahu." John watched for Len's shift in mood.

"I guess I was hoping she would stay here with me..." Len looked at his boss, "Us?"

John smiled, "Your mom still needs time. I feel like even though your father is gone, she hasn't really found the peace that she deserves. I wouldn't even attempt asking your mom out until she was a hundred percent ready."

"Perhaps I can help my mom with that," Len said as he admired his boss beaming at the thought.

Trotting down from the steps of the main office, holding his megaphone up in the air, John corralled the swarm into a neat couple of lines, like a procession, and sent everyone off to their rooms to unpack.

***

The summer went off without a hitch, flying by at lightning speed. The campers all sang a farewell to Len since it was his last summer as a counselor at Camp Pi'ilewa. They cried knowing that when they return the following summer, the scary stories wouldn't be the same, if there were any scary stories at all.

Mercy was a lot more mobile by then and she had a new found appreciation for all the work that was put into running the camp. "You have this whole thing all sorted out, don't you?"

John blushed, "It's nothing, really."

"Don't be modest. It takes a strong man to lead the way you do. It's 'very attractive'," Mercy poked fun at the Head Camp Counselor. "You know what else is 'very attractive'? A man who can confidently wear rainbow pattern swim shorts!" John turned around stupefied, "Relax, John. I knew the E.M.T. wasn't trying to hit on me when he asked if *I* was the 'very attractive' woman in need of assistance."

John slumped over and Len slapped him on the back, "Give the guy a break, Mom! He's been holding a torch for you since the first time you dropped me off at camp."

John looked at Len perplexed, "Wait! How did you know that!?" He hid his face thinking he couldn't handle anymore embarrassment.

Mercy's eyes moved toward the head counselor, "Geez, John! Why didn't you say anything?"

"Have you ever seen yourself before!? Talk about out of my league." John was shocked at what he just said and wished he could take it back.

"Well, that was awkward," Len went behind the counter and pulled his diary out from his mailbox. "Shall we do this before some other tragedy hits us?"

Mercy, John, and Yvonne sat at the fire pit awaiting Len's momentous occasion. He stood in front of the fire's light flipping through the pages of his journal, remembering all the hurt that had brought him to this moment. He thought about all the growth he made with the help of his family encircling him. He took a deep breath and closed his eyes while turning his face to the heavens.

"Mahalo!"

Tears trickled down as he exhaled, "Everyone here has made sacrifices in keeping me safe, strong, and prepared for the dangers in this world. I used to think that only one person could do that, and when I met Kawika, I changed my perspective. He made it difficult for me to accept anything else, or anyone else, as a viable source of knowledge in my upbringing. While I am indebted to that man for saving my life on many occasions, for making the ultimate sacrifice in the end, I know that I have found the same kind of love and devotion from everyone here."

Len tore his journal and threw a nice sized wad of papers into the fire as he looked at John, "You have educated, saved, and touched so many lives in your career as counselor at Camp Pi'ilewa, me included. There is *nothing* I could ever do to repay you for that or for saving my mom a few months back. Maybe, if she lets you, Mom will let you save her again. I love you, bossman!"

John's eyes were wet, "I love you too, kid."

Len turned to Mercy as he ripped another portion of his journal and tossed it into the flames, "Mom. You gave up *everything* because of me."

"I would do it all again if I could," Mercy interrupted.

"You sacrificed your sanity, the best years of your life, which most regrettably caused you to put your passion on hold. You kept me fed, sheltered, and safe from harm… mostly. You know that I already love you more than anything, so I would like to ask you to please stop worrying about me anymore. Go and fulfill your dreams knowing that I can handle whatever is thrown at me."

With tears in her eyes, Mercy nodded, "My boy, all grown up."

Len looked at his mother and smiled, "I am sending you on a mission. I want you to go back up to that campsite where we saw Dad. I'd like you to tell him what happened here. Tell him we did what he asked us to, tell him I forgive him. Then, get him to explain himself to you. Ask him why he abandoned us. You deserve to hear the truth from his mouth."

Len cast the remainder of the diary in the pit and looked at Yvonne, "I wanted to wait a few more years, until your graduation, but I think now is as good a time as any." Len dropped to one knee, "Yvonne Bush, will you marry me?"

Kanahā kūmāha

Yvonne sat quietly adoring the gleam in her engagement ring from the moonlight of Nuʻuanu. Her windbreaker cracked in the frigid breeze that moved though the forest and over their campsite. Her partner fumbled through their tent like a rummaging raccoon.

Mercy shook her head, "Well, that was irritating!"

"Did you find it?" Yvonne watched her soon to be mother-in-law clicking her flashlight on and off.

"Hmmm, I don't remember if I put fresh batteries in this thing. Oh well! Too late now," Mercy grunted and started her small solo hike. She noticed that the forest was actually quite noisy and was amazed that she was able to fall asleep the last time she was there with Len.

When she got to the downed tree that Kaulana's remains were hidden behind, Mercy sat and soaked in the ambience. She thought about all the things she wanted to say to her husband, and all the things she *needed* to say to him. The hurt and the pain he put her through for all those years, left to raise their son all alone.

"Why do I let him make me so angry!?"

"Probably because he has never deserved you."

Kaulana stood at the edge of the horizontal tree trunk. Mercy was in shock. "You have to admit though, we needed to be together to have Elenor. That kid is something." He made his way beside his wife, "May I sit?"

Mercy moved over in disbelief that Kaulana was there. All the questions she thought about had vanished the moment he appeared. Mercy handed a freshly wrapped custard danish to Kaulana. He took it from her hand.

She asked, "How is this possible?"

Kaulana chuckled, "I'm sure Elenor has already told you about what makes this particular night so special." Kaulana could feel the repressed frustration emanating from the woman sitting beside him, "I'm sorry, Mercy."

"For what?" Mercy's face was strained, "You have a lot to explain, Kaulana! But, before I get your side of the story, your son wanted me to share something with you. He found out what he needed to do. He returned the sacred lei to its rightful place. And, he also said he forgives you. Let me just say, I believe he was a lot more accepting of your misdeeds on our family then I am. You will need to provide me more proof to get me onboard. Call me immature." Mercy crossed her arms, "So speak!"

"I was always looking for ways to make you feel special." Kaulana's opening statement did not help his cause. "Do you remember the time I went with Alika scouting for locations for that movie? I don't remember which, but we came across Camp Pi'ilewa. I went up the mountain and Alika went down to the lake. I didn't find a place to film, but I did find a beautiful scenic spot up there. I thought I could bring you there for our anniversary. That sunset was just gorgeous, Mercy." Kaulana could see his wife was waiting for an actual reason.

"Anyway, the sun filled a hole in the side of the mountain and something caught my eye. I could see the niho palaoa necklace resting on the bones inside the hole. Now, I know I shouldn't have done it, but temptation was too great. Instead of replacing the rock that slipped away from the burial's opening, I grabbed the niho palaoa that was inside the cave and took it as my own. Soon after, a legion of voices slowly cropped up saying that they curse me. It drove me to near insanity. I brought the lei here and sold it for a small fortune. I made a deal with this guy down River Street, in China Town. He took it from me, but he didn't take the voices.

The voices would call out to me at night. I begged them to leave me alone. I said I no longer had the niho palaoa, that they should go to the collector who bought it. They filled my head with deranged scenes of yours and Elenor's deaths. They wanted me to hurt myself. I thought I was going mad, so I left you and our boy." Kaulana could see a fire burning in Mercy's eyes.

"I used the money I got for the necklace, the money meant for us, to fly over here to reclaim the item, to set things right, but the guy wouldn't let it go. I couldn't bare the voices, so I checked myself into the mental hospital to get relief. I did not get any. The voices made me sour. I could not come back to you or Elenor until I found peace." Kaulana wrung his hands. "Good news finally came in the form of the mysterious death of the man I sold the necklace to. I was able to reacquire the necklace through not so legal means."

Mercy couldn't believe how despicable her husband was.

Kaulana added, "I found someone knowledgable about spirits and he said I could find ali'i up in Nu'uanu. I came here, camped out, waiting for the spirit of royalty to come, so I could apologize for my digression. I wanted so much to come back home, Mercy. You've got to believe me.

"When the marchers came, I kneeled in front of them with the necklace in my hands outstretched. I felt the sacred item leave my possession. My head fell silent! The voices were gone, I was cured. Now I could come back home to my wife and child.

One of the men in the procession came over and squeezed my face tight, pulled it upward and forced my mouth open.

The ali'i smiled as he lowered the lei into my mouth and the man that held my face had let go to ready his spear. He was about to impale my heart. I swung my fist fast and hard not believing I would make contact, but I buried my knuckles into the spearman's knee. With that I got up and ran. The next thing I knew, I felt a sharp pain in my lower back. My legs went numb and I fell. I hit my face against the ground and the necklace that hid inside my mouth made its way partially down my throat. I panicked and struggled to get away. When I realized I was suffocating, it was too late." Kaulana turned and looked at the dirt behind the place they sat. "I was here for a long time. I wandered these woods looking for a way to get home. But it wasn't until you called out for me that I was able to make my way to you."

"I called out to you? Psh! Yeah right!" Mercy waved her hands, "No way, no how! Why would I?"

Kaulana couldn't believe how much he ruined his relationship with Mercy. He did not realize his time after dying was fleeting in comparison to the amount of time Mercy struggled on her own as Len grew up. "It was after you learned Elenor was applying for camp counselor. You called out for me and I heard you. I found you fast asleep in your bed, having a nightmare." Kaulana explained, "After I learned where you were, I tried my best to help you and Elenor. I would try to give you signs throughout the day and I'd move our son's journal when I had enough strength to."

Mercy's eyes widened, "That was you? And, that was you at the laundromat!? You jumped at me from the drier knocking my head against the floor!?"

Kaulana stood to his feet with his hands raised, "Whoah! No, that was not me! There was something else looming over you both. Something very evil. It knew I was trying to help you, so it was trying to block me. I was too far away to overpower this thing. I tried everything I could, believe me!"

Remembering how Kaulana punched the night marcher, Mercy balled her fist and cracked Kaulana in the arm, "You didn't try hard enough, you bastard! If you had just left that burial cave alone everything would be so different right now!"

Kaulana tried to reason, "I was doing what I thought was best for us! I couldn't give you everything you deserved! You deserved so much more from me-"

"You were enough, babooze! Your son had a huge hole in his life because of you! I had no one to confide in! Pi'ilewa was all because I couldn't watch him at work!" Mercy had tears of anger trickling down her face. "Your choice just made everything all that much harder!"

"I see that now. I am so sorry, Mercy. But you are still proving yourself to be someone I never deserved. For what it's worth, I think you raised a damn fine young man on your own." Mercy turned away and he continued to say what he needed to, "I love you. I always have and I always will. I hope one day you can forgive me for all I've done to hurt you and Elenor." Kaulana turned from the tree and started to walk away.

Mercy stood up and called out to her husband, "What's next for you!? What do I tell Len?"

"Tell him that he is the only man that he needs to gain acceptance from. I know he already accepted my apology, but tell him that I'm sorry. Tell him I'm so proud of his accomplishments." Kaulana raised his hands toward the sky. Pahu beat rhythmically through the cold air. "I'm going to start my long journey into making things right with the ali'i. It was a terrible thing I did to them as well. I'm finally going to do something selfless for once in my life, or life after death anyway."

The spirit procession appeared and Mercy watched them move through the area as if they were on a mission. After the marchers dressed in ancient garb passed by, Mercy could see men wearing clothes of many different eras following close behind. Kaulana bowed his head waiting patiently for the end of the line.

Finally, the last group of the phantom train approached filled with people of a variety of ages and quality. Kaulana stepped forward and was accepted into the spirit ranks.

The Huaka'i Pō disappeared from view and Mercy spoke to her husband for the last time, "Good bye, Kaulana."

***

Yvonne leaped in fear when her partner made her way back to their camp, "Good grief! You scared me!"

"Why are you so jumpy?" Mercy was concerned.

Yvonne looked around the forest, "While you were away I could hear drums beating off in the distance. It was wigging me out."

Mercy sat beside Yvonne and hugged her, "Well, we're safe now, sweetie. At least out in this forest, we're safe."

Kanahā kūmālima

A loud ringing sent a hoard of bodies pouring into the halls of Lunalilo High. A few lingering students sat in front of Len's desk listening to his personal experience with the night marchers.

"So, the moral of the story is to show some class. Don't be proud, or vain. Be humble and be respectful."

Kaimi responded, "Wow, das crazy. T'anks fo' da story, Mr. Kahi! Was killah!"

"It was my pleasure. I was so happy to share it with you," Len smiled.

Wili asked, "You get any stories about da kine, people getting possessed?"

Len squinted his eyes and puckered his lips, "I may have a story or two about that subject, but it's getting late and I need you boys to pack up your things."

Wili begged, "Aw, come on Mr. Kahi, at least tell us how da possession story ends jus' incase we get da choking ghost tonight!"

"Just remember... respect, gentlemen. It's all about showing aloha. Okay, you kids better get going. Study for your test on Friday."

Kaimi grabbed his backpack and dropped a shaka, "Shoots! See you tomorrow, Mr. Kahi."

"Hey! Don't forget to finish your homework, boys!" Len sat at his desk watching the last of his students leaving for the day.

He leaned back in his seat and thought about everything that he experienced throughout his life and how it was a miracle that he was still alive. He saw that miracle as a gift, a gift that was meant to be shared. He was in a position to spread his knowledge, spread his wisdom and provide a safe space for his students to work their troubles out. He also used his interactions with his students to learn as well. He knew the youth had much to share and he treasured that infinitely.

***

Len returned home from a long day at work to a delightful aroma. "Yvonne, baby what are you cooking? It smells divine!"

She made her way out of the kitchen holding their baby boy in one arm and a wooden spoon in the other, "Spaghetti of course! I'm teaching the munchkin how to cook early so he can take over."

Len threw his keys in a small porcelain dish, "Is this all the mail from today, babe?"

"Yup, yup!" Yvonne called back in confirmation.

Len smiled at a post card from California sent by his mother, "Hey!" He yelled out loud, "Mom got the part!"

"Oh!? Great! Maybe after she makes her millions she can come back here and babysit for us!" Yvonne laughed at the absurdity.

"Don't even jest," Len made his way into the kitchen where the smell of basil and garlic made his mouth water, "you know I'm not going to hear the end of it if she misses any opportunities."

Len pulled up a letter from the Hikina 'ohana.

Yvonne could see something was bothering her husband, "What's the matter, hun?"

"A letter from the Hikina's, well, Frank Hikina. Dear Mr. and Mrs. Elenor Kahi please join us in the celebration of life…" Len's eyes blazed through the writing. He turned the invitation toward Yvonne flashing a beautiful photo of a young woman smiling, "Cheylene Hikina's funeral. She finally came home to her father."

Yvonne looked disappointed, "Oh no! I have to work the emergency room this Saturday, Len! I'm so sorry, I can't go with you."

Len smiled through his sadness, “It’s fine, me and the munchkin can pay our respects. We’ll stop by the emergency room with lunch afterwards.”

“Please don’t go to that deli you love so much, Len!” Yvonne licked her fingers, "You know the one, Uku Paila Deli! You always have trouble digesting that food. If it actually *is* food.”

“Oh, but it’s so delicious!” Len cried.

Yvonne slapped Len in the gut, “Forbidden! That hole in the wall is going to put my husband in a hole in the ground! Kawika needs his daddy!”

Hope

Frank Hikina stood beside his daughter's coffin addressing those who came to pay their respects to the young woman.

"Mahalo to all of you fo' coming an' showing yo' aloha an' support fo' me an' my family," Frank stopped for a moment truly understanding that he was the last of his immediate family. The kahu placed his hand over Frank's shoulder to send him mana.

"You all know Lou-lou, my wife… uh, my late wife, tried her best to make da community aware of our behbeh's disappearance. I t'ink dat da good lord took Mary-Lou, to ready a place in heaven for our girl. I would like to t'ank Detective Brent an' Detective Reed fo' not giving up on finding Chey. She was such a good girl, a quiet girl, she nevah made it hahd fo' us. She was so helpful to me an' Mary Lou, I really believe God sent us an angel, 'ānela mai ka lani. I am still in awe at how she looked when she was returned to me. It's like she nevah aged a day."

As Frank concluded his eulogy, Keoki, squinting through the bright sunlight, looked over at Detective Barshaw, "I feel uncomfortable, sir. It just doesn't feel right that Mr. Hikina believes his daughter is in that casket. He gave up his plot for that *thing*!"

Brent leaned over, "Okay, kid… I get it. You're upset, but this isn't for us now is it? So pipe down! Show respect for this man. He went through too much and he needs his peace."

Keoki pouted, "It isn't right."

"Ugh!" Brent was annoyed by Keoki as usual, "If I told you I will give Mr. Hikina my plot, would that make you feel better!?"

Keoki looked at Detective Barshaw, "Why, where's your plot located?"

Wili slapped Keoki, "Sssssh! Brah, I tryin' fo' listen!"

Kaimi saw what his brother did to his best friend and elbowed him, "Wili! No be laddat!"

Reed could see that the small group was attracting some odd looks.

Barshaw barked, "Enough already!" He squeezed the boys closer into his space to show the congregation he was quieting them down.

"Mahalo Frank, for allowing us to know your daughter, Cheylene, more intimately. Your love for your 'ohana is undeniable." Kahu Piha began closing the celebration, "Please bow your heads, e pule kākou."

The young girl standing beside Reed pulled on his arm, which caught Len's attention, "Uncle Boro, can I go down there?" She pointed toward a shady tree that was near a wall of interred urns.

Reed looked over at the location and nodded, "Sure, honey."

The voice of the kahu could be heard, "I ka inoa o ka makua, ke keiki a me ka hemolele, ʻāmene. With that, our celebration is completed. Please join Frank at the meeting place for refreshments and some time to talk story. Cheylene will be buried after everyone makes their way off of the burial site."

Frank made his way toward the detectives, "Mahalo, again to you boys for finding my baby girl." He looked at the three boys squirming in the midday sun, "Got some glazed donuts at da hale ʻāina if you guys like."

Barshaw looked over at his partner, "Ready?"

Reed pointed his thumb behind, "I gotta grab my niece first. Meet you guys there."

"Alright, I'll take these knuckleheads over to the hall." Barshaw scooted up a path with the boys slapping at each other.

Frank placed his hand on Detective Takao's arm, "Reed. I like give you dis." Frank handed a notebook that was hiding inside a manila folder to the puzzled officer. "It's strange, I see my angel in my dreams sometimes. I no take deez visitations lightly. So, when Cheylene pointed dis book out to me from her shelf, I knew dea was some kine impo'tance. Maybe it's somet'ing you might undahstan' moah den me 'cause I heard yo' name when I woke up. Found da book exactly wea she showed me in da dream."

Frank made his way to a cart that was there to take him to the reception, "See you!"

Len stopped Reed for a moment. "That's funny. I had a notebook just like that when I was a kid, like *exactly* like that." Len shrugged, "Probably thousands of journals that look like this one I'm sure."

"Oh yeah?" Reed was intrigued, "Let's take a look." The detective opened the diary and found Cheylene had created some kind of story. Scattered between the pages were journal entries.

Len was taken aback, "Wait, please tell me this notebook did not come from the office of Dr. Campbell."

Reed flipped the book back to the front and saw an inscription on the back of the cover. It read Property of Dr. Henry Campbell. A memory of the good doctor stopping by the house looking for his brother's mother-in-law popped into his mind, "Well, unless there's more than one Dr. Henry Campbell on the island, it appears you are correct. You two have history?"

"Dr. Campbell gave me a journal just like this when I was a patient of his." Len shook his head at the thought of seeing the book he remembered burning all those years ago. "He was my therapist."

Takao was surprised, "I didn't know you needed therapy."

"It's not really something I like to dredge up from my past." Len took a hold of the book. It gave him the chills seeing the young woman's intimate thoughts, "This is so surreal."

"Give me a second will ya, I can't see my niece." Reed ran over to the tree down the hill.

Len looked back into Cheylene's diary/story and skimmed through the pages finding things jumping out in her words, holding his attention.

"Hey, Len I'd like you to meet my niece!" Reed had a huge smile on his face.

"Hello, young lady! I'm Elenor Kahi. I'm your uncle's friend," Len stuck his hand out.

The young woman shook Len's hand with her very soft fingers, "I'm Promise. It's nice to meet you."

Reed squeezed her close, "She's transferring to Lunalilo High, her parents need some time to sort through some things."

Len nodded, "I know what that's like, Promise. I can't wait to see you in school, my dear." Len made a face that said he needed to tell Reed something in private.

Reed scooted his niece off, "Honey, why don't you go ahead to the hall. Go find me the most sugary glazed donut, okay? I'll meet you there."

"Okay, Uncle Boro." Promise made her way slowly across the cemetery talking to herself.

Reed bounced his head, "You got something?"

Len answered with his hairs standing on end, "I should say so!"

Reed could see the chicken skin running up his friend's neck. "That bad, huh?"

Len turned the book facing the detective, "Cheylene wrote a story describing the disappearances of the children from our community years ago."

"Hold on!" Reed's eyes rounded, "I know these names, this boy was my first missing person's case!"

"There's no way Cheylene could have documented that ordeal from a decade ago, right? Didn't you interview her?" Len was trying to get to the bottom of this revelation.

"I had no idea she was friends with these kids!" Reed took back the journal, "Cheylene was the missing link all this time!? Maybe, with this journal, we can finally bring to justice the person responsible for the abductions and mutilations of those teenagers!" Reed's skin had now puckered at the pores making chicken skin appear all over his exposed areas.

Len was astonished, "Hang on a second, did she add a title to her story?"

Reed made his way through to the left side of the notebook falling upon words written in large, bold letters. Len's heart skipped a beat as Detective Takao read aloud, "Manapua Man down Manahuna Lane."

THANK YOU!

Mahalo nui loa!

Aloha to you my dear friend,

We hope you enjoyed reading this mo'olelo, story, as much as we enjoyed creating it.

We would greatly appreciate it if you could continue to support us by leaving an honest review of this book on Amazon.com.

If you don't have the time to write a review, you may also choose to click a "Star" rating which only takes a few seconds.

In either case, please use the QR code below to find our Author Page and tell us your thoughts.

With much love and thanks, Del Aragon

Find us on: @Del Aragon @del.aragon

Glossary

Aloha: Love, respect or compassion
A hui hou: Until we meet again
'Aikānaka: Man eater
'Āina: Land
'Ākala: Pink, as a color
Akua: Spirit, divine or supernatural
'Āmene: Amen
Ana: Cave, grotto or cavern
'Anakala: Uncle
'Anakē: Aunty
'Ānela: Angel
'Ano'ai: Greeting, salutation
Au/Wau: I or me
Auē/Auwē: Grieve, moan or express "Oh dear!", "Alas"
'Aumakua/'Aumākua: Deified ancestor(s), family protector(s)
'Awa: Sour, bitter or the piper methysticom
Eia: Behold, here or present
Eō: Call, to call out or answer
Haku: Braid, compose or invent
Hala: Pandanus Odoratissimus or screw pine
Hale: House
Hāli'i: A covering, spread
Hāmau: Hush, quiet down or silence
Hana: Work, job or to do something
Hānai: Raise, adopt or foster
Hanale: Henry
Hao: Scoop or dig
Haole: Foreign entity, arrogant or ethnically caucasian
Hapa: Half or in part
Hāpai: Pregnant, carry or lift
Haupia: Pudding, type of dessert
Hiki Nō: Alright, ok, it can be done
Hō'ihi: Respect or sacred
Huaka'i: Travel
Huhū: Mad, anger or wrath
Hūi: Halloo, yoo-hoo and hey
Hulō: Hurray, hurrah or cheers
Hūpō: Foolish
Ihe: Spear, javelin or dart

I mua: Forward, progress or advance
Ipo: Sweetheart
Iwi: Bones of the deceased
Kahawai: Stream
Kahiko: Old, ancient or a time long ago
Kahu/Kahuna:
Kākau: Write, mark or carve
Kākou: We or us
Kalo: Colocasia esculenta or taro
Kālua Pua'a: Pig roasted in an underground oven
Kama'āina: Native
Kānaka: Human being
Kāne: Man, race of man or Kāne himself
Kaona: Innuendo, hidden meaning or double entendre
Kāo'oloa: Ghost procession
Kapa: Clothing or bedding made of wauke or māmake bark
Kapu: Forbidden, sacred or prohibited
Kēia: This
Keiki: Child, kid or little one
Ki'ipōhaku: Petroglyph
Kīkepa: Sarong
Kinolau: Shape-shifter, having many forms
Koa: Warrior, brave or military
Koko: Blood
Kōkua: Help or assist
Kolohe: Rascal, mischievous or naughty
Ko'olau Poko: Windward part of the island
Ko'u/Ku'u: My/My(affectionately)
Kukui: Candlenut
Kula: Academy, school or place of learning
Kumu Niu: Coconut Tree
Kupua: Half-man half-supernatural, demigod
Lāhui: Nation, tribe or race of people
Lani: Sky, heaven or very high chief
Laua'e: A fragrant fern
Laulau: Wrapping, bundled food in taro leaves
Lei: Flower garland
Liliko'i: Passion fruit
Loa: Long, tall or excessive
Loa'a: Find
Loke: Rose
Lōlō: Brain

Lomilomi: Masseuse or massage
Lua: Pit, hole or toilet, or a type of martial art
Luawai: Well, pool or pond
Mahalo: Thanks, gratitude or regards
Mahina: Month, moon or farm
Mai: Come or when in front of a word it becomes negated
Maile: Alyxia olivaeformus, a kind of shrub
Maka'ala: Alert, vigilant or watchful
Makai: Lowlands or seaward
Māka'i: Police, guard or inspect
Makaloa: Cyperus Laevigatus or perennial sedge
Make: Die, dead or deceased
Mālama Pono: To take the utmost care of
Malihini: Foreigner
Mamo: Descendant or black honey creeper
Mana: Spiritual strength
Manō: Shark
Maoli: True, native or indigenous
Maopopo: Understand, realize or clear
Makua: Parent or care giver
Makuahine: Mother
Makuakāne: Father
Manapua: White bun with char siu inside
Māua: We or us
Mauka: Uplands or inland
Mea'ai: Food
Menehune: A people of Hawai'i, mistaken as leprechaun like elves
Miko: Seasoned with salt
Mokupuni: Island
Mo'o: Lizard
Mo'olelo: History, tale or legend
Mo'opilikua: Dinosaur
Mo'opuna: Grandchild
Mo'owahine: Lizard woman
Naupaka: Scaevola, a kind of shrub
Niho: Tooth
'Oe: You
'Ohana: Family, relative or kin
'Ō'ia: Gore, stab or pierce
'Oi'o: A departed chief and his company or ghost procession
'Ōkole: Bottom, buttocks or anus
'Ōlohe: Hairless, bare or brindled, or skilled in lua

Oli: Chant
'Ōma'o: Green
One Hānau: Birth place
'Ono: Tasty or delicious
'Ōpae: Shrimp
'Ōpala: Trash, rubbish or waste
'Opihi: Limpet
'Ōpū: Stomach, belly or womb
'O wai: Who
Pāhoehoe: Cooled lava that has a smooth surface
Pahu: Drum, barrel or box
Pa'i: Slap, spank or hit
Pā'ina: Party that includes a meal
Pakalana: Chinese violet telosma cordata
Palaka: Block print textile
Palaoa: Sperm Whale or whale tooth pendant
Pau: Done, finished or the end
Pia or Hēpia: Pale yellow or starch derived from arrowroot
Pīkake: Jasmine or Peacock
Piko: Navel or bellybutton
Pilikia: Problem or trouble
Poina: Forget, forgotten or absent minded
Pō: Night, obscurity or the realm of the akua
Pōloli Loa: Extremely Hungry or starved
Pono: Just, fair or moral
Pōpoki: Cat
Pua: Flower or baby/child
Pua'a: Pig or pork
Puka: Opening, vent or hole
Pule: Prayer
Pūlima: Wrist
Pupule: Crazy, reckless or wild
Tītā/Kīkā: Sister
Tūtū/Kūkū: Grand parent
'Ulu: Breadfruit
Ulua: A type of deep ocean fish
Wahi: Place, location or site
Wāhine/wahine: Women/woman
Waiū: Milk or the action of milking
Wala'au: Talk, speak or converse
Waoakua: Highlands reserved for supernatural beings
Wili: Wind, twist or screw

Acknowledgment

First, we'd like to thank our father in heaven, without whom we would not be here. Almighty God, please, continue to grant us all your light, love and leadership.

To the mākua and kūpuna that have passed on their knowledge. Your wisdom has strengthened the lāhui!

Pops, Grancie and Debbie... we could not have done it without you. We will cherish the love you have shared with us, remember fondly our travels together and are forever grateful for all the support. We love you.

Kō māua 'Ohana, we hope you have enjoyed the journey thus far. This is only the beginning.

To the people reading this book, our labor of love, a huge thanks to you all for your tremendous support.

Warmest regards,

Del Aragon

Del Aragon

Del Aragon is a creative team of the ʻOhana that shares the same family name. Together, Kiara and Gabriel pair to bring forth their best creative literary works of both fiction and non-fiction genres that deal in entertainment as well as education, inspired through the values gifted to them through their Native Hawaiian upbringings and family traditions.

Gabriel was born and raised in Waimānalo on the island of Oʻahu. Living a life through creativity, Gabe loves expressing himself through the fine arts, music, story telling, and film and shares his knowledge with the youth he interacts with as an art instructor. His moʻolelo come from a history of personal experiences that range from bizarre to life altering. He is a proud father of two beautiful girls and the husband to a genuine angel.

Kiara was born and raised in Kailua on the island of Oʻahu. Her upbringing was fortified through her daily life as ʻŌlapa of Pukaʻikapuaokalani Hula Hālau. She has dedicated her life to educating children, not only as an elementary school teacher, but as a loving mother of two precocious girls. She absolutely adores traveling and the thrill of visiting new places to take in the sites, flavors and culture. She is also an avid reader.

Available Now...

Book 1

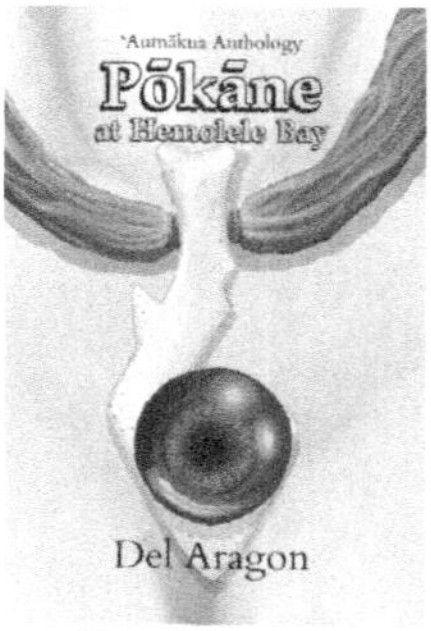

Pōkāne
at Hemolele Bay

Book 2

Mo'owahine
of Makalike Bridge

Book 3

Huaka'ipō
up Pi'ilewa Point

Coming Soon...

Manapua Man
down Manahuna Lane

Made in the USA
Middletown, DE
17 March 2025

72791173R00204